PRIORY

Oliver Hardacre Book 1

BECKY WRIGHT

Published by Platform House
www.platformhousepublishing.com

Copyright © Becky Wright 2021
All Rights Reserved
www.beckywrightauthor.com

ISBN: 9781092807630

Book & Cover Design © by Platform House
www.platformhousepublishing.com

CONTENT WARNING:
This contains a scene of sexual assault.

Mitzi, Kay, Vini and Zach
for your love of a good ghost story,
love Mum

PROLOGUE

We should start with *once upon a time*. It is fitting for a story with foundations built so long ago. Except, I've never been one to deceive a reader, so it's best we start here.

My name is Oliver, and I write.

I walk in the past surrounded by the memories of others, their lives, and deaths. Not the famous or people of historical significance, but ordinary men—those who have moulded our paths; those whose footprints lie within each worn cobblestone; whose hands shaped the door jambs and handrails; who wandered the same streets, lanes, and dirt tracks, the routes our modern lives take us today. Though some are now shadowed by contemporary architecture, stark reminders of our current technology, the ground they rest on is the same.

Have you ever touched the wood of an old door, stepped into the cool shadows of a timeworn hallway, and sensed them—those who were there before you? We leave behind a residue, a trace imprinted on the fabric we touch, the places we frequent. It is this very thought, the need to discover more, that makes my heart beat with a rapid thump, keeps my hot blood pumping.

When that first compulsion to put pen to paper swallowed me whole, it was to note history. A desperate need to document the past, my surroundings, and the place I had called home: Yorkshire. I have now spent many years researching, years of in-depth study into sites of preternatural interest along the length and breadth of the country—to be precise: spirits, ghosts, whatever you like to call them. The subject has always split opinions, but even the most sceptical mind expresses its curiosity about that age-long fascination of what lies beyond the veil of death. A mystery that may never be solved.

For more than half my life, I've been putting words to paper, compiling a measure of my thoughts on the subject. The paranormal and supernatural are good bedfellows for history. There is no pinpointing what led me down this precise path; a fascination far beyond the natural curiosity for such things is more a desperate need for answers, as if my sanity depends upon it.

My early career was cemented by historical facts and digging into the pasts of haunted locations. Now I am known for historical mysteries. Are they fiction? They are, except there is one underlying aspect to my whole career that has stayed under lock and key until now.

The truth.

This is *what* I am, but not *who* I am.

Before you read on, you should know this: the story that lies before you has lain hidden in the obscurity of my childhood memories. I tried to escape, thinking I could outrun it. There is no outrunning your heritage.

I am the last Hardacre.

PART ONE

THE PRESENT
Winter

ONE

'Hello, Mr Hardacre?'

My hand left my laptop to answer the call, passing straight through my mug on its way. Hot black coffee slopped over my lunch. I cursed under my breath and threw my soggy sandwich in the bin, quickly followed by handfuls of brown tissues. I balanced the phone on my shoulder as I attempted to mop my desk.

'Hello…?'

'Oh, sorry,' I replied, moving the earpiece to my other ear as I headed to the kitchen to wash my hands. 'Sorry, can I help you?'

'Hello, Mr Hardacre?'

'Yes…' I replied hesitantly. No one called. I got emails, hundreds of them, but no one rang me. I should have put the phone down right then; my instinct should have told me nothing good would come of it.

'Mr Oliver Hardacre?'

'Yes,' I said more firmly. That blasted name sent chills.

'Ah, good. I am Mr Fisk of Beamish, Talbot & Fisk Solicitors. We are dealing with—' He paused.

I waited for him to regain his momentum, trying to shrug off a sudden apprehension. 'And what can I do for you.'

'You are a hard man to track down, Mr Hardacre.'

'Am I?'

'In truth, we had all but given up when…' The rustle of paper and tapping of a pen—*tap tap tap*, in time with my pulse. I pushed the heel of my hand to my temple. 'Would

1

you have a few minutes you could spare me, please? I have things I need to discuss with you?'

'I'm free. Go on.' My pulse began to quicken.

'It has been a long time. Years. We almost gave up hope in finding you. Until the letter, anyway, and… your latest book. Such a coincidence, though are they ever really those?' He gave a low, gruff chuckle that snorted down the phone. 'Please forgive me, I've wandered from the matter at hand. Let me get to the point.'

I wished he would. I was still looking at what was left of my lunch at the bottom of the bin, feeling my stomach growl. I gulped down the last dregs of coffee. I needed another—I'd been awake since 4am. Two mugs of coffee wouldn't cut it.

'I am rather busy,' I said. 'If you could get to the point, I would be grateful.'

'Of course. You are a busy man, I understand that. For many years—several decades, in fact—we at Beamish, Talbot & Fisk have been dealing with an estate. I joined the firm some years ago, by which time this matter lay dormant. Always eager to get my teeth into a challenge, I took up the gauntlet with new vigour to find a relative. To find you, Mr Hardacre.' His hurried words quickly dried as he waited for me to join the conversation. 'You see,' he continued, 'we have something for you. Something that has been in our possession for many years.'

I perched on the edge of my desk, my empty coffee mug still in my grip. 'Are you sure you have the right man?'

'Oh yes, without a doubt. I am here looking at your website.'

'Ah, I see.' My cheeks coloured. I put my mug down and moved the phone to my other ear, running my finger along the inside of my shirt collar.

That sensation of unease that I knew so intimately was creeping its way beneath my skin, a feeling that had lingered as a child when I awoke from a nightmare. That one

2

nightmare, the only one I have ever had, the one that never left—the one I'd had last night.

'So, let me get back to the matter, Mr Hardacre. I will need you to come down to the office at your earliest convenience if you please. Also, bring some formal identification—just for the legality, of course.' A cough followed an uneasy laugh. 'Not that there's a colleague in the office who doesn't know who you are.'

'Could you please tell me how you got my number?'

'Oh dear, oh dear. Please forgive me. After the letter, I assumed. I thought, in the circumstances, it would be prudent to speak to you directly rather than reply to your letter.'

'What letter? I haven't written to you, nor have I received anything from your firm. To be honest, Mr Fisk, I am more than confused by this whole thing. Could I please ask you to explain what you have for me? I am adamant you have the wrong person.'

The solicitor said nothing for a few seconds.

'Mr Hardacre… Oliver. Do you mind if I call you Oliver?'

'You can call me whatever you wish if you get to the point.'

'I and all at Beamish, Talbot & Fisk were sure you knew the matter after we received your letter last week, Oliver.' He swallowed loudly. 'I have the letter in my hand as we speak. I was about to pen a reply when I remembered a colleague is reading your latest book. We are all fans, you see, and after scrolling your website this morning, there was no doubt. So, here we are.'

Was this some weird way of getting a signed book or interview of some kind? My reclusive nature was common knowledge—well, it had been until recently. Trawling my website wouldn't have brought much joy, especially with one photo taken about fifteen years ago. So, why this charade? My mind wandered, grasping at all these loose ends, and I found myself at the patio doors leading onto the terrace. Beyond that, the cliffs and sea. It was cold today. The sea thrashed the beach, and a low mist lay over the pier. This was my haven, my world. How dare this man, Fisk or whoever he was, invade it? I felt tainted. I could—should—hang up right now.

'Oliver, are you still there?'

I didn't answer, but a deep sigh gave me away.

'When would you like to come down to Suffolk to sign the papers? Would this week be convenient? I think the sooner we can finalise this matter, the better, especially after so many years.'

'As I have made it clear to you that I have not written to you on any matter,' I declared, 'you must have the wrong person. What's more, you haven't given me any clear information, so I'm taking this call as a hoax. Now, if you would excuse me, I'm a busy man.' My finger was on the button to end the call.

'Please, *please*, forgive me.' There was more than an apology in his tone—it was apprehension. 'Yes, I can see how this may seem a little out of the blue, but as I have said, I have your letter here. This matter has been in our hands at Beamish, Talbot & Fisk for forty years. We've been solicitors to the family for many decades. There are no other living relatives. We are positive after forty years of search. This belongs to you. I must urge you, Mr Hardacre.'

What was I meant to say? After last night—restless, filled with nightmares—I should have known somewhere in my core that today would bring something peculiar. I never imagined Suffolk would call me back in one way or another.

I placed my hand on the patio door; moisture formed beneath my palm on the cold glass. Wild winds whipped at the garden furniture and upturned the odd plant pot. My hand was on the handle before I knew it, and I walked outside. Winter was calling its greeting; no trace of autumn left.

'Oliver? Are you still there?

Mr Fisk's voice seemed a world away, a place I didn't want to visit. My childhood belonged in the past. I'd put so much distance between then and now that I'd forgotten the intensity of pain. The keenness to do so had locked away all those memories in some box somewhere. Only, the night, the dark, and the thought of winter brought those memories out. Winter always unlocked the terror box.

'Oliver?'

'Yes, I'm still here,' I shouted over the wind. I ran back inside and pushed my back against the closed doors, the rush of wind still in my ears. 'I can't do this.'

'Oh, I assure you, the signing of a few documents is all I need.'

'No, I mean, I can't come down to Suffolk. I don't wish to sign anything. Whatever it is you have there, I don't want it,' I declared swiftly, striding back to my desk.

'I must urge you to rethink,' he ushered, his tone an octave higher.

'My life is here, I want no part in this matter.'

He sighed—a slight shuffle of papers. I pressed the phone a little firmer to my ear with my shoulder as my hand went to my empty coffee mug.

'Very well, Oliver. I understand.'

'Thank you.' I exhaled my words as my shoulders eased. 'Good day to you, Mr Fisk.'

'Could I please, if you have one more moment, ask you a question? I understand how busy you must be, of course.'

'Um, yes, okay. What is it?'

'Reading down to the last paragraph...' The rustle of shuffled papers flowed down the line. 'You mention your brother?'

With that one word, my life spun like a cyclone.

TWO

There was no denying the brisk chill that swept up from the rolling tide as it reunited with the rocks. The sun had set, and the evening yawned into darkness. Still, I sat on the decked terrace wrapped in a trusty blanket, bobbly, fuzzy, and littered with holes—the one I'd grasped in my tiny fingers that first night here in Whitby.

It had been dark, the sea wild like an untamed beast rising to swallow the cliffs. I'd listened to the wind whistling through the little window of the attic room so long ago. And yet, my heart drum in that familiar march, rapid as it did that night. I suffered the fear of that small boy again.

If I could just stay, lock all the doors… not that anyone came to visit. No wife, no children, no family left. I had few friends, all of whom were through work. Were they real friends? I was a loner, a reclusive writer well known for my slightly eccentric hermit life. With no skill of peopling at all, I was not known as a people person. I preferred history and those who still lived there, with no care for what anyone thought, dealing with work through emails, phone calls if I had no choice.

My agent once made a surprise visit out of sheer frustration as I kept cancelling appointments. I had gone down to London in the early days with trains, taxis, hotels—the stuff of nightmares fit to put me in an early grave. The entire trip causing me nothing but a heart-stopping trauma. I have since firmly anchored my feet to my tiny piece of Yorkshire coastal land.

The wooden lounger creaked as I shifted to retrieve my glass from the table beside me. I wrapped the blanket closer around my shoulders, grappled with the edges while juggling with the tumbler. I'd planned to buy new garden furniture ready for the summer, something stylish I'd seen online, but I never had, just as I hadn't for the four previous years. It was becoming a tradition. Obviously, I was meant to keep this rickety lounger. What was the point of a new one anyway? The salty sea air would see to its new varnish soon enough and bleach its richness as it did everything else.

I loved everything about the sea, about Whitby town, of being windswept and weather-beaten. It reminded me I was still alive.

But what I valued most was my anonymity.

My glass sloshed, the contents swirling a little too near the rim. It was my third gin, at least a double—I didn't measure, the bottle poured just fine. No doubt it wouldn't be my last of the night. It blurred the sharp edge of the past and everything it brought, the misery of it all being that I just couldn't remember it in enough detail to reconcile my pain. The memories and stories of others? Yes, I remembered all those like they were my own. The only real memories that belonged to me were of when I arrived here in that winter—that desperate winter of despair, dramatic as it sounds.

I had been only a child, a young boy packed off in a whirlwind. A muddle of harried voices, large hands taking mine and leading me into a vehicle, a train, then another car. Hours and hours in the back, watching the darkness blur past the window while I gripped the blanket, now as familiar to me as my own skin. It was only in the cold light of the winter morning that I looked to see its colours: a vibrant mix of wools crocheted into an ever-decreasing pattern with a dark-red centre. It was my centre, my core. Desperation and loathing. Fear and panic. Pain and grief. I couldn't put a name or understanding to those emotions back then. They stemmed from events I'd somehow, with a need for survival, washed from my memory, which left only the faded impressions of a tin of polaroid images. For a child, to put words to such a thing was unfathomable. Even as a man, these forty years later, I can't find enough of those memories to make any sense of them or to speak them aloud.

I had been questioned. People, one after the other, face after face. Some I vaguely recognised, some total strangers in uniforms. I had said nothing. I had no voice. There were no words or explanations to convey, so I remained mute. It was much later, when many days and nights passed in a distortion of restless sleep and unconscious waking. When the sea air had filtered my lungs, purifying me somehow, that the words returned. But I remained adamant—I remembered nothing.

My foster family had been kind, forgiving. More than that, they had been understanding. It had been the seventies—boys like me with nothing; fell through the net all too often. I'd been fortunate to find a family rather than be placed in an institution for such kids. I've since heard the horrors of some children's homes of that era, watched the news, read of the abuse and neglect. I'd been lucky, if only after unmentionable and unrecallable horrors.

I never called them my parents, and they never insisted I did. It didn't make them any less. Vera and Bob, both locals and hardworking habitual creatures in their middle years. Loyal, trustworthy with no children of their own; I never asked why. Their dwelling had been a small terrace house nestled on a narrow road along the East Cliff, near the old steps up to the church and abbey. An old fisherman's cottage, with a whitewashed exterior. Bob and I repainted it every couple of years. My efforts were probably more a hindrance, but Bob lavished me with his most valuable commodity: his time. First, the cottage's tiny window frames were green, the shade of geranium foliage to match the ones Vera planted in baskets either side of the front door. Then, sometime in the mid-eighties, Vera decided to repaint them all in cornflower blue. I saw that colour, the vivid shade of August skies, when I closed my eyes with thoughts of her.

Vera was always cooking. I'd arrive home from school to a waft of frying fish or a stew. 'Get those shoes off before you go any further, young man,' she would shout. In my grey school socks, I stood at the bottom of the tiny staircase, holding the door open with my elbow as I flung my shoes up the stairs with my school bag in some meagre attempt to reach the top. One shoe would inevitably tumble back down.

They had been proud people, my folks. Bob had been a baker, rising before dawn each morning and whistling a tune as he put on his shoes and closed the front door with a soft thud that rattled to my tiny attic room. Sunday afternoons, he would lounge in his brown leather armchair the colour of toffee you had held in your hand for too long. The sun streaming in through the parlour window at the back, casting him and his chair in a beam that made my heart swell.

Outside those whitewashed walls, my childhood from then on had been as good as could be expected. I disappeared into myself, calling on fictional characters for friendship, burying my head in any book I could find. The kids at school left me be, as much as the odd name-calling was being left alone. But they hadn't attempted to offer friendship, for which I'd been grateful. *The changeling*—that was what most called me, including adults, some to my face. More imaginative kids had come up with a more descriptive narrative: *the ghost boy*.

Those first few days here in Whitby—never leaving my attic refuge, wrapped in my newfound friend—I had looked in the small wooden mirror that hung on the wall opposite the window. I hadn't noticed at first; its carved frame was all I saw, but there was a familiarity that kept dragging me back to that mirror and its precisely carved acorns that covered every inch of the polished wood. That fact had started a desperate churning. I spent hours staring, tracing my

9

fingertip over each acorn, wondering why the mirror stirred something dark deep inside my gut.

That was when I first *saw.*

The sun had drifted. The late afternoon glare had caught in the corner of my window and sent a shaft of bright orange light onto my hair, clarifying my reflection. I saw more than just me. There was a silhouette, an outline of a memory. I wiped my hand over the glass surface and peered further into the mirror. It stirred behind me; I didn't turn. I knew I wasn't alone. Then the shadow disappeared as I ran my fingers through my hair and wondered what was different. It was one of those moments when you know something is amiss, only you can't put your finger on it. Then, when I stepped back from the mirror, it hit like a thundering blow:

My hair was no longer the dirty brown of a dead mouse I had kicked around in the fields. It was white.

The ghost boy.

In my university years, Bob once told me that those kids were just too scared to come near me. 'I can only imagine the stories that must have spread around those kids of seven and eight. The sort that chills you to the bone.' Bob had eyed me over his pint as the words slipped in the smoky pub air. I hadn't risen to it or given him any more than I had done for over a decade. 'Aye,' he continued. 'But look at you now, my lad. All grown up. And clever, mind. Not that we doubted that of you. We knew you'd turn out a good'n, never mind the past.'

I stared at him then, unable to respond. What a childhood history to carry around on my shoulders. Bob, he'd had no idea.

I'd heard my folks discuss the matter on occasions. How I came to be there, and the circumstances. They called it the *Happening*. How I happened to be in the sleepy seaside town perched on the Yorkshire cliff when I belonged among the rural folk of Suffolk. I told them repeatedly that I had no memory of it, when in truth, it was not entirely so. I wondered if it would have lessened the burden had I told someone the snippets that hung like stray threads. As my years grew, I was glad I never had. I'd saved them that, at least.

I'd lost both those dear people in my early twenties—a freak car accident. The facts were unclear, only that they had been heading into Suffolk. At least they had gone together. I found consolation in that. Never having to live without the one that made you whole... I knew that agony. It never stopped ripping at your soul. Now I was alone again, and truly this time. No one to rush me off in the middle of the night. No blanket to bolster my grief.

I overheard a voice at their funeral, which I'd organised in the local pub. The voice mentioned Suffolk. I stood behind a pillar around the corner of the bar, listening. Then, quickly, an uneasy sensation crawled down my spine—I knew that voice. It struck with awareness so vivid it flashed red before my eyes. But it was more the darkness that began to burrow beneath my skin that made me move; I couldn't listen any longer.

'Oh, Oliver,' she had said. 'I didn't see you there. You won't remember me.'

But I had remembered her. And it had come to me then, crashing down like a freezing wave over my head, ready to drown me.

'Mrs Scarfe?' I stared at a jagged slice of my past in the figure standing in my present.

'I wasn't sure you would.' A slight hint of something extra left her lips with those mundane words.

'Why are you here? I don't understand.' The more I glimpsed back into the past, the more confused I became. The face I recalled was younger, but her flash of red hair and large eyes hit like a bullet. The main issue I had was placing her in any kind of scene or location. Instead, the red-tinged image was hovering, disconnected.

'Vera was my sister.'

Those words dug out my heart with a spoon. The day I had said goodbye to the best part of my life—that I remembered, now had me greeting something vastly different. A cruel trick to play when I was already grieving.

I never set eyes on Mrs Scarfe again. She had written twice over the following couple of years, the general enquiring after my health and wellbeing, which felt misplaced. Even though I had tried to answer her, my letters had fallen flat. I'd never sent them. It was safer to bury past connections where they belonged: in a deep hole with Vera and Bob.

Enough wallowing.

Staggering from the garden lounger, I gulped down the last of the gin. Leant on the door, pushed my forehead to the frame as a wave of sickness swamped me, dragging me back to the phone call somersaulting my thoughts, churning my stomach.

What did this Fisk have that was so urgent?

And my brother?

Why had I agreed to catch the train down to Suffolk the following day? Not one word Fisk had spoken made any sense, not in the real world.

The moon was high by the time I stumbled inside. Relieved that I'd already packed a holdall, I slumped into bed. The room spun around me as my insides burned.

THREE

The night brought nothing but a bottomless void. The morning, no room for reflections amid the abrasion of gin—a small mercy I was thankful for as I awoke a little before six. The train was not leaving until 7:30, so there was time for a much-needed mug of black coffee.

I should have known better than to drink. It never boded well with my concentration the next day. As a writer, it was a lesson I'd learnt early on. Those years after losing my folks, finding myself alone with all the memories of them in each strip of wallpaper and fish supper, it had been easy to lose myself in the obscurity of alcohol, though it had soon become apparent that to succeed in life, I needed to take control, even if it was in small measures.

Fictional characters once again greeted me with open arms. This time, they were my own. I filled pages with the troubles of others; there was no time to wallow in mine. Success found me, and in turn, I found a way to live another life—many lives. It was easier dealing with the horrors of others. There would be a resolve in closing the book. For better or worse, everything always ended. My life, on the other hand, was not as kind.

Reality does not always give you the key to unlock the answers.

The time to open that box of terror seemed to have found me. There was nothing for it but to switch to autopilot. If I thought about it any longer, I would talk myself out of it. I checked I had my mobile phone and wallet, patting down my tweed jacket pockets three times to make sure. I grabbed my keys and holdall. With the key in the lock, I stood on the stone front step of the cottage they had raised me in as a wisp of morning air brushed my ear. I heard Bob's voice: *Time to sweep away all those cobwebs, Oliver. Go be the man you are, not the boy you were, my lad.*

The Yorkshire morning wore a brisk chill along with the early sea salt. The smell was now part of me, and I was as much part of the cliffs, harbour, and sea. The fear that threatened to choke me every time I swallowed grew with each step towards the railway station. I could turn back. I should. If there was a letter or something for me, couldn't the solicitors deal with it? Send me whatever it was and the papers to sign?

I stopped before I crossed the bridge; I saw the station, didn't need to get on a train. Why go all the way to Suffolk to sort this out, *if* there was anything to sort? Doubt still niggled at my throat. Nothing good would come of it.

There's no memory of getting to the station, the walk over the bridge, coursing the path around the harbour, or buying my ticket. The first realisation was the bitter sting of bile rising in my throat as my stomach lurched with the first motions. We were off. The calmness of Whitby I'd come to know was swiftly being left behind, growing ever smaller in my wake. I was being summoned. I felt it.

The journey would have been a mundane affair to a seasoned traveller. To me, it was close to torture with the fear of missing my next stop or boarding the wrong train. I gripped the timetable in my fist for most of the way, and three stops later, I climbed aboard the last one. This was it: Peterborough, platform six. I would reach Bury St Edmunds in a little over an hour. It was midday, my stomach was angry. I would get something to eat before heading to the solicitors' office. It would be somewhere in the town centre— I would stop by a coffee shop on the way.

With the promise of a quick lunch, I lifted the collar on my jacket and rested my head against the seat. Sleep took me as swiftly as the train.

Our skinny legs ran in shorts that skimmed scabby knees. We were at the tree. We sprawled on the grass under the limbs of the great oak. My brother lay his head back on clasped hands to rest on a tree root.

'Come on, I'll race you up the tree.'

His bony legs dangled from the main branch, which reached out farther than any other—a long, twiggy finger extending towards the house.

My lip trembled as I reached up to the first branch. Before I could get my feet higher than the gnarled root, it began. It was slight at first—a tiny judder.

My brother stood on the colossal bough; his arms stretched to a higher one as the rubber soles of his wellies gripped the bark. 'Look at me,' he called down.

My heart pounded, but it wasn't fear of my brother falling. It was something else, something far worse. Something deadly.

'No, don't do it,' I shouted.

I let go of the low branch and fell back a couple of steps. My brother stood above me, stock still, his eyes locked on something below him... but it wasn't me.

There was something eerie about his stillness. His mouth began to move in silent words, but he wasn't talking.

He let go of the branch, and his arms dropped by his side. He was going to fall.

Then it began to tremble. Each coarse vein in the bark, each old knot of the great oak tree shuddered and shook. Acorns sprinkled over my head. Again, I screamed for him to hold on, to come down, to be careful.

His face grew vacant.

I screamed as whispers surrounded me from the leaves, the branches, the acorns: Clever boys. Remember, two are more than one. One be bound, the other lonesome.

Sweat beaded as I buried my face in my hands. The same nightmare. My only memory of my brother amongst the rubble of my past. Was he to haunt me forever, even after all these years? I supposed the answer was *yes*, especially now. Suffolk would only make the matter worse. *It will get harder before it gets better*, Bob had said. I had to be stronger than I had been.

The train pulled into the station. The coldness hit me as I descended onto the platform. I hitched my collar a little higher around my neck, cursing the chill. 'Should have worn a bloody scarf,' I mumbled.

The station was busy — families, couples, suits on business. I hadn't expected it to be so crowded.

Whether Bury St Edmunds was as I remembered, there was no saying, as I couldn't recall it at all, well, not in detail. Mere sparks of memories more like faded, double-exposed photos, each recollection layered over another. Yet, an intense familiarity struck me hard in my chest as I took each step. Young Oliver had left from this station forty years ago; although, it was not the station or a memory that stirred me like a handshake from an old friend. It was the voices in my head. They were growing louder, more urgent, more vital.

I wanted to go home.

You are *home*.

I refused to listen. They knew I was back; of course, they did. They had been calling me since that phone call. It was their doing.

'Mr Hardacre?'

I spun to see a gentleman, his hand out in front of him and his face wide with a grin.

'Oliver? I took the liberty of finding out what time you would arrive, so here I am.'

'Mr Fisk?'

'Please, call me Nick,' he declared, shoving a hand in my direction.

I struggled to cover my shock as I took his proffered hand. From the phone conversation and merely the tone of his voice, I had pictured someone older.

'Please accept my apology and surprise,' I said. 'I was not expecting...'

'Well, I thought it would be advantageous in the circumstances.'

I thought it was an odd choice of word. It must have shown in my knitted brow.

'It's just that I expected you would be keen to… get to it. I took the liberty of booking you a room in the local inn for convenience.'

'To be honest, I imagined finding the nearest place to the station, a bed and breakfast in town. Because I came by train, you see? Well, obviously… If I'd driven down, maybe that would...'

I was at a complete loss with this Fisk. Such an odd character. I felt somewhat dislodged, floating outside my comforts. My empty stomach leapt.

'I need to eat,' I said.

'They offer a superb lunch—all homecooked, as you would expect. My car is outside. I shall drive you straight to The Old Oak, let you settle in and eat.'

Those words drove a shiver down my spine, raising the hairs on the nape of my neck, which in turn hurled me back to the vision of my brother and that bloody tree.

'Where is the… inn?'

'In Raynham. Our office is in the village too, so no need for you to stay in Bury. Too many people. Far too many.'

He whisked my holdall from my hand. It seemed pointless to argue, so I followed his feet as my eyes stared at the ground. There was dread in looking up.

I was being dragged back to the past.

FOUR

The village of Raynham was small with a high street of timber-framed buildings at its centre, a varied pallet of muted plaster façades. Traditional Suffolk pink with blackened beams nestled easily next to Victorian red brick. My feet paused mid-stride as my eyes caught the rooflines, a jumble of heights and materials, thatch set against pantiles. History lived here; century layered upon century.

I had prompted Fisk to head straight to his office. A blasted migraine was already bashing at my skull, threatening to break in. Prolonging it would only have aggravated my blood pressure. We stopped outside a building, which wasn't much more than an arm wide and a deep shade of custard yellow. It was a contrast with its black timbers, solid wooden door and small window. It sat back a touch under the jettying of the upper floor as the beamed framework frowned down over the pavement.

'Here we are.' Fisk took my elbow. I flinched, wondering at the gesture. 'Over here.'

I stood in the middle of the narrow road, a scattering of shops either side huddled between painted houses. A green car faced me. The square bonnet and headlights hitched themselves to an old memory. The driver—a young woman— eyed me as her fingers tapped the steering wheel. There was more there, but I couldn't place the thought. It was whisked away as she beeped her horn. I mouthed an apology and paced backwards out of the road. The woman gave a quick nod with a curt smile. She waited a moment, then revved the car back to life and drove off. I studied the car as it faded into the distance, the sun glinting on the chrome bumper. It stopped hard, its brake lights glaring red, and two young hands waved from the back window.

'Oliver? Are you quite well?'

Sweat beaded on my forehead. It seemed unnecessary to answer, his voice some vague disruption to the moment. When the car vanished around the sweeping corner by the pub, I finally followed Fisk into the reception area of the solicitor's office. My hand rested on the wood, mottled with centuries of patina. The black hinges creaked as the heavy door closed and blocked most of the sunlight.

'Through here,' Fisk said. 'Let's go into my office. I will get some coffee arranged...' He stood lost in thought a moment, his eyes wandering the plaster beamed walls. 'Ah, Mikey, there you are. Some coffee, please?'

A patch of black hair appeared around a doorframe, followed by a young face. 'On it!' The reply was a little more relaxed and informal than I expected. Fisk responded with a quick nod and slight laugh and turned back to me.

The door handle hovered in Fisk's hand. 'Shall we?'

The office sat at the back of the building in a modern extension... or as modern as the late 19th century was. The ceiling was higher in here. The large window allowed light to filter across the oak desk.

Refreshments arrived on a silver tray: two large china mugs along with all the usual paraphernalia. I eyed the plate of biscuits. Could I resist a digestive for the sake of politeness? The growl in my stomach got the better of me, and I threw all niceties to the wind.

'Oh, go ahead, please,' Mr Fisk said. 'You must be ravenous. I could get Mikey to pop out, get us some lunch from the bakery over the road—nothing extravagant but wholesome and homemade. That's what counts, after all.'

'Please, there's no need,' I insisted. 'I can wait until later.' In truth, I was now too nervous to eat.

Fisk hovered by a large cupboard that stretched the whole wall. 'Now…' He turned away and vanished behind a door, then reappeared with a cloth bag. 'As I said on the phone, we have something that belongs to you.'

He placed the bag on the polished desk and sat opposite me. The sunlight cast a halo about his head. I squinted and moved my chair to one side a fraction to adjust. Our eyes fell onto the bag again. It was coarse linen, probably black at one time but now grey, flecked with age spots, and a musty smell akin to incense. Its tang clung to the back of my throat.

'As a matter of interest, I have a spare set of keys to Hardacre,' Mr Fisk said.

I held up my hand and closed my eyes a second. 'I have no intention of going to the Priory.'

'But your letter… and since you're here, surely…?'

'Under no circumstances,' I added and sat back in my chair, my arms crossed.

Curiosity. I'd seen that look many times, but not in recent years. Something about the strength of it sent an uneasy bolt my way. Perhaps it had been easier to dismiss it all when I was a child, easier not to answer the adults. My behaviour was excused as trauma. Seeing the look that always followed my determination not to speak of the *Happening* only made me uneasy. Guilty.

'Let us return to the matter at hand then,' Mr Fisk said. 'There's no hurry, after all. For the moment, I need you to have this.'

The cloth bag jiggled on the desk as Fisk rose to retrieve a custard cream. He dunked it in his tea and placed his other hand over the bag as if to spur it into life.

What the hell was in there?

'Before we get to that'—I nodded at the dusty object staring at me— 'you mentioned a letter, and more importantly, the matter of my brother.'

There, I'd said it. His image had been circling in my head since the train journey.

'Maybe we should go over your letter first. Yes,' Mr Fisk spoke more to himself than to me. 'I know. You are right, we should,' he mumbled over his shoulder.

Drops of coffee sprinkled over the polished surface as Fisk shut the desk drawer. I pulled a tissue from my pocket to mop up the mess. When I looked up, he held a crisp white envelope with a decorative stamp of a large Leonardo da Vinci sketch, like the commemorative ones I had bought last February.

I took the article, it dangled from my fingers a second, I brought it close. I recognised the envelope— watermarked with the local Whitby printer's logo, identical to the stationery I'd used for decades. The handwriting was mine.

'I don't understand.'

Fisk looked confused. 'What?'

'I didn't send you this. I hadn't even heard of you or your solicitors until you called me. So, how is it…?' I knew I had to open it to see what was inside, but I couldn't. 'What the…'

'It arrived in the post last week—on Monday, I think it was. Nothing unusual, I can assure you. It was funny though—my colleague mentioned your book the day before. He just finished it, you see. *Behind the*—'

'—*Ancient Doors of Suffolk*.'

'Yes. Well then, the rest, as they say, is history, if you excuse the pun.' Fisk chuckled.

I could look at this envelope all afternoon or I could just read the bloody thing. The paper was thick and crisp. It was my stationery, my personalised header printed at the top of the page, and my writing.

'How...?'

Word, phrases, they are my tools; but this… this was alien to me. It was undoubtedly written in my hand, though there was no recall ever seeing it before.

My eyes flew over the first two paragraphs. They were quite ordinary besides their content:

I would like to arrange a visit to Hardacre Priory. I understand that you are the acting solicitors for my ancestral home and have been for many years.

It went on to mention the new book and finished with:

I would be grateful if you would contact me at the above at your earliest convenience.

It all sounded like me, but… I glanced at the envelope's postmark. Whitby; dated last week.

'I have no idea how you got this,' I began, wanting to add more but words were lost to me.

Then, Fisk lightly touched the paper over my arm. 'When I spoke to you, I referred to the last few lines. There…'

I sat forward slightly and brought the letter closer. Scribbled in biro like an afterthought, it read:

Please sir, I must know about my brother. No one will tell me and I'm so afraid. Please could you explain what happened? I think you are the only one left who can help. I must know before it is too late, but please, it must be our secret, or I shall be in such trouble. We all will.

The paper fell in my lap as I slumped back in the chair. The soft-padded leather was a welcome comfort as my migraine finally broke and split my brain in two. I pressed my fingers to the pressure point at the bridge of my nose in a vain attempt to ease it, but I'd left it too long. The throbbing had taken root.

'I'm not entirely sure that I can help you with your brother, but I can help with the other matters.'

'I said no.'

'I see.' Fisk sipped his tea and took another cream-filled biscuit from the plate. 'I could take you to Hardacre Priory. We could go this afternoon… No. I think, by the look of you, the best thing would be a hearty meal and some sleep.'

'Some paracetamol too,' I mumbled.

'Right. That's that sorted; the rest can wait. We need to get you to the Great Oak to be fed and watered.' Another chuckle. 'Ah.' He opened a drawer, rummaged around in it, muttering to himself before presenting me with a packet of painkillers. 'Here, these will help.'

I popped two out of the blister pack and downed them with the last of my coffee, then rested my head against the leather chair and closed my eyes. Just for a minute or two, enough to let the pills settle.

I was at home, the sea visible from my bedroom window. I pressed my nose to the glass and stared out at the blue. Condensation bloomed with every breath and gathered at the tip of my nose. That sensation on the back of my neck had been more relentless of late. It lingered there longer today and raised every hair.

In the corner of my eye, I saw a shadow. I spun around as the round oak mirror on the opposite wall juddered.

'Go away!'

I slapped my hand to the back of my head and smoothed my palm over my shirt collar. I still wore my school uniform even though I'd been home for at least an hour. I hadn't spoken to Vera when I stormed through the front door, simply shrugged in answer to her usual, 'how was your day, love?' I'd taken the stairs two at a time and flung my school satchel onto my bed. My shoes had landed somewhere on the other side of the room.

If I could just look at the sea, I could forget the day I had. The torment and constant name-calling didn't always bother me this much. There were times when I could push the voices out, give them a look of if you do not leave me alone, I shall— *What would I do to them? Nothing, probably. But they didn't know that. The stories about me were enough to make them wary, but was I capable of such awful things? Could I kill?*

Even now, after an hour of trying to calm my breathing, my heart was racing. Whatever was standing behind me, I wished it would just leave me alone.

When I came to, a soft grey blanket lay folded over my knees. I couldn't have been out for long—my coffee was still tepid.

Fisk stood in the doorway. 'Ah, you're back with us. I have spoken to the landlady over at the Oak. Your room is ready, and there's still time to get some lunch. Homemade cottage pie is always a good choice.'

My voice seemed to have vacated, leaving me with the energy to merely nod.

'That's okay,' Fisk said. 'There is no rush. I told them we'd be over at some point this afternoon.'

My eyes scanned my fingers for the letter. It was back in its envelope with the address forward, resting against the dusty cloth bag. I'd forgotten about that thing.

'What is it?' I asked.

'Sorry?'

'In the bag. What is it?'

The curiosity had caught me in its net and was pulling me in. I drained the last drop of coffee and needed more.

Mikey slid into the room past Mr Fisk and placed a large mug in front of me. 'Thought you could do with another.'

'Thanks,' I said. 'Appreciated.'

He left, humming to himself.

As I put the mug to my lips, Fisk opened the cloth bag. Dust particles followed by the musty smell of age rose between us. I covered my coffee with my hand.

'Oops, sorry,' Fisk said. 'It's been a while since this has seen the light of day, as you can see.'

'What is it? Why do you have it?' I asked.

'Well, as to what, I'm not entirely sure, but it's been with us for longer than anyone knows. The oddest thing is that there's no documentation for it. Everything, as you can imagine, has some kind of document or other to identify the item and nature of its occupation here in our safekeeping, so to speak.'

None of that information made any sense or any difference to me in the slightest. I was still none the wiser.

'I think you should do the honours. It's yours, after all.' Fisk pulled away the old cloth and reached in to retrieve a peculiar leather object. He placed it on the desk in front of me. 'There. It wasn't until the book that we thought to look at it again, and then the letter…'

'The book.' I sat forward, realising I had shrunk so far back in my chair that I was virtually one with the leather.

'I read it—well, we all did. I didn't see the connection until now. So, I have to ask: why Hardacre?'

Fisk sat down hard. The gesture had a determination I hadn't seen in him before. He steepled his fingers, tapped his hands on his chin. I knew what was coming next.

'Before you say it, could I please reiterate my intentions to you? I have no desire to visit the place.' I sat back in my chair and mirrored his gesture with a deep sigh. 'I've spent a long time—a *very* long time—trying to put the past behind me. But unfortunately, history has a way of peering around the corners when we least expect it. I've steered clear of the place for decades. Until now.'

'So, why now?' Fisk asked. 'Why use the name now?'

If I had the answer, it might have saved a lot of recent anxiety. The brunt of it was suffocating, brewing to the point we were now facing.

'The book wasn't my idea. You're probably aware that I've stayed away from Suffolk in my career, for good reason.' I closed my eyes and rubbed my temples. 'Given the nature of my subject matter, the notoriety that Hardacre Priory holds within the paranormal field, I have distanced myself from that place using my pen name. Having my connection to the Priory in print would have dragged me to Suffolk a long time ago, as it has now.'

Why had I used Hardacre and not my pseudonym for this book? The truth was that I hadn't. It had been proofed; I'd checked it myself. So, why hadn't it been noticed when the print run was delivered, the bookshop stock distributed? It had stared in bold, red letters when I opened the box to sign the limited numbers: *Oliver Hardacre*.

'It wasn't my choice.' I left the matter there and looked at the leather item.

'Of course.' Fisk's eye twitched with a slight frown, but he shook whatever thought it was away. 'We were surprised to find the section of the Priory quite short compared to other places in the county.'

'We?' I quizzed with a raised brow and tentatively pressed the hot mug to my lips.

'Raynham is a small village,' he countered with a flourish of his hands.

'If I'd had my way, Mr Fisk, it wouldn't have been included in the first place, despite its picture on the bloody cover.'

'Please, would you call me Nick? I feel we've come a long way since the telephone conversation. *You* have come a long way.' He smiled, easing the commitment behind his resolve a tad, but not entirely. The smile soon fell, and a steelier expression replaced it. 'Before you go any further, may I say something?'

I nodded. 'Go ahead.'

'You have been on an extraordinary journey. I don't mean returning to Suffolk; I'm referring to life.' Leaning forwards, elbows resting on the desk, he placed his hands either side of the leather object and pressed his palms onto the desk's surface. 'Not everyone is given a gift or curse of a family legacy such as Hardacre Priory. And, of course, you see it as a curse, don't you?'

I nodded again. The urge to add some sarcasm was too divine on my tongue, so I bit the impulse back. Fisk eyed the object, and a frown formed on his otherwise relatively smooth forehead. He was a conundrum, a young man with the intellect and personality of someone at least twice his age. I lost myself for a moment, watching him until he picked up the object and turned it over in his hands. Shafts of afternoon sun danced over the surface.

'There!' I leapt towards Fisk. My hand touched his as the object fell to the desk. 'Look! What's that?'

'Ah, well, what do you know?'

I picked it up, inspecting a small wax seal a little closer. Warmth from the sun softened the leather in my hand.

'How old do you think it is?' I asked.

It wasn't much longer than a handspan and no thicker than a few inches; whatever was inside had been tightly wrapped in leather, bound with a thin length of leather cord, and sealed with a wax stamp. The seal was worn, a little smooth and cracked, but intact.

'What am I to do with it?'

'That, I don't know.'

I placed it back on the desk and pushed it slightly away from me. I glanced at the letter. 'And what am I to make of that?'

'I don't have the answers you need,' Fisk said. 'I do have a solution that may help you find the answers yourself.'

'Look, I understand you're only doing your job, but I'm eager to get back home as soon as I can. That book has cast a shadow over my life, and with this and that letter... I need to get back home. Nothing good can come of any of this, that I do know.'

'Cast a shadow? Surely it opened a window.'

Something in those words scared me. I needed to get through the day and on the train home, then I could forget the whole thing. The book was out now. All the pomp was over, and I'd come out of it relatively unscathed. Fans and readers had taken the name change well after several articles and online interviews. I hadn't expected anything to bring me back to Suffolk.

Perhaps I'd underestimated Nick Fisk. All I could do was follow that queasy sensation in my gut. How much did he know? No more than what was in the book. No more than anyone else. I'd given nothing of my life away, hadn't included the detail of my living at the Priory. People had made a connection, but I stayed well clear of my relationship to that damned place.

However, this was Raynham, and Fisk was a local with a clear interest in the Priory. So, what were the stories of Hardacre Priory that truly flowed through generations? It was one thing documenting the history and transgressions of my ancestors, but gossip was another thing.

And unfortunately, gossip was more effective at concreting perceptions than fact.

FIVE

Despite Fisk's insistence, I turned down a lift to the pub. I knew where it was: at the bottom of the high street, no more than a few hundred yards away. The sunlight had hit the hanging sign as the green car rounded the corner and out of sight. As I thought on it more, it became clearer that Fisk was unsure about leaving me to my own devices.

My room at the Old Oak was the welcome slice of solitude that I'd been craving since I shut the front door of my cottage. I'd only left that morning, yet, in the cold light of evening, it may as well have been the last century. The dire awareness that the longer I was away from Whitby, the more a distant memory it would become shot panicked shock waves through me. I was beginning to feel like I'd never left Suffolk in the first place. The familiarity of the very air solidified my childhood.

The mood was different down here. It wasn't merely the people, the accents, the buildings—there was something in the atmosphere. It smelt different from back home, and it filled my head with those dark memories I'd locked away. That car, the letter, even Nick Fisk placed the key in my hand.

I hadn't mentioned the green car, or more significantly, the impression it pressed upon me. I wasn't sure how such a thing would be taken or understood; however, after having spent those two hours in Fisk's office, it was clear it wouldn't have been such an odd topic. There was, after all, a certain ambience to the Priory. It held an ominous fascination for everyone who knew its centuries of tales. Moreover, Fisk knew more than he was saying, of that I was certain. My fear was that I wouldn't be able to resist the Priory's lure. Could I resist turning the key, would I unleash whatever memories were buried inside?

Time was slow in Suffolk. Whitby would never hold the title of Most Fast-Paced, but here in the countryside, there was no marking the hours other than where the sun hung in the sky. It was low now, and although it had been a cold day, the winter sky had been bright. The afternoon had been swept away by the impending night's onslaught, harbouring its darkness and cold winds.

I'd eaten dinner in my room away from the crowded bar-restaurant. I'd considered the cottage pie but decided a simple sandwich and a side of chips would be easier. I had also turned down the offer of coffee—almost unheard of, but with the headache still hammering at my skull, water was my best bet.

I'd been lying on the bed for the most part of an hour, and the blasted migraine finally eased. I flicked the switch on the kettle nearby, ripped open the coffee sachet, and tipped the brown granules into a mug. If I were to suffer a winter night in Raynham, I would do it armed with caffeine. There would be no proper sleep anyhow. I'd stay awake all night if I had to, sleep on the train back. My ticket was an open return, but I had every intention of being on the first early train. And now, the thought of meeting with Fisk for morning coffee wavered my resolve. If steadfast tenacity was ever required, it was now, and I needed it in spades.

The bound leather object lay on top of my open holdall with the letter next to my phone. The urge to throw them both straight out of the window was almost suffocating.

I kept going over the afternoon with Fisk, desperate to grasp something I was missing. We had walked to the office door and said our pleasantries. After young Mikey cleared the coffee tray, Fisk gently closed the door behind him and turned, his hand on my shoulder. I'd already tucked the letter into my bag after he'd insisted on returning it. Then, he had made an odd remark: 'I have no need for the letter, but you, Oliver, you *both* do.'

I hadn't risen to it, but I had taken in every word. Except for the thought of its content and origins, which were too disturbing to process, Fisk had shed no more light on it. I'd gone over it twice more, traced my fingers over the ink. It was mine, of that there was no doubt—I used a particular turquoise ink that I purchased by mail order. But the blue biro scrawling...

The leather object was another matter. Fisk had been reluctant to let it go at first and had eyed my hand as I held it palm up, waiting for him to hand it over. 'Keep it on you,' he'd finally said. 'Best to keep it safe.'

Instinctively, I unzipped my holdall to place the object inside. Fisk grabbed my hand with a warning look. Not sure how to respond, I'd opened my jacket and popped the object close to my chest. It jolted me with a firebolt shock, ceasing my breath, then it was over. Within that second, it took hold of me, almost bonding to my very skin and bone.

'That is best, Oliver. Keep it close.'

Persistently, Fisk mentioned the Priory as my foot hit the path outside the solicitors. 'I shall bring the keys with me just in case. You never know—a hearty meal and good night's sleep can work wonders for the soul.'

'I assure you, I won't need it. Just a lift to the station if you could? Or I'm happy to get a taxi. I don't want to put you out.' It may have left my lips as a warning. If it had, I didn't apologise, and Fisk didn't seem to mind.

'No, no, it's no bother. I'd like to see you before you head back, maybe get you to sign my copy of *Behind the Ancient Doors of Suffolk* if you would oblige me?'

I softened a little. 'Yes, of course. It would be my pleasure,' I sighed. 'Except, I must stress the need to return to Whitby as soon as possible. I have a looming deadline.'

'Yes, of course. These bestsellers don't write themselves, do they?' He smiled then. 'There's no need for rash decisions surely, is there? I will meet you at The Old Oak in the morning, bright and early. We can discuss it again then.' He pressed his hand on my shoulder, then patted my chest over the pocket. 'Just remember to keep it close. It's worth bearing that in mind.'

Fisk disappeared back behind the door with a solemn smile, closing the street and me off.

Looking like a man out of time, I stood there unable to move, my back pressed to the small solicitors' window for support. A few locals passed by, not one batting an eyelid. I could have been invisible. I pulled my jacket collar tighter around my neck, touched my chest to check. It lay next to my heart, my rapid beat a tangible hammering.

I undressed, pulled back the thick duvet, sat on the bed sipping my coffee. It was hot, which was welcome. I nestled back against the pillow. I craved oblivious sleep, though in truth, if I dared at all, it would bring no peace. I held a deep-rooted fear of winter nights; the nightmares had followed me down to Suffolk. This was where they had formed. They had merely returned to roost.

SIX

Going down for breakfast had proven something of an event. Word travels fast in villages like this, and the local radio station had marked me as a celebrity staying at The Great Oak. I am no celebrity, but as far as the locals were concerned, I'd written a bestseller about the area's most celebrated haunted locations, even if the Priory only featured in one meagre chapter. That was the *celebrity* in this context. I was the mere channel, but I'd been cornered in the restaurant.

When I left my breakfast table, dozens of locals and tourists holding copies of *Behind the Ancient Doors of Suffolk* had gathered in the bar. Some carried paperbacks of previous history books and novels. I imagined the village bookshop had made a roaring trade this mundane Thursday morning. As long as they didn't request a book signing later today, we'd be okay. It wasn't that I didn't enjoy meeting readers and signing their books—they were the reason I'm able to write. I actually love hearing their thoughts and beliefs, especially their accounts of hauntings. It makes my blood pump a little faster. It's that I'm not particularly good at meeting people and making small talk.

I've been asked several times over the years—with every new book, to be precise—to do readings and book tours. My agent has stopped asking me now. I had done one early in my career. It was a small affair in hindsight, though, at the time, it was as daunting as jumping off a cliff with no more than my boxer shorts to break my fall. Facing the room of readers, fans, and a select few of the paranormal sector had started all

33

right. I had taken guidance from the shop owners, a large established independent store on three levels, but fallen flat on my face when it came to the reading. I stumbled over words, even those I created on the page.

This particular book was set in a manor house in my hometown of Whitby, one that had burned down in the 19th century. It had been my first novel. Until then, my writing career had been consumed with nonfiction histories. Not much had been documented on the manor, most of its story entangled in the nets of legend, tales passed through generations.

I'd stood in front of the crowd of eager ears and piercing eyes and stumbled over dates and names, strictly because of dreaded nerves. I was called out by a prominent parapsychologist who dissed my novel and said it wasn't history but a sheer fabrication, a sham. It hadn't been my finest hour. Explaining my sources had always been a sticking point. I ended the event early with emphatic apologies to the crowd of dedicated readers and fans, who had simply come to get their copy signed. It so happened the local press caught the story the next day, but the parapsychologist came off far worse. Rather than harm my status and then non-existent name as a novelist, it boosted my reputation in the genre. It was an overnight bestseller, and even marked a ghost tour around local sights named in the book: St Mary's Church and Whitby Abbey.

After that, I'd been adamant that putting myself in that situation again was a definite no.

Deep breaths, lots of smiles, and a steady hand would get me through this breakfast crowd before Fisk arrived. I smoothed my sweater sleeves around my shirt cuffs, fixed my smile, and made my way over to the landlady. Josie had introduced herself when I arrived—confident but not pushy, she was in her forties with shoulder-length red hair and lipstick to match. Pretty. Striking.

'Good morning, Mr Hardacre. A pen with your coffee this morning, I think?' Josie smiled. 'I took the liberty of making you a cappuccino. Does that work for you?' She winked as she touched my forearm. I looked at her polished red nails on the knit of my black cashmere sweater.

'That's very thoughtful, thank you.' Heat rose around my collar. I didn't have time for this. I smiled, careful not to make eye contact, and headed to a square table with a white cloth and one of the tall-back dining chairs pulled out ready. Josie had thought of everything, hadn't she? That made my skin prickle.

'There you are. Do you mind if I call you Oliver? I hope that's not too familiar,' she winked.

Josie placed the large cappuccino on the table, with two chocolate finger biscuits resting on the saucer. She pulled a silver Parker pen from her jacket pocket. It dangled from her fingers as she waited for me to take it.

'Thank you, that's considerate,' I whispered, casting an eye to the waiting crowd who were beginning to quieten down, their excited chatter dispersing in the dark panelled walls, leaving me feeling exposed.

'Not at all. It's not every day we have anyone of real fame in our sleepy little village. You know how it is around here, Oliver.'

I couldn't help looking at her then. There was a tang of something in that last line. A knowing. But she just smiled back, her red lips parting in a beam that reached her eyes. I glanced at the pen. As I went to take it, Josie closed her fingers around it and watched my hand as it awkwardly hovered between us.

'I'll have it back once you've finished with it.'

I withdrew my hand, feeling somewhat abashed by the remark. She smiled softly with something unsaid on her upturned lips.

'Silly.' Josie placed the Parker on the table in front of me. 'I'm just teasing you, Mr Oliver Hardacre.'

My hand laid flat over the pen in an easy gesture, but there was no mistaking the steel rod it thrust up my spine. I pressed my back against the chair.

'Thank you for letting me use your pen.'

She nodded, glancing at my fingers and tapped my hand. 'Of course.'

I didn't count how many books I signed. How many personally inscribed dedications I wrote. My face ached from smiling. I'd run out of small talk, my mind an unusual buzz from the endless conversation, although, I must confess, I *had* enjoyed it. When the book was released, my biggest fear was the backlash, the suggestions, and downright accusations of it being fiction and not factual history at all. Maybe in any other town or village in the country, it had been greeted by scepticism, but the villagers of Raynham knew the history they were part of.

I drained the last drop of my cold coffee, clicked the Parker pen, and imagined the look on Josie's face if I slipped it into my pocket. I couldn't help smiling as I rose from my seat and pushed the chair back under the table. I noticed a woman on the other side of the room with an anxious look and a well-read copy tucked under her arm as she leant against the bar Josie stood behind. Something so familiar about them both.

'Go on,' Josie mouthed to the woman, pressing her hand on her shoulder.

The woman took an audible breath as if bracing herself. I felt a pang of immense guilt at wanting this all to be over so I could head home to Yorkshire. I waited, but she didn't move. Okay, there was nothing for it—I would go to her.

'Hello,' I mumbled. 'So many people. I had no idea.'

The woman looked directly into my eyes, nailing me to the spot, engulfing me with a desire to shrink down inside my sweater.

36

As she went to speak, the grim expression fell to reveal a gentle smile. 'Hello, Oliver. I don't think you'll remember me, but...'

The thunderbolt hit me square on, firing memories at me from every direction. I no longer stood in The Great Oak; I was back in the rustic seaside pub in Whitby, the grief-stricken feeling of loss heavy in my chest as the vision of Vera and Bob flooded in, swiping my feet from under me.

'Mrs Scarfe?'

'You do remember. I was hoping you would, but time passes so quickly, and it's been so many years. You were only a young man then.' A mortified look fell over her face. 'You're still a young man, of course.'

'Oh, Mum, stop it,' Josie said. 'It's just our Oli. Don't go all gaga because he's a big celebrity author now.'

I gripped the edge of the bar. Josie's words, with a twinkle in her bright eyes, didn't sink in until the door slammed behind us.

'Goodness, it's windy out there. The heavens are sending a warning, of that I have no doubt. It's a harsh one coming. The skies are clouding over.'

'Ah, Nick. You missed all the excitement this morning,' Josie announced with a laugh.

'The book signing by a local author, was it?' Fisk headed towards the bar, winking at me as he did.

'Our Oliver has been obliging us with his time. Quite the hit, especially with all the ladies.'

I gazed at Josie, then at Mrs Scarfe. I blushed. 'I'm sorry, I'm confused.'

'You really don't remember me, do you?' Josie asked incredulously. I felt my face redden under her gaze.

'I... you are Mrs Scarfe's daughter?'

'Of course, I am, silly. I know it was years ago... I thought you'd remember.'

Guilt and embarrassment—all the emotions I avoided— were overwhelming. This was why I didn't people well. I was sure it was showing on my face, too.

Josie grabbed my hand. 'It's okay. I have changed a lot. But you…' she teased, leaning closer, her eyes twinkling as they creased a little at the corners. 'Yes, still the same boy in there.'

I couldn't tell if that was a compliment. Something about the whip of Mrs Scarfe's head in Fisk's direction told me it was nothing of the sort.

'Well, I just caught a couple of people holding copies of your latest book on my way in. They looked mighty pleased with themselves.' Fisk glanced Josie's way. 'And on that note… One more to sign, if you don't mind after the morning, you must have had?'

I took the hardback copy, opened it, and clicked the pen.

Fisk turned to Mrs Scarfe. 'You got yours signed, I see.'

'Oh, not yet. Sorry, Mrs Scarfe,' I apologised, closing the cover handing Fisk the book back. 'What would you like me to write?'

'Oh, I don't need it signed,' Mrs Scarfe said, her cheeks pink. 'I didn't come to get it signed. Of course, that would be nice, thank you.' She handed me her well-read copy.

'If not to have it signed, then why did you bring it?' I asked.

Mrs Scarfe hesitated as she looked from me to Fisk, her eyes narrowed. She lingered a little longer on his. 'Because I need to tell you something.'

The winter's chill of that night forty years ago was as vivid as Mrs Scarfe's face as she stared at me. The look in her eyes said far more than her words. There was a panic behind them that her voice didn't let slip. In that instance, I was a boy again with all those fears crawling up my arms until horror's devious hands were around my throat, ready to choke me.

Only, it was another's face I saw, another's sad eyes.

I needed to get out of there. The dark panelling was swallowing me like all the morning light.

'Oliver has no time now,' Fisk said. 'Don't you need to get back?'

I swung around to see his face turned from mine, my eyes fixed on the book in his hands. The image of Hardacre Priory stared back at me from the cover. In an instant, the book was no longer in his grip but flying across the room. It struck the mirrors behind the bar. Optic spirit bottles smashed into shards, splintered glass tore through the air. A shower of sticky, wet liquor spattered every surface.

Josie screamed. 'What the hell?'

'It wasn't me.' Fisk's voice trembled. 'I don't know what happened.'

Josie grabbed some bar towels in a meagre attempt to mop up the mess. Long shards of glass still bombarded the bar in a relentless assault.

'No! Move, now!' My voice wasn't my own, even as I shouted over the smashing glass.

Rows of bottles flung themselves off the mirrored shelves. Spotlights exploded one by one with flashes of fluorescent sparks.

Josie scrambled out from behind the bar with her arms wrapped over her head and threw herself into her mum's arms. Fisk pulled the women to the far wall. The small leaded windows gave little light to the darkened room, but there was no mistaking the devastation.

I had no reasoning for what I did next, nor could I explain the voice that whispered somewhere inside me, urged me, compelled me. Yet, at that moment, it was the high-pitched cracking that splintered my nerves.

I threw a glance back to the others, seeing nothing except fear, confusion, and pulled my mobile from my pocket. Swiping the torch app, I pointed it towards the long mirror. Most of the surface was dashed with small, shattered areas, but a crack had started from the far-left side. It slowly split, rupturing into fragmented veins. Holding my phone out, I walked around the wooden bar, anxiously pointing it towards the mirror, revealing a shattered reflection of myself. I reached out.

Without comprehension, I pressed the tip of my forefinger to the cold glass. Every instinct told me to pull away; instead, my finger whitened under pressure. Then it grew wet. Red droplets dripped onto the mixed puddles of potent liquor. I pulled my finger through each sharp break, tiny fracture of the broken mirror. The sensation of my ripping flesh jolted up my arm. The sound of splinters cracked beneath the pressure in my ears.

'Oliver, stop it.' Mrs Scarfe ran towards me, pulling at my arm. 'Look at your hand.'

Though loud in my ear, her voice was nothing more than a distant murmur compared to the deafening screams in my mind. I saw her reflection beside me, a face of panic. But I no longer saw me, Oliver—the man I had become—but the terrified boy of that night forty years ago. Mr Scarfe saw it too. She pulled away and dropped her hand. My arm fell, spraying a single strand of red specks over the front of her dress. I stepped back from the glass, my elbows on the bar behind me, and took in what I'd done.

The mirror was cracked from corner to corner, a long splinter of broken glass smeared with blood.

Fisk's hand was on my shoulder. 'I think we need to leave.'

I'd never heard desperation sound so urgent.

He pulled my arm. 'Now.'

'I don't understand,' Josie cried. 'What have you done?'

It wasn't until I saw what was on the mirror that her words began to have two meanings. I hadn't only followed the fracture with my finger, but my blood also highlighted words in the cracks:

You killed him.

SEVEN

I held the bandage tightly around my finger. The white dressing grew red as I squeezed. Thankfully, the pain numbed a little more. The real agony was that those words had unlocked something bleak, something terrible. Memories are like vultures: they circle their prey, bide their time, then strike when you are most vulnerable.

I had been bundled into Fisk's car. He was driving, and we were alone. I supposed Mrs Scarfe and Josie were clearing up the mess. Guilt was palpable on my skin. I felt it as I ran my fingernails over my neck, trying to scratch away the sensation I was being watched. The eyes that were on me now had been watching me all my life. I would never escape them.

'I have your bag,' Fisk said. 'It's on the back seat. Did you pack it properly?'

I didn't answer. My mind was still repeating the bloody words.

'Oliver? Is it in your holdall?' Fisk pulled over on the quiet country lane. 'You remember the item I gave you?

The mechanical ticking of the indicators aggravated my nerves.

'What?'

'Okay, Oliver. This is really important. Please. Is the leather object I gave you in your holdall?'

I frowned. 'Um, yes. Yeah, I think so. It should be.'

'Good.' Fisk frantically revved the car as we sped off. His shaking hands gripped the steering wheel. 'Good.'

'What about the bar, the mirror?' I asked. 'Is Josie okay?'

'They are fine.'

'Oh hell, the mess. I need to pay for the damage.'

'It wasn't your fault, was it? In truth, I…'

Neither of us spoke again for a while. I closed my eyes and allowed my mind to wander anywhere other than here. The thought of being back on that train home to Whitby warmed my cheeks. Vera's face flew into my head, a familiar vision that appeared whenever I needed comfort. She had been good at that, had always known when I needed it or when to leave me alone with my demons. But this time, it wasn't the face I recognised. It wasn't her customary smile that dimpled her left cheek.

'How well do you know Mrs Scarfe?'

'Gloria? Well, I've lived in Raynham all my life.'

'That's not what I asked.'

Fisk turned left at the next junction. The forefinger on his right hand twitched as he pulled on the steering wheel. We swerved into a concealed driveway, and he turned off the ignition. The engine died, plunging the car into a silence that made my ears buzz.

'Why is that?' Fisk asked.

'I remember her.'

There wasn't so much hesitation as deliberation painted on his face. I saw the look in his eyes as he arranged the words before they left his lips.

I'd done my fair share of people-watching to collect characters. Nick Fisk was one of those. There was an oddity, an eccentricity, about him that I couldn't put my finger on. Not that I was one to talk—I'd been described as far worse over the years. The more I was with him, the more I wondered about his motives. Was I unnecessarily suspicious?

I nodded to encourage the words he was holding on to. 'Gloria?'

'Oliver, Raynham, despite the ample size of the village, is a small place when it comes to its traditions and beliefs. Things are handed down through generations, you see.'

He unclipped his seatbelt to face me. For the first time, I properly saw the age that sat behind his young disguise.

'I know many places like that,' I affirmed.

'Precisely. Places like ours aren't unusual. Villages all over the country have their own legends. You've lived in Whitby most of your life. You know what I mean about legends and folklores, don't you?'

I nodded.

Fisk took a deep breath, filling his chest to concrete his convictions. 'Did you know I've read all your books? Every one of them. I know full well that you comprehend the power that places like Hardacre Priory possess. You, of all people, recognise the magnitude of that. Outsiders may not understand. To them, a book like *Behind the Ancient Doors of Suffolk* is a fantasy, talking of ghosts and curses, feeding the appetite of those who relish the lure of the supernatural. We both know it's nothing of the sort. You're not an outsider, so stop thinking like one.'

'What are you saying?'

'Do you really need me to spell it out? You see them, all of them. That's how you write their histories. I'm right, aren't I?' Fisk pushed his hand to his forehead. 'You're a Hardacre—the *last* Hardacre.' The blood-smeared graze on the back of his hand peeked out from under his jacket cuff. 'It's been a long morning, hasn't it?'

'I don't know what happened at the pub,' I said. 'I can't explain it.'

His gaze pierced me, a swift knife through my skull. I stared at him, and his eyes bore back.

'When will you acknowledge the power this place has over you? It's always been there. I know it, and so do you.'

43

'That's why I'm going home—I don't belong here anymore. I may have spent my boyhood here in Raynham and Bury, but the Priory robbed me of my childhood. I won't give it, you or anyone the satisfaction of robbing me of anything else.'

'So, what's your plan then?'

'I'll return to Yorkshire on the early afternoon train. I'll go home to my normality and my life,' I sighed, then inhaled sharply. 'I have work to do, a deadline, a book to finish.'

Fisk shook his head. 'When will it sink in? This is your home. This is where you belong.'

My heart thumped against my ribcage. I felt betrayed.

Sweat was mounting under my shirt collar; I felt the heat rise along with the anger. I unclipped my belt and swivelled in my seat to see out of the car windows. We were surrounded by fields on two sides, with the narrow road winding off in front of us. What glowered at me through my window seized the air from my lungs. It had me in its grasp just as it always had.

I grabbed my jacket and closed the car door behind me, and stood at an old crossroads. We parked in what was once the entrance to a drive, a clearing, a narrow roadway that disappeared into the bare trees. Opposite, a dirt farm track divided the barren fields as far as the eye could see, all painted with an endless expanse of steel-blue sky. No thatch or tile roof to split the view. I filled my lungs with the brisk air and took in the scene of my youth. And just like that winter I remembered, the sky was growing dark with threatening clouds. The east wind whipped the hem of my jacket, and I pulled the collar up close around my neck.

Fisk stood within the opening of his driver's door, hesitation thick on his face. I nodded.

At the entrance to the narrow drive was the great oak tree that featured as the backdrop to my nightmares. It served as the landmark of horror more than the Priory did when it came to my brother's memory. Every winter, midnight images of its lumbering boughs and twisted limbs reached out to me. There's no describing the sensation that filled me, consumed me whole. I knew all its secrets.

And it knew all of mine.

Fisk's shoes fell in line with my footfall. My feet had taken me around the oak tree, my hands skimmed the trunk's bark. It could have been witnessed as a tender gesture reminiscing in the laments of a missed childhood, but this is *my* story, not that of a typical youth who had rambled through woods climbing trees. There was nothing affectionate in my touch. It was filled with nothing other than loathsome contempt.

The need to place myself here was so strong, but the compulsion to dig my nails into the tree took me by surprise. If I could have made it bleed, I would have gashed it open, torn it branch from branch. To hear its cries as it had heard mine might have soothed my soul just enough.

My eyes travelled up to the thick bough that hung overhead. It pointed in the direction I had to go. I saw us then: two boys playing in its shadow, collecting acorns from the mass of fallen leaves and tiny twigs. Had we been as innocent as we had imagined ourselves to be? We'd been ourselves, doing what came naturally… and all those terrible things that came unnaturally.

'Oliver.' Fisk held the leather object in his outstretched hand. 'I took the liberty. I think you will need this.'

It was true. Whatever was under this age-old leather wrapping was fundamental. It held power. To deny it at this point would have been imprudent. I had sensed it as soon as it met my chest in my breast pocket. A power seeped from it, and it was taking something from me too. It kept calling me. I tightly closed my hand around it. As it melded to my palm, my heart quickened. Fisk's eyes widened. His head whipped up to the top of the vast oak tree. The land trembled beneath our feet. All those memories of my brother flew from the top of the branches, crashed down over me, stealing my breath. I fell to my knees. Bone-chilling cold travelled up my legs into my hands. I gripped the leather object tight—I wouldn't let go.

Thick branches twisted and snapped. The brash wind whipped leaves up from the ground; a dense whirlwind of debris swirled around us, keeping us fixed.

'Hold on to it,' Fisk shouted over the wind.

I nodded; my eyes closed against the spiralling leaves with the leather clenched in my fist. I couldn't fathom what I was holding, but my instinct swore I'd never give up another thing to this damned place. From within my soul, from my very lineage, I knew it was imperative to my survival, whatever this was. Without it, I would perish like the rest of them.

Fisk reached for me; his arms stretched as far as humanly possible. His fingers grasped at the air as he staggered towards the vortex.

Scrambling to my feet with my hands pressed to the earth, I pushed the object into my jacket pocket. My fingers found the vast tree roots. I dug my nails into the bark, stripped away the thick green mulch and moss, and found a foothold between them. My brother had climbed this tree that day. The fear had been fierce in my chest; I'd watched in both awe and contempt of his dexterity. To have him here with me now… I shook the idea from my head. I was here because of us.

'No.' The sound came from my lungs as a rasping, desperate cry. My fingers found Fisk's in a knotted attempt, and he pulled me into the clearing.

The creaking, twisting of brittle branches, the rushing wind—it all fell silent. All that coursed around us remained suspended in the atmosphere, a motionless sight of impossible measures hovering in the chill.

I fell to the ground, my hand pressed to my pocket. Numbness tingled through each limb as I tried to breathe.

'It knows I'm back.'

'I can see that.' Fisk knelt on the ground and patted my shoulder. 'But you're not alone, Oliver.'

'I wasn't alone last time. I had my family.'

'Yes, you did, but I wasn't implying myself. I was referring to that.'

Fisk pulled the leather object from my pocket. Holding it up in front of him, he walked towards the tree. I waited, but I knew it wouldn't rise to the gesture. Fisk shoved the object at the tree as if to taunt it, to garner some reaction. Instead, the suspended debris, the array of winter-worn sticks and greenery silently fell to the ground. The wind ceased, and the great oak regained its composure.

'It wants me,' I said. 'And it's annoyed that I'm armed.'

EIGHT

What we witnessed isn't easily explained. Occurrences such as this don't often happen, those snippets in time when we imagine the possibility that the supernatural, the paranormal—whatever you like to call it—exists. Often, we dismiss these as mere tricks of the brain, flashes and sparks of miss-signals, miss-communications between the grey matter. Few people accept them for what they are. When they happen, it is vital to take note; and there was no mistaking the ominous nature of what we had witnessed.

Evil lay at the root of this, and it had risen to greet me.

I'd written as much. My book was a document of these unexplained happening. The section on the Priory's history, the truth as I knew it and stories, I'd felt first-hand. In my dreams, I had witnessed the validity of all those generations who had suffered before me. When writing, I put aside the fact that I had memories that belonged to my forebears; they flowed in my blood and out through my fingertips. The irony was that my own memories were no clearer than mud. Putting my feet back on home soil only cemented my certainty that I was about to throw some clarity on my memories—a prospect that terrified me to the core.

'So, what now?' Fisk handed me the leather object, his hands on his knees to catch his breath. He eyed me over his brow. 'Do you want me to drive you to the station?'

'The answer should be *yes*, shouldn't it?' I said. 'No man in their right mind would want to go any further. I know what lies beyond this point. The oak tree is just the edge.'

'That didn't answer my question. You do have a choice.'

'Do I? To be honest, I'm not sure I have ever had a choice over any of it. Life keeps throwing me curveballs. The past has a habit of catching up with me.' I ran my fingers through my hair, relieved I still had any. 'Gloria is a fine example of that.'

Fisk's brow furrowed. He stood and rubbed his hands together for warmth. 'What has Gloria got to do with your past?'

'She was there. So was Josie, though I can't recall her. Vera, the woman who took me into her home and raised me as her own, was Gloria's sister.'

'Oh, I see. And what does that mean?'

'It means that I never really left Suffolk. That my new life in Yorkshire has always been tethered to my past. I never outran it.'

'Maybe you're reading too much into it.'

'Perhaps. Except, we both know that's unlikely. So, if I went back now, ran away again, it would be pointless, wouldn't it?'

Fisk nodded with a swift smile. 'Sooner or later, it would catch up. You're no longer Oliver Hardacre, the outsider.'

'Exactly.' I placed the object next to my heart.

'Well, come on then,' Fisk said. 'I suppose if you've made up your mind, there's no time like the present.'

'Are you coming with me?'

'I've come this far. What kind of man would I be if I just left you here? Especially after witnessing that,' he exclaimed, pointing to the tree, shaking his head.

'A sane one.'

'Quite.' Fisk glanced at his watch, then at the sky. 'It's a little past eleven—not that you'd guess by the look of it.'

The steel-blue sky was dark, a few shades gloomier and thick with thunderous clouds blocking the sun. We were still standing in the great oak's shadow. Fisk's car and the road were visible from here. Beyond it lay the barren fields. There hadn't been another car for at least ten minutes as we stood talking; we were utterly alone in the ominous, deafening silence.

We looked at each other for a few moments, pondering on the next move. Aware of the sudden temperature drop, I shivered, my teeth chattering inside my skull. I patted my breast pocket for reassurance and walked to the old lane.

'You have it safe?' Fisk asked.

Feeling my resolve, I nodded, then retrieved the leather object from my pocket for a second check. I held it between us. The storm clouds split in two — not with the expected rain, but with sunrays. A shaft of blinding gold light hit the leather object and cast it in a warm amber glow, clarifying the seal; every line, every carved contour of the wax matrix refined until it was as clear as on the day it had been made. I'd seen it before.

'Well, will you look at that? This day is getting more...' There was a laugh in Fisk's hesitation.

I smiled in return. The hairs on the back of my neck stood to attention. The eyes behind me, those that were always watching, came closer.

We headed towards the lane, leaving that wretched oak at the crossroads. The sun was bright on our backs, though the ground grew frosty with every step. The debris that would have been a crispy russet only a few weeks ago was a decaying brown and rotting underfoot, edged with glistening white frost. I kicked at it. My toes dug into the mulch as it grew brittle under my soles.

The frost grew slowly at first. Despite the heat of the morning sun, I watched as the leafy ground of the lane whitened before my eyes, a carpet of frozen vines and roots. With every step, coiled creepers and knotted roots unravelled creaked and disentangled to allow us in. Frost grew underfoot until anxiety froze my heart.

We were being invited.

Life outside the Priory's boundary vanished in our wake. More terrifying was the realisation that we were heading into a place that marked itself outside of time and normality. I feared Nick Fisk wasn't fully aware of this matter but kept my thoughts to myself. The reality of it would soon rise to challenge our convictions—something that the solicitor had in bounds. I, on the other hand, feared I had lived the past forty years in hiding.

Several minutes of walking passed without a spoken word between us, yet my thundering heart against the object's warm leather was prominent. The land was white as far as we could see. Trees that lined the lane were no more than sticks that reached up to the murky clouds, piercing the sky with bony fingers. The thick bramble ground untwisted with every step, moving, alive even though it spoke of death.

I have tried many times to put this feeling into words. Coming face to face with the horrors of my nightmares isn't an easy thing to describe. Words fall short no matter how many times I edit and rewrite them. A child's vivid imagination is likely to replay a moment in time, snippets of something so terrifying with an intensity much darker than reality. It would be forgivable to think that revisiting those memories as an adult would shed light as only a rational mind could.

Forgivable, but wrong.

With the lane now far behind and Fisk by my side, I stood in the overgrown entrance driveway to my ancestral home.

The ground was now covered in ice. Beneath it, I imagined the gravel I'd known as a child—the sharp, grey stones that orchestrated grazed knees. The landscape around us was low and barren— wild lawns of long ago, sparse, and white. The whole aspect that filled our eyes was one of brash coldness. Central to all stood the ominous structure of Hardacre Priory.

Before I could think of what lay on the other side of those stone walls, I pressed my hand to the old wooden door.

Fisk rushed to my side, rummaging in his pocket. He placed the key in my hand—the blasted key I'd been dreading to hold.

'Can you hear them?' I pressed my ear to the door.

My companion answered with a shrug and vague look of confusion.

The key slid into the lock, melting the frost around it as it did. My shaking hand turned the iron ring handle until the lock's heavy bar on the other side clunked.

I stood on the brink, my feet on the worn stone of the deep porch. The door opened inwards with so much ease I wondered if something pulled it from inside.

I smelled the decay—it filled my head—yet all I saw was the lurid image of my crippled childhood. Entering the Priory's halls was an open invitation—not for me, but for every ill wish, vengeful thought, and wicked deed that ever existed.

PART TWO

THE PAST
September 1979

NINE

Nancy pulled on the handbrake, exhaled, her leg quivered as she eased her foot off the pedal. Cursing under her breath, she gazed up at the view she had been dreading.

Their destination boldly sat on its foundations, solid and tolerant of its surroundings without embracing them. It was doubtful it had ever been one with the landscape. Maybe it had sat at peace in its first incarnation, but no longer. Now it was a building at odds with nature—flora, fauna, and human alike.

Twisted brick chimneys rose like serpents from the grey stone walls and bit at the indifferent sky, while leaded windows stared across the grounds with cataract eyes. They sliced the reflection of the grim steel atmosphere and none more so than the rose window framed by a steep gable. The round stonework framing its silver eye glared with defiance, a statement of *how dare you look at me? How dare you be here?*

This was Hardacre Priory.

After snaking its course, avoiding dips and holes along the narrow lane, the car came to a stop on the broad stretch of the stoned drive. Filthy, sparse gravel littered with clumped, dead weeds wound towards the vast entrance. No foliage as far as the eye could reach. Instead, bare trees lined the boundaries like skeletal soldiers standing their ground. Whether they guarded the house or those who visited was unclear but stand their ground they did with their fingers outstretched in a warning.

The keys jangled in the ignition as the radio blared from the newly polished Hillman Avenger, its metallic olive paintwork the only green in the landscape. It was modern and out of place against the imposing stone edifice and the vast expanse of unwelcoming nature.

Two small pairs of hands wiped the condensation from the windows as both sets of eyes gawped at the austere exterior. It was bigger than anything they'd ever seen and as gloomy and miserable as their nightmares. Not a cloud in the sky today—their mother had said this as if it were a blessing. Here there was neither summer nor the start of autumn. The icy cold of winter hovered overhead like a beast biding its time until it was ready to strike.

These two didn't know why they were here, especially now. After all the tears of the last couple of months, after everything they had lost, all they wanted was to go back home. But that was gone now too. Sold to a couple with no children. A couple from London with smart clothes and smart voices, using words these two didn't understand or cared to. Who would play in the backyard now and talk to old Mr Beardsmore through the broken fence? Who would water the strawberry patch at the bottom near the tree swing? No one— they knew that; hadn't needed to be told. Their home had *gone to the dogs*, as Dad would have said.

'Do not move, do you hear me?' A deep sigh followed, quickly catching the question before it turned into an order. 'Please? Do this for me, you two, will you?' Twin heads nodded. 'I'll be back as soon as I can. Stay here in the car, okay? I need to have a quick word with your... Just stay in the car.'

The engine's rumble stopped beneath the radio's blare. The driver's door shut a little too briskly, sending a judder through the car. Nancy stood a second or two, looking back at everything she had left in the world. That car, as frivolous as it had seemed when she bought it, held all she had left:

those boys. And despite the secrets, the pain, the death, and loss, surely, she was doing the right thing.

That fear crept over her shoulders every night when she lay alone thinking about the choice she had made. Now it sat on her shoulder, a dark angel waiting to take her too. *It is as it should be.* She would rebel against that statement for as long as she breathed, no matter how much she dodged it every step and every choice along the way, and there had been many. *To the ends of the earth*, she had vowed *before they ever set foot here*. Yet here they were. And there was absolutely nothing she could do to stop it.

Soft, wayward strands of mousy brown hair. Dark eyes that drilled into her heart every time they looked her way. Her boys, her twins, a mirror image of each other, they were two halves of one whole, and as a whole, they were every bit the same as their father. They were just boys; they didn't deserve this, any of it, yet she knew the worst was still to come. They would be tested, all of them.

'Curse you, you bastard,' Nancy muttered, pulling the collar of her red coat about her throat, tugging the belt tight around her waist. 'May you rot in hell for this.' She kicked the gravel, settled her leather boot hard on the ground, and marched to the front door.

Elliot sat back. The tan leather creaked as he pushed his feet against the back of the front car seat. He thudded the soles of his new trainers in rhythm with the radio—a determined *thud* with every word.

His brother hadn't moved, his face still pressed against the cold glass and his eyes cast high staring back at the round window. Moisture ran down to his chin as Elliot nudged him.

'Oi.' Still no movement. 'Oliver!' Elliot shouted, jabbing his elbow into his brother's ribs.

Oliver slowly turned; his moist fringe stuck to his forehead. Rather than respond, he looked past Elliot out of the opposite car window towards the gardens to the trees. To the oak.

It had caught him on the drive up the lane, hooked his thoughts with its long-reaching branches. It wasn't the size of the tree that had caught his attention, even though it was the biggest he'd ever seen. Of course, they had trees in town—the park had lots—but this was more than that. Mother had braked hard as she turned onto the narrow lane where the tree dominated the crossroads. He didn't know why, but she had pulled the handbrake, her white hands gripping the steering wheel. Oliver had felt it: the great lumbering boughs of the oak twisting and creaking towards the car. Its long, pointy branches had peered through his window as if it winked at him.

Mark me, it said. *Mark me, boy.*

It knew him, and he knew it.

Nancy pushed on the door; it creaked with a low groan, not so much a protest as an enticement. It was large and dominating, like the building it lay admission to. This door had hung as the entrance to the Priory for centuries since the beginning. It had borne witness to every visitor, friend, or foe. Now it was dark, riddled with the sin of all the hands that had touched its iron ring handle.

And it was pulling her in.

She wouldn't succumb to the bait, but it had hit her as soon as she turned off the village road and onto the lane: their arrival had been noted.

Nancy wrapped her fingers around the edge of the door and took a tentative step inside onto the black-and-white tiled floor. Wintry light filtered into the area before her. She winced.

A tall male figure stood to one side; his hand swept the way before her. 'Welcome, Mrs Hardacre. Lady Hardacre is waiting in the drawing-room. Would you like to go through?'

Nancy flipped her hair over her shoulder as she glanced back to look at the car. The boys were still in there. They hadn't moved. The music was still blaring, the car juddering with its rhythm.

'Be thankful for small mercies,' she breathed and pushed the door just a touch. 'My boys are out there. I don't want to leave them outside too long.' The fleeting thought of them all camping in the car was pleasing. She could find a quiet country spot. They could hide. No one would know.

Ludicrous. She scorned herself for the notion.

'I thought it best to settle things first.' She stared into the shadows as she waited.

'Through into the drawing-room, madam.'

Nancy turned from the tall shadow figure and followed his gesture towards the heavy carved door.

'So, you are all here.' The voice came from inside.

'Not all of us.' Deep sadness slipped from those words in hot tears, yet Nancy sniffed them back and stood fierce.

'No, not all of you.'

'Can I come in?'

'Of course. You have always been welcome here, my dear.'

That was a lie.

'Let Dawson get your things.'

'No.' She caught her breath before an extra wave of panic rode in. 'No, it's okay. The boys are still in the car.'

'Whenever you are ready, my dear; however, you won't let them sit out there getting cold now, will you?'

Nancy stepped over the threshold and left all her confidence behind her. A shuffle bought the voice and face she had been dreading to see clearer.

'I remember the day you left. I never thought I would see you set foot on the grounds again, let alone through these doors. Your arrival has been quite a sensation in these halls,' Lady Hardacre stated.

'I'd no choice, really, did I?' The hot retort came far too easy. 'You saw to that.'

It needed no reply. Lady Hardacre's expression spoke of abandonment, of lost promises and grief. Then the face turned from hers. 'Come on then, let us get you settled in. This place has no time for regrets, yours or mine. They get lost between the cracks in the floorboards.'

Nancy followed her farther in. Her heart was pounding, resisting all that felt natural and good. She turned back to check the door was still ajar and watched it a moment.

For God's sake, keep it together.

She had done nothing but curse the air blue for these past weeks. How could he have done this to her? It wasn't her own pity that made her angry but the thought of her boys having to go through the inevitable, which she had done her damndest to avoid for almost a decade. They had vowed that this was the last place the boys would go, no matter how it turned out. He had promised her. After everything, the past had come back to haunt them all, had taken him away and left her to ramble alone through the mire that would be her future.

Nancy followed the old woman deeper into the drawing-room. Lady Estelle Hardacre hadn't aged in the past ten years; Nancy saw no change at all. She even wore the same rose-pink floral tea-dress she had worn to welcome her that first day so awfully long ago. The slow gait of her stride was as weak as ever yet hadn't deteriorated as Nancy had expected. What had she presumed to find? An older and more withered Estelle, perhaps.

Estelle gazed over her shoulder a moment, her blonde hair scrolled in coils like always, her eyes just as sharp.

Nancy paced the room. She couldn't bring herself to look at Estelle's face—it made her skin bristle. There was guilt there, although the repulsion was too intense. It was, after all, a mark of this house and the way it crippled its occupants.

Nancy kept her eyes down, regarding every scratch and scuff on her brown leather boots, each abrasion a reflection of the scars her heart bore. She was a woman in pieces.

'Will you please sit down?' Estelle insisted. 'Pacing the floorboards won't help. You will wear out the Persian.'

Estelle moved slowly, shivering in the cold air from the windowpane as Nancy approached. They stood and gazed out into the white vista, timeless and bleak. The stark reality of the shiny green car and the two boys, the last Hardacre generation, stared back.

'I won't let you have them,' Nancy said.

'I have no intention of doing such a thing. They are my blood too.'

'You won't have that either.'

'This is their home, Nancy. It's where they belong, you know that. Always so melodramatic. You have not changed, have you? Grief has not mellowed you; I see.'

'*Mellowed* me? How bloody dare you.'

The instinct to run was tangible, but Estelle gripped her hand and pressed Nancy's palm to the stone windowsill, keeping her put.

'I have never been particularly good at apologising,' Estelle said. 'Please remember that they are not always my words.'

Nancy knew it was true, no matter how much she resisted.

'It will be as it always has been,' Estelle said. 'You know I have no control over matters.'

There was a pacifying residue to those last words. Nancy doubted it was genuine regret or remorse for the old wound. If she allowed herself to think on it, she knew that this old and frail woman had no way of altering what was to come any more than she could change generations and centuries of history. To think on that fact for too long only bought other emotions. Nancy wasn't ready to dampen her anger, mollify herself to a more temperate mood. Maybe she liked the rage. It kept grief away from her door along with the wolf.

'I'll arrange some tea,' Estelle announced. 'Some hot chocolate for the boys—all little boys like hot chocolate. Are they coming in?'

'They don't like it.'

'Don't be silly. Every boy loves a mug of cocoa. Just like their father.'

'Oh, dear God. Don't even think about it. How dare you? You know nothing about them. They are mine; do you hear me?'

Nancy felt it bubble inside her chest. She pressed her hand to her throat. The walls were folding in on her as they had that first visit. The very skeleton of the house heard and recognised every one of her emotions. It had leaked into her skin that first day, and she'd done her damndest to cleanse herself of it ever since.

'Fuck you…' Nancy scanned the walls. 'And your curses.'

'Oh, my dear. This will not help, will it? Now, we had best calm down.'

'How can I be calm?' Nancy's hands whitened at the knuckles. Her fingers gripped the top of the ornate radiator. The old paint peeled off the metal ridges, and shards dug up under her nails. Tiny beads of blood pooled at the ends of her fingers. She lifted her hands as scarlet drops hit the windowsill and the floor. 'It's so cold. The whole damned house is always so bloody cold.'

Estelle sighed so audibly Nancy felt the rafters rattle in disgust at her arrival. The Priory hated her as much as she hated it, and that was what she feared the most—that deep down, far more than oak and plaster lay within these walls.

'Look.' Estelle's grip was tight.

Nancy edged a little farther into the stone casement window.

'You go fetch the boys in. Get all your cases from the car while I get Lizzie to warm the pot. Tea will help.'

'You really don't get it, do you?'

'Or perhaps something a little stronger? I will drop a little in yours.' Estelle eyed her, cautious at first until it weighed Nancy down. 'I know why you are so angry. I wanted to, but I couldn't. You know that.'

'Your own son,' Nancy spat.

'I cannot leave the Priory.'

'Not even to say goodbye? Your only son lies rotting in the earth, and you didn't even have enough heart to be there.'

'There is no place for me out there. Not now. My time has passed.' Estelle stared out far beyond the boundary of the grounds. Her gaze reached into the past, where the ghosts of all who had gone before her hovered.

'I needed you,' Nancy said. 'We all needed you.'

'It wouldn't allow me to leave.'

'It's a house, Estelle! Just a bloody-goddamned house that's fit for nothing more than the bonfire.'

Nancy stamped her foot on the floorboards. The sole of her boots smeared the beads of blood into the woodgrain. She slapped the stone window frame, let the unnatural cold seep into her palm until it scorched.

'I'll burn the place to the ground before I end up like the others.' Nancy searched every corner and shadow. 'I shall destroy you just as you have destroyed everything I love. I will watch you burn.' Nancy's heart pounded, her fists by her side. She closed her eyes and breathed deep to stop the pain in her chest. Grief hammered to get out.

'Calm, now.' Estelle put her hand on the wall. Her long fingers gently tapped the muted plasterwork the colour of soft putty.

A shudder struck them both. Tiny fragments of stone fractured and fell onto the windowsill, rattling the leaded windowpanes. A crack, fine as hair, appeared in the ceiling. It rose at the base of the grand chandelier, which hung with wisps of grey cobwebs. A slow meandering course of fractious veins spread until they stopped. Nancy took two steps from the radiator, searching Estelle's features for a response. Estelle closed her eyes and placed her hand on her cheek. Nancy strode a few feet farther into the room. She turned on her heels a few times, almost spinning on the spot, but her eyes never left the ceiling.

'Can you see that?' she asked. 'Tell me you see that too.'

'I shall arrange that tea,' Estelle softened. 'We need to warm up. Go fetch the boys in, my dear.'

'What? Stop it, Estelle!'

Estelle left the room, closing the door behind her. Nancy glanced to the car, her twins still inside. At least they were out there.

The house didn't allow her attention to sit elsewhere for more than that moment. It called her back, her eyes fixed on the cracked plaster.

Above her head, high in the once ornate moulded plasterwork, a web of cracks teased her. She had always known its game, even when the Hardacres of true blood pretended they did not. She had felt it from the moment she took her first step onto the grounds as a young, naive teen, in love and afraid of losing the boy she wanted. The house had felt her and she *it*. She knew its game, and it never played fair.

Nancy raised her hand above her head; squeezing one eye shut, she pointed, tracing the fractured lines with a forefinger.

It wasn't a crack. It was a warning.

'Don't put your feet on the furniture, don't talk with your mouth full, and do exactly as you're told. Can you both do that for me, please?'

Nancy followed her boys through the enormous open door, the white daylight giving way to the gloomy shadows of Hardacre Priory. She heaved three leather suitcases over the threshold. The heel of her boot caught the stone step and sent her a few feet into the hall, where she landed on the cases.

Breath caught in her chest. She held back the tears and grit her teeth with a careful look at her right palm. A long abrasion, the breadth of the inside of her hand, glared red. It traced the length of her lifeline. She laughed at the irony.

'Mum?' Oliver scrambled over the heaped cases and caught his mother's hand in his. 'You all right?' His nose creased. The edge of his lip quivered at the sight of the blood.

'I'm fine, love, just a scratch.' Nancy rose to her feet and slowly twisted her ankle to check movement. She grimaced at the pain. 'Please be careful too. This place is old.'

Two heads nodded, though only one pair of eyes met their mother's—Oliver watched her, his forehead wrinkled. All she saw was their father. But not the Andrew who'd loved and laughed, but the one he became that last day. Her eyes fixed on his for a few moments until his little head nodded and his unruly mop of mousy hair flopped over one eye. She smiled. Maybe the first genuine smile she'd been able to conjure for months. Then, as soon as it arrived, it disappeared with the image of that morning.

'Elliot?' Her eyes flicked to her eldest. He was older only by thirteen minutes, but it may as well have been months, he held a maturity, a defiance to him that his sibling didn't. 'Did you hear what I said? I mean it.'

'I heard you.' His eyes, darker and sharper than his twins, had wandered to every wall, nook, and dusty corner of the entrance hall, right towards the wide-sweeping upper gallery landing.

The house was larger than anywhere they'd ever been. With black-and-white Victorian tiles, the entrance hall had an expanse greater than their whole house back in town. A myriad of carved wooden doors spurred off from all sides. The smaller one, which lay in shadows near the sweeping staircase, caused the hairs on the back of his neck to prickle.

Nancy felt the questions seeping from their skins. There was nothing like the curiosity of a seven-year-old, and her two had it in bounds. From the moment they could mumble nonsensical sentences, they had flourished, feeding off each other and all they met. They both bore a vast vat of curiosity forever needing to be filled. Now here they were with more than a lifetime's worth, and yet, silence.

She had made assumptions; it was true. How could she not have? Their young lives had been halted by the loss of a parent. She related to them with her own grief. Although she had lost her parents in her teens, the pain was still raw, an open wound that never healed. To reason such pain was easier for a grown-up to comprehend. But, in truth, the more her mind wandered to that early spring morning, the less she found a reason. Her precious boys had no real understanding of what had occurred.

'They may revert inwards to hide for the need for self-healing,' the therapist had said. She had sat in her high-back, tan-leather chair, swivelling on its shiny chrome base while tapping the top of her notepad with her pencil. She had nodded with pursed lips at regular intervals with no real help offered. Nancy had had no time for her; the sessions had ceased as quickly as the spring rain. They were her boys. She knew what was best…

And it wasn't hiding from their grief that brought on their silence. In this house, it was something else. They were at the mercy of this place, its history and all that came with it.

All because Andrew had been too weak to deal with it.

TEN

Oliver had barely touched his cocoa, whereas Elliot had stuck his finger in twice, swirling it around the inside edge until the brown skin that had formed puckered on his finger. Mum would normally have turned her nose up in silent scorn with a wide-eyed warning.

Mum had told them to sit on the settee, still. She made a great deal of fuss over it, repeating the word over and over like an order—because it *was* an order. She had become moody since Dad died. She never smiled. Oliver always thought how pretty she was with her long brown hair and golden eyes. Dad had said once how he'd lost himself in those eyes. Oliver had no idea what he'd meant. Something about love, he imagined. Sometimes when she smiled, he saw that she was beautiful. Now her eyes were grey, dull, and empty. Lifeless like Dad's body.

Oliver knew her sadness. It seeped into his skin when he looked at her. Those first few nights after Dad had died, he'd lain awake when the world was asleep and watched Elliot in the next bed, willing him to wake up; he never did. But he'd heard Mum. She never slept. Her back-and-forth footsteps in her bedroom became a rhythm, a repetitive thud, that gently lulled him to sleep…

Much like the pendulum of the grandfather clock next to the settee did now. It sent shivers through him.

Elliot sat closest to it—he had made sure of that. It felt like it had been waiting for him. The rest of the room had almost faded away from sight, leaving him and that clock. Elliot had pushed him onto the settee, kicking the back of his knee on purpose. Oliver had scrambled onto it as far away from the clock as he could get.

The settee was hard, a shade of gold like the setting sun— warm but leaving at any moment only to be greeted by darkness. Oliver ran his hand over a blue cushion with long tassel corners. It was not soft as it should have been. Cushions were supposed to be comfortable; all it gave him was distress.

They nudged each other with their bony elbows when the old lady entered the room. There was a stoop to her shoulders and an arch to her back. Her thin arms seemed unnaturally long as she leant on a wooden walking stick, but her eyes were bright, and so was her dress. One mug in hand, she whistled through the door, the tune entering before her. She left the room to repeat the journey, each time with just one mug.

'I do not get many visitors. I could have asked Lizzie to bring us tea but thought I would quite like to do it myself. It is an occasion after all,' she muttered, as much to herself as to them.

Occasion. The old lady had given special attention to that word, and so, too, had the boys. *Occasion* usually meant a birthday or special treat, not this.

Oliver glanced at his mother, who stared at the ceiling with glassy eyes like his action man, waiting to strike if needs be. Not once did she offer to help bring the drinks in. So unlike her. Mother was a nice lady, always helping the neighbours, chatting to the other mothers at the school gate. She often popped to the shops for old Mr Beardsmore, too. Now she barely said a word to anyone except Elliot and him. She was angry. This old lady made her even more so.

Elliot bashed his feet together to annoy his twin, which jolted the settee. 'Is there a telly?'

The old lady pondered a while until the boys saw a twinge of a smile on her mouth. 'There is.' A full smile now. 'I imagined you might like one. It is set up in the old study. It has not been used as such for decades, so a television room for you boys will put it to good use. Not too much, mind.'

Nancy gave a curt nod to the boys.

'Thank you,' they said.

'But there will need to be some rules too,' she added. 'The Priory is old and needs to be treated with respect.' The twins glanced at each other. 'There are some things that you must never do, and some that you must always.'

She sat in a high-back armchair. It reminded them of one they'd seen in a shop window on the way through the village. Mum had said it sold antiques, though they didn't know what that meant. Oliver imagined it meant *old stuff*.

'You must promise to do exactly as I ask.' Her face became stern, and her blonde hair had dimmed a little in the chair's shadow. Its high sides closed in as she sat back, her hands clasped in her lap.

She didn't look scary but quite pretty, so why did her face send shivers over Oliver's skin? Mum always told him to trust his instincts if something felt wrong. She looked at him now, and Oliver nudged his twin, who jumped.

'You are very welcome here. This is your home—that is the most important thing. Within the walls, inside the house, you are safe as long as you remember to treat the place with respect.' The old lady's eyes cast high to the ceiling. The boys followed them and saw the fractured crack in the plasterwork. 'You are not the only children the Priory has seen, after all. There have been many children here.'

His mum's eyes flashed her way. 'They will behave themselves.' She shot them a cautionary stare. 'Won't you?'

They quickly nodded.

Elliot shuffled, eager to go and escape into Scooby-Doo. Anything to bolt. Oliver, however, was far too intrigued as the old lady traced her finger over a worn stain on the leather arm of her chair. It looked like a heart. Over and over, her finger trailed until she clapped and pressed her hands to her lips.

'Is anyone hungry? Lizzie can arrange some sandwiches for supper before you settle into bed.'

'Please,' replied Elliot. 'Do you have peanut butter? The crunchy one?'

'I think we can find you some.' The old lady beamed as she rose from her chair, with tiny steps wandered to the window and then back to the fireplace.

'Thank you, that would be good,' his mum said. 'I'll get our stuff upstairs.' She looked like she wanted to get out of there. Oliver saw beads of sweat on her forehead as she trailed her finger over the graze on her palm.

'Oh, no need, my dear. Dawson and Lizzie have arranged them already. We were expecting you, after all.' The old lady smiled. Mum didn't. Oliver saw her lip turn up like the time he'd brought worms in from the garden or Dad bought a cup of whelks at the market.

The maid appeared with a tray of sandwiches, china tea plates, and a large sponge cake. Wide-eyed, the boys took their plates and piled them high with peanut butter triangles. Elliot dived in, his mouth full when he gulped down some orange squash.

Oliver, however, couldn't take his eyes off the old lady with the odd face. They'd been told to call her grandmother, but they didn't know her. They'd never met her or been to this house. She didn't have the grey hair that lots of old people had. She was old, he could see that, but at the same time, she wasn't. He felt it behind her eyes, much like when he and Elliot had dressed up for Halloween last year. Elliot had worn a horrible werewolf mask, hairy with big teeth. It had scared Oliver when he first watched his twin walk down the stairs. He had to look hard at his eyes to see Elliot. Grandmother was the same. Maybe this was a mask too. Perhaps she was young under there.

Mum had never spoken of her. The first they heard of her was when Mum had hauled the suitcases out of the loft and thrown them onto the beds.

'Pack your stuff,' she'd ordered.

The boys had done nothing for a moment or two, confused.

'For a holiday?' Elliot had asked when Oliver went to open his mouth. He'd known there was more to it—it had been brewing in Mum's eyes like a heavy storm since the funeral.

'Not a holiday, no. Just pack a case each. We leave first thing.'

They had spent a few nights in a guest house in town. The owner had been an old school friend of Dad's, Mum had explained. They'd gone back home, but not to stay.

The boys had been told to go play at the bottom of the garden. Mum had stayed in the house and looked out of the front room window. Oliver hadn't seen the couple from London arrive until Mum followed them around the garden. The lady with her posh hat had pointed at Mum's peony shrub and turned her nose up, making arm gestures that made her look like one of the men he'd seen on TV who wore yellow jackets and signalled planes to land. The posh couple had bought the house. Oliver had heard Mum cry that evening. He'd walked up the stairs and seen her sitting on her bed, a pile of soggy tissues by her feet. He hadn't said anything, just sat beside her, his young arm wrapped around hers. Mum had rested her head on his and gripped his hand.

'It will be all right, Mum.'

'She's going to pull up the peony, Oli.' She'd cried harder. 'And they aren't that posh either.'

Oliver squirmed on the settee and shoved the lumpy cushion behind his back. He'd been watching the old lady, her slow steps; she didn't sit or look at Mum. Instead, she paced the room, first to the window with her palm on the cold glass, then the fireplace, her back to the flames. Now she stood before the boys, her hands clasped in front of her.

'You can call me Nan if you like, or maybe Gran. I do not mind, whichever you like best.' The old lady smiled as she said it, but there was a strangeness to the words as if they meant something entirely different.

The twins didn't answer, though Oliver nodded slightly. Elliot was eyeing something that hung above the fireplace.

'Ah, the swords. A tempting sight for young boys, I know. I remember your—'

Elliot didn't notice or care that she broke off, but it only made Oliver more curious. If she was their nan, then she was Dad's mother. Oliver knew it was rude to stare, but it was difficult to keep his eyes from straying. Every time they did, she was watching. Something about her eyes made him want to hide, a familiarity that clutched his heart and squeezed it until he felt sick.

With a great urge to run away, Oliver gripped Elliot's hand. But then, his eyes caught the clock in the corner. It stared back at him with its bland, white face and almost unmoving hands. Oliver glared at it until his eyes burned as he waited for the minute hand to move. But it didn't, and yet the pendulum swung until his eyes closed.

The hot cocoa went cold, and the sun sunk in a stark glow over the far trees.

Oliver awoke in the dark. His eyes desperate to adjust, he grappled with the layers of blankets with no recollection of how he'd come to be there. His memory was vague and white—white landscape, white sky, white face of the staring clock. Panic climbed from his chest to his throat and drenched him as if he were about to be sick. He remembered the feeling, and it gripped him as it had before, taking hold until his body shuddered and sweat dripped from his forehead, his breath quick and shallow. But Mum had been there before, holding him tight, whispering to calm him. They'd sat until the sun rose, until the hand he held stiffened and went cold in his trembling fingers. In his other, he'd gripped a tiny shard of something that had fallen from dad's hand while keeping his eyes on his dad's blank stare.

The memory was still raw. He clenched his eyes so he wouldn't cry.

'Elliot?' he called.

He listened but only found silence.

They hadn't made it upstairs when they arrived. There'd been no tour of the house, no exploring farther than the massive room with swords above the fireplace. The lumpy blue cushions on the settee were all they'd seen. He knew little about the house, hadn't known it existed until a few days before, yet he was tucked into a bed in a dark room he'd never seen. Fear scuttled spider legs over his body; panic of what lay within the blackness rushed at him.

'Elliot, are you there? Please?'

Oliver scrambled out of bed, wrestling with the sheet over his chest. It gave way, and he fell to the floor with a smack. For a second or two, he sat waiting for the sound to dissipate into the air. He willed an answer from his brother, a hint to know he wasn't alone. Surely the noise had woken him.

Oliver thought of Dad again. He should miss him. Everyone assumed he did. Part of him was relieved. That part, he hated. Dad had betrayed him, let him down. Mum was angry, and she hated the place and the old lady—Oliver knew that much by looking at her face. She had tried to hide all the disappointment at first until she no longer cared. The pain had been manageable. Everyone felt sadness and misery when someone died, didn't they? But that hadn't lasted long with Mum. Maybe that had rubbed off on him. Elliot never seemed to notice anything, but then Elliot hadn't been there that morning. Only Oliver had seen what had happened.

'Are you awake?'

Nothing came back. The house was soundless, a dense, ear-numbing, unnatural quiet.

They had lived in town where it was busy. Their house had been one in a long terrace just off the main road that drove straight into the town centre; the hum of cars was a steady flow through the night hours. It was comforting to know that others were out there, that he wasn't alone. He had Elliot, of course, so he was never truly by himself.

Oliver wanted to go home. The lump in his throat threatened to choke him; he bit back the tears as he got to his feet.

The floor was cold. Tentatively, he took a step, then another. His toes touched the rough edge of a carpet. He half-heartedly called out again. There was no point—Elliot, wherever he was, wasn't within the dark walls. The skin of his neck bristled. Rubbing his hands over his arms and feeling the flannel of his new pyjamas—printed with knights on horseback, dragons, and castles—Oliver thought of his mother. She'd let him choose them. Elliot had The Incredible Hulk, his favourite. He watched every Saturday evening right in front of the TV, slumped on his belly and his legs crossed behind him.

'You will get square eyes sitting that close,' Dad said.

It didn't matter now; he hadn't watched it since.

The pyjamas were warm, but Oliver shivered with cold sweat, slowly dripping down the crevice between his shoulder blades. Mother had got him undressed and put him to bed, even if he couldn't remember any of it. So, that meant everything was all right. He was safe, wasn't he? She was somewhere inside this house, tucked up warm in a bed. No, she wasn't. Oliver knew she would be pacing the floor, just like she had every night since.

A small light caught his eye. Focussing hard on the far side of the room, he headed towards it. The low glow seeped in under the door. Within it was a shadow.

Someone was there.

Oliver pressed the back of his hand over his mouth and held his breath. The shadow moved and took the light with it, leaving nothing but obscurity to grow at his feet. He felt his twin, his voice in his head and a shudder of fear creeping beneath his pyjamas. Where was Elliot?

As rapid as the pounding in Oliver's chest, the sweep of light returned with quick footsteps. With sweaty palms, he reached for the doorknob, his hands fumbled over the door, trying to find it. As his fingers met the cold metal, a fierce bolt shot up his arm. It flung him back, and he landed flat on the floor. The air was sucked from his lungs. He felt panic, fear, the air thick with dust closing in to choke him. He was no longer in the darkness of the bedroom but curled up tight inside a small black hole as a voice whispered in his ear.

Oliver screamed, curled his arms about his head to block out the voice.

'Leave me alone,' he wept.

With slow, deep breaths, the room opened. The shadowy corners fell away beyond his reach. He felt small, lost, and forgotten.

'Oli?' A beam of light hit his toes, with a gentle creak, the door opened inwards. 'Come, look what I found.'

Elliot, torch in his hand, stood inside the open door. He flicked the light over the space, which sent a yellow glow into the room just short of his twin. Oliver stared with one hand over his eyes. The Hulk stared back. He leapt into the hallway towards Elliot, gripped his arm and his shoulders. The repressed fear that had slowly edged its way beneath his flannel pyjamas swamped him, and the tears flowed.

'Where were you?' he bawled. 'Why aren't you in bed?'

'Oliver.' Something odd edged his twin's voice.

'What?' He stood back a pace, trying to find Elliot's face in the gloom. The torch pointed at the floor.

'You need to come, see what I found.'

In the deep darkness, the twins crept down the narrow staircase to the main gallery landing. A glint of cold light skulked in from an open door at the end of the hallway.

Elliot nudged him, his face hidden behind the torchlight. 'I think that door was closed when I first came down. Quick, before someone sees.'

'Who is it?'

'I don't know. The old lady, maybe?'

Oliver could do nothing but follow; his feet fell in his twin's steps whether they wanted to or not. They stumbled down the sweeping staircase, their hands skimming over the age-smooth bannisters.

'Down here,' Elliot whispered, his fingers over his mouth to muffle his voice. He swept the torch over a carved door panel. Smaller than the wide door of the drawing-room, it sat along the far wall, in the shadow of the upper gallery landing. 'Come on.' He pulled his brother closer.

The door gave way with a gentle creak as both boys tumbled into the room, then swiftly closed behind them. The torch sliced through the darkness. Oliver grabbed it and waved it around the space, so the thread-beam streaked the walls. It wasn't big like the room with the swords but still bigger than their old living room.

'Why were you down here?'

Elliot shrugged. 'Dunno.'

The torchlight found an old settee, a chair with a small round table, and a brass lamp on a pile of books. Oliver clicked the switch under the orange tassel lampshade, and now the room glowed with unnatural warmth. A tiny chink of light through the curtains was the only distraction from the panelled walls. Oliver almost tripped on the edge of the thick rug as he ran to the heavy curtains and dragged them open. The window was black. Nothing lay beyond the glass, only his reflection.

'This is a bad idea,' Oliver whimpered. 'We shouldn't be in here. I don't like it. Why were you in here?'

'Yes, we should. Look, there's the TV... It's gonna be our room, I suppose.'

'I still don't like it.'

'Look.' Elliot ran his fingers over a low panel on the wall behind the door. It gave a soft squeak as the old wood rubbed on the floor. Then, after a *thump*, it gave way. Both boys sunk to their knees and peered down into the hidden space.

'What do you think it is?' Oliver asked. 'A cupboard?'

'Don't think so.' Elliot leant a touch farther as the darkness swallowed his head.

Oliver grabbed the back of his brother's pyjama top. 'Don't,' he yelped. 'It feels wrong.' Fear engulfed him again, that sensation of being lost and forgotten. 'We need to leave right now.'

'Look at this.' Elliot pulled something free from the cavity. 'Why would it be down there?' He turned to Oliver and showed him the small object.

Elliot ran his palm over the surface, wiping away dusty cobwebs and spider corpses. He held it up, so his face stared back. The round mirror rested easy in his hands, his fingers gripped each side as he pointed it towards the lamplight. The frame was carved, back and front with acorns and oak leaves. He turned it over, and again his own face looked back.

'It's the same both sides, see?'

Oliver took it, rotating it in his hands. It was heavy as if pushing his feet into the floor and sinking him into the carpet. His leaden limbs crumbled. He flung the object and pushed it away with his foot.

'It doesn't feel right.'

'It's just a mirror, Oli.' Elliot grabbed it and held it up between them.

Oliver sat forward, squinting as he levelled up to the mirror. He stared hard. Behind him was no longer the orange light of the tassel lampshade or the black reflection of the window. It was now daylight, bright and welcoming. Yet as he moved, there was something else. It darted in and out of view, almost playing with him. It grew thick and black, a swirling shadow without definition or shape. It swallowed the light until it had eaten it whole, leaving nothing behind but the bones of darkness.

Hidden in the shadows of the forgotten corners of the panelling stood another boy. Samuel had watched from the round rose window as the car had crunched through the gravel. He had not been alone in his interest, their curiosity as keen as his. It had been some years since there had been such an arrival. The oak tree had told him they were coming — these curious twins, the boys of winter. One would have been enough; Samuel knew that well, all that was ever needed, but here again, were two.

He pushed his hand to his heart and willed it to beat so he could steady the sickening panic that rose in his throat. He had no control. What was to be, was to be, whether he had his say or not. No one would listen — it had always been the same.

An arm wrapped around his small shoulders and coaxed away those terrible memories. 'You cannot save him,' they said. 'This story will play out just as yours did.'

'It still does.'

The arms held him tighter. There was a lost lingering of warmth. 'Try not to fret so, child. It will only make it worse.'

'Am I to live in this forever?' Samuel asked.

'No, dear child. Not forever. Just until their story ends.'

ELEVEN

'Elliot, go on back to bed. Heaven knows why you two are down here when you should have been asleep. It's not safe to wander around in the dark, especially in the middle of the night.' She would have scorned them both, but the look on Elliot's face deflated her.

Oliver lay on the floor, curled into a ball as he always was. Elliot sat beside him with one hand on his brother's forehead, the other clutching something close to his chest.

'I'm sorry, Mum. We're both sorry.' There were lots of tears. Elliot's face was wet, his eyes swollen red. 'I couldn't wake him. Is it like Dad?'

'No, of course not. That was different.'

'I thought he—' Elliot wiped his cuff across his runny nose. 'It frightened me. It's like when Dad—'

'It's okay. Everything is all right. I'll get him back to bed, don't worry. But I need you to go straight back up now. I don't want anyone catching us up at this hour. Be quick.'

'We won't lose him like... Dad?'

'Don't even think about it. It's just...' She didn't know what it was. Was it this house? 'Oliver will be fine, now go to bed.'

Elliot eyed her with a strange hesitation. He felt the words she held back; she didn't need to speak them. Instead, he squeezed an arm around her waist and kissed her bare shoulder. 'I love you.'

'I love you too,' she answered. 'Why are you down here, anyway?' He wore that serious look she'd seen a lot lately. 'No matter. Just as well that I was. Now, to bed.'

He scampered off with the speed of a rodent rushing under the skirting. His hurried footsteps above her head halted on the turn of the staircase, his soft footfall on the landing. She held her breath, knew where he stood, felt where his eyes were scanning, then heard the faint click of the torch switch and his feet scurry up the next flight of stairs. She exhaled, rolling her shoulders.

Nancy lifted her youngest off the floor, limp and heavy. Was Oliver different to Andrew? The similarity hadn't escaped her, but now the awful comparison hit her like a ton of bricks. What had they been doing, wandering these halls in the middle of the night? This was no place for games. She had to make her boys understand that there were rules. It was the only way to keep them safe. It wasn't a childhood she had envisioned, but it was what Andrew had left them.

'*I had no choice, Nance.*'

'Go away,' she cursed; clenching her eyes, she was in no mood for such fancies.

'*You must know that I had no choice. You must listen to me.*'

'I said go away.'

Not tonight. Not here. This place would only amplify those emotions. Nancy hugged Oliver a little tighter; she wouldn't allow the same for him.

'*You shouldn't have brought them here.*'

'You saw to that though, didn't you?

'*Sorry, Nance.*'

'What for? Leaving me? Bringing us here?'

With a wistful sigh, she felt the cold breath on her neck. An arm eased her into an embrace. She held her son closer, cradling him and desperate to block out the longing that took her every night—the longing to be no longer alone.

'*He always was such a little thing. Unlike his brother.*' His tone changed. She opened her eyes, expecting nothing but air, only to find his silhouette. '*Always so beautiful.*' He reached for her face, teasing a strand of hair away from her eyes.

'Don't be so cruel. Go away. You're not here.'

He released her and paced a silent step back into the room. There was a realness to him that stirred all those memories that mocked her.

'You're not here, Andrew,' she snapped. 'I've had enough of your pitying whispers. Get out of my head.'

Nancy stumbled away from the window and fell onto the chair. She remained there a while, coaxing free the sweaty hair that stuck to Oliver's forehead. The familiar tang of guilt gripped her gullet. Oliver was slight, it was true—not in size, but in his nature. His skin was clammy, pale in the soft morning light that edged over the horizon.

There had always been a delicateness, a sensitivity, to their second-born that had seized her breath more times than she could remember. He had a sight beyond natural vision. He felt others pain, was open to emotions and anguish like an angel resided in this child of winter. The night they were born, a wild snowstorm had cut them off, leaving her and Andrew to bring two tiny creations into the world alone. A light, brighter than any she had seen before, had blinded her when Oliver arrived. A serene silence had fallen on her as he slipped from her body. A gentle calm had washed the room and swept away the deep howls of the storm winds that had filled the house for hours.

And then they'd been there—two tiny mites.

No mother should compare her children but love them the same. She tried, God knew she did, yet her boys were a breed apart. A shadow inhabited Elliot—a knowing like his brother's, but it held darkness she feared. Many times, she had watched from the corner of her eye, caught glimpses of his stare, and almost heard his thoughts. Pain struck her heart with the guilt. It was wrong that she was afraid of her own child. What horror could a boy of seven possibly cause? The shame of it had lain heavy on her shoulders for all these years.

Being at the Priory now, she would know once and for all if what she feared the most was well-founded.

Oliver stirred in her arms; she clutched his hand a little too hard. She hushed, rocking him as she had when he was a baby. She ached for those days, for those simple, almost carefree moments in the early hours when she'd held her newborn. Tiny, innocent, and vulnerable. She had been needed then. Maybe Nancy needed him more than he needed her. Oliver had slept soundly until 3am, the same every night, had held each other until the sun came up, two kindred souls.

Elliot, on the other hand, had repelled her touch. He had needed little attention beyond feeding and changing. She had caught Andrew standing in the nursery, his hands hovering over the cot, and fear had rampaged through her at the possibility that he might hurt a child she'd carried for nine months. Every night as Andrew had turned from the room and wandered back to their bed, she had ached with grief of a different kind. She'd seen that look in his eyes, blank and glazed. It was that look that had taken him that last day. Maybe his end had always been mapped. There was no way she would allow the same for her boys.

A bright sunbeam touched her face. Closing her eyes for just a minute, she could see Andrew standing before the window. *You should be sorry for leaving us.* But her thoughts fell into the bottomless pit of her despair. Andrew cared no more now than he had done that last day.

Oliver stirred again. She carried him to bed after he had fallen asleep. Estelle had eyed her questionably, but Nancy had offered no reply. He wasn't like his father. He wouldn't suffer that fate. Not ready to share her fears with anyone, she locked them away in her box of denial with so much of her life. She would live a lifetime in hell before she confided in that old woman.

Their relationship hadn't started on the right foot if it had begun at all. The two had been at a stalemate from the moment Nancy had arrived at the door. Now she was a mother herself, a sliver of her soul understood, even if she loathed herself for it. Andrew had been Estelle's only child. The Hardacre dynasty suffered more than its share of woe. Children didn't fare well within these walls—a desperate reality Nancy was beginning to feel for herself. Why had she come here? No wonder Andrew had longed to leave despite the Priory being his legacy, his responsibility. So, too, was the curse that soddened its very foundations. Nancy had swanned in, flaunting her beauty like a red flag, opening the door wide for escape. She'd never forget that word: *escape,* from what she hadn't known at the time or even cared. She'd fallen in love, and that was that.

Nancy pulled Oliver closer and shifted him over her shoulder, padded through the grand hallway and up the staircase. Eyes bored into her skin. Her foot left the last tread of the first flight and came to rest on the thick carpet of the gallery landing.

It was swift. A flash of movement quickly explained away if she'd been so inclined. Except, this was the Priory, and all who knew it knew better than to underplay the games that were commonplace within these walls.

'I'm not afraid of you,' she asserted through gritted teeth, her son gripped tighter to her chest.

It slipped into the shadow of the old carved chair; age darkened the engraved back and arms. It nestled along the wall between her bedroom door and the next flight of stairs. Her legs were shaking as she stared into the darkness. Oliver stirred in her arms as she clung to him too fiercely. The chair joints creaked as if *it* sat down. It said nothing, of course, but she felt its intentions. It made them so brutally clear.

'You will not have him too. He is mine.'

The Priory heard. It knew her heart. It pummelled the air onto her skin with a mirroring beat.

Nancy slid her foot forwards, edging closer to the gallery bannisters as far from the chair as possible. A wisp caressed her leg and gently wound a tendril around her ankle, pulling her towards it. She stumbled. One hand left Oliver's back to steady herself, the other struck the chair, and her shoulder whacked it hard. Pain shot through her arm like a hot poker as she grappled to keep hold of her son.

'Damn it,' she whimpered.

'Mum?'

'It's fine, Oli darling. Let's get you to bed.'

Her chest screamed as she tried to move, every muscle burning, Nancy's body gave way, and she sank to the floor at the foot of the chair.

It was still close. Breathing on her. Watching her. Her eyes searched for any movement as it loomed overhead. Its coils lingered about her shoulders, travelled down to her hands as she gripped her son. It teased at her fingers, prized them away one by one from his warm flesh. Nancy thrashed at the air with her free arm, swiping in the darkness. But it had no form. It couldn't be attacked or escaped.

She got to her feet, made it to the stairs, all the while staring into the pitch black. It stared back; felt it right up in her face, looking through her eyes deep into her soul.

You have two. What is one for the sake of the other?

Nancy's bare feet pounded up the last staircase. Reaching the bedroom door, she threw herself in and flung her foot to bang the door closed behind them. Her fingers frantically searched for the bedside lamp. With eyes the size of saucers, Oliver jolted in her arms, fear and alarm fresh on his face. Nancy hushed and checked his twin was sleeping. Elliot didn't move. He faced the wall, though she felt the air shift when he opened his eyes. She let him be. For the next few moments, Nancy hurried around the room, checking the window latch, under the beds and inside the wardrobe. She knew the absurdity of it—what inhabited this house didn't hide beneath beds.

Oliver shuffled under his covers with a confused look when he laid his head on his pillow. 'Did you put me to bed earlier?'

Nancy wondered if she should tell him. 'Of course, love. You fell asleep on the settee; I didn't want to wake you.'

'Okay.' He rubbed his eyes and yawned away any other questions he might have had.

'Settle back down. You need some sleep.' She left other words unsaid. Instead, she tucked him in, the crisp sheet smooth under his chin.

'Too tight.'

'Sorry, darling,' she lulled. The quiver of her lip was fleeting, but he'd seen and returned it. 'I love you.'

'Mum?'

'It's all okay. You need to get some sleep now.'

'Mummy, I don't think it's safe here.'

'Safe?'

'The house, it doesn't want us here.'

Such a sad look on her dear boy's face. How she wanted to wipe away all the pain, bundle it up and throw it into that deep hole with his father.

'It's just a house, love. Don't think any more on it now.' She soothed her palm to his cheek, coaxing all the bad dreams from his thoughts.

'She's Dad's mother, isn't she? That old lady.'

'Your nan? Yes, she is.'

'She knows what happened—So does this house.'

'No more. You mustn't worry about any of it.' She pressed her finger to her lips, her eyes lingering on the door.

Nancy closed the door behind her, letting it come to a natural rest with a small gap. She stood there waiting, listening before summoning the nerve to head back down.

It was waiting for her.

TWELVE

As he lay awake, Oliver sensed the presence waiting at the bottom of the staircase. His mother's panic, her fear, it was too heavy in his chest to sleep. The events of the night were vague, a floating image like a bubble on the breeze he just couldn't catch. As his eyelids closed on the darkness, another presence moved closer. It felt lighter, a tangible hand that tightly held his.

He mumbled his brother's name from beneath his bedcovers. It left his mouth in a croak, barely audible. It wasn't Elliot—he wouldn't be holding his hand but kicking the bed. *In jest or play*, he always said. Though, as Oliver thought on it more, he'd seen a change in Elliot since they'd arrived at the Priory. It had been quick and so subtle. He couldn't think what it was, but his twin was different even if mum hadn't noticed.

'Hello,' he tried again, this time with a little more certainty.

Attempting to pull his hand free, Oliver scrambled to sit though it held him fast. His body began to shake, tremble, his skin tingled with pain as if in a deep, violent fever. He'd felt it once before, last summer when Dad had still been there, and life was as it should be. The doctor had come, taken Oliver's temperature and checked the angry pink rash that had spread over his pale body. Mum had said he was sick and needed to stay in bed, no school, and no play. Confined to his bed for days with little to no energy, he had drifted in and out of sleep. There had been visitors. They'd come in the middle of the night, some only for a moment to check on him, smile at the small child, lay a cool hand to his forehead, while others had waited with him, sat beside his frail form until the sun rose. One he remembered—a man in a long, black dress who'd said nothing just prayed by his bedside.

Mum had discarded the notion in her usual casual manner: *you were just dreaming, darling. There was no one there, I checked.*

Dad had waved a hand in dismissal, smiled, and ruffled his hair. *We're just so glad you're feeling better, champ. Had us worried there for a bit.'*

It wasn't until Elliot glanced his way with a look of thunder that roared so loud, he needed to cover his ears. Oliver had glared, stripped back those fierce layers his twin wore so thickly to find something vastly different beneath. *Don't let him come back, Oli.*

Resolve pumping with his blood, Oliver tugged his hand away and pushed himself up to sit properly. His head pressed back against the wooden headboard. He stared around the room, avoiding the direct sight of the small figure who sat on his bed. A slight glow of light sifted through the curtains and fired a dart of clarity.

'Good morrow, Oliver.'

It wasn't the one who had visited before. This was a child, a boy no older than he.

'Hello,' he replied with a finger to his lips. 'We mustn't wake my brother.' It was better to keep it secret. Perhaps it was the fright he'd seen on Elliot's face before, the change in him… the change in himself.

The boy nodded.

Elliot stirred, rolled over under his thick eiderdown, and mumbled, 'No, Dad, please no.'

Oliver held his breath, his finger still on his lips as he waited for Elliot to settle. Relieved, Oliver turned back to the boy. He was gone.

✝

Oliver awoke to shards of cold light slicing the wall and the air bitter on his cheek. With his back to the window, he pulled the heavy blanket around his neck. Elliot, buried under the eiderdown in the opposite bed, shifted a little, followed by a grumble and a snore. A chest of drawers stood between them. It was the same treacle brown as his brother's bed. The headboard was tall and carved, and the footboard matched. Oliver had no energy to see if his was the same. He imagined it was. Almost everything they had was a mirror image of itself, much like them. But this should have been different. This wasn't their bedroom at home, yet the very air in this house held the inexplicable feeling that this was all for them.

A deep yawn took him. It was too early to get up. He cast his eye over to the clock on the wooden drawers. Its round, white face said 6.35, yet its ticking said something else. It whispered, called to him from inside the clunking workings, the noisy cogs and springs inside the blue metal case. Oliver reached out towards the black hands but pulled away at the last moment. It was one of the only things of his past that had come with them. It had been Dad's and looked every bit at home in this room.

It all felt wrong.

'Elliot? Elliot!'

His brother sighed and rolled over, pulling the sheet over his head.

Oliver settled back on his pillow, wishing the tension in his neck to ease. *Go back to sleep*, he willed as the image of his dad floated in.

It had been dark when he found Dad in the middle of the garden wearing nothing but his pyjama trousers. Oliver felt a shift in the air. He'd awoken to a silent house, known something was wrong because his heart pounded in his ears. Panic took root, grew from his toes, working its way up until the need to scream filled his throat. It had taken no more than a minute to find Dad outside, barefoot on the lawn near the peony bush.

Oliver called as loud as he dared with a glance up the stairs, hoping not to wake anyone else. Dad hadn't turned or answered, just stood stock still with his back to the house. Oliver called again, shouted this time. He should have run to the garden to see what was wrong, but he just couldn't move his feet. Instead, Oliver stood with his bare toes gripping the backdoor step, his arms stiff by his side as he watched Dad fall to the ground.

The bedroom at the top of the house relaxed. Along with the beams and rafters, floors and walls, the Priory sighed. It was as it should be. These boys, these twins, were finally where they belonged. They lay in matching beds, caught in dreams, with gentle breaths and steady heartbeats. These beds had belonged to many Hardacre children but never to ones as significant as these.

Neither child had noticed the carved wooden box that sat in shadow just behind their father's travel clock. This box was no bigger than the timepiece and identical to the beds with intricately carved foliage. And its dark intentions. The box opened just a fraction. Every chiselled oak leaf and tiny acorn on each bed became more distinct, more sumptuous in their ancient sculpting. Rising from the wooden surface, minute coiled creepers wound from their engraving and entwined with these boys of winter, slightly at first—a mere strand of hair, a touch to their skin. Slowly. Carefully. There was no need for haste.

And from the confines of the wooden box, a single strand slipped, ominous and needy. Which boy? One to be bound, and the other…

THIRTEEN

The kitchen was the warmest room in the house, but even here, Nancy's skin tingled as goosebumps rushed up her arms. It was an illusion due to the egg-yolk-yellow walls that sat behind the wooden cabinetry. The only room in the house that sat at odds with the rest of the place, though she couldn't say why. It was part of the original kitchens with a great open fireplace, working spit, and hanging rack that lay unused now, neglected like so many other corners of the Priory.

Lizzie hovered at the deep sink at the far end of the room. Vaguely aware when she'd entered, Nancy now felt her, the peculiar way the whole place charged with her presence. Her long skirts swished the old floor tiles as she instinctively headed to the stove to make tea. Nancy carefully walked to the table, keen not to disturb the air, and sat opposite Estelle.

'Tea, my lady?' Lizzie asked softly.

The earthenware teapot came to rest on the table atop its cork mat.

'Thank you, Lizzie,' Estelle answered. 'I'll pour. You go finish what you were doing.' There was a fondness in her tone that would have touched Nancy if she'd been in her usual temperament, whatever that was.

'Thank you, my lady,' Lizzie said. 'I never seem to finish that...' She wandered off along with her words, lost on the cold air that hung low over the table.

Estelle lifted the pot and held the lid as she poured. Nancy watched, tracing the long hairline crack from the chipped spout.

'Why on earth don't you buy a new teapot? This one looks like it's about to crumble with the next cuppa.'

'What? No, don't be silly. Our Brown Betty has been with me since...' Her eyes fell on the crack as she placed the teapot back down. 'This was a wedding gift. It belongs to the Priory as much as I and Lizzie.' There was a hint of a smile; even Nancy felt the warmth of those sentimental memories.

Nancy perched on her chair. 'I've put Oliver back to bed for a while. Hopefully, he'll sleep a bit. It was a long night. As long as Elliot doesn't keep pestering him to get up...'

'Try not to worry. It is a new place for them. They will both settle; it may just take a little while.' Estelle reached out her hand and passed Nancy the sugar bowl.

'There will need to be rules.' Nancy twisted her hair over her shoulder and stretched her neck, releasing the tautness settling in her shoulders.

'They are just boys,' Estelle said.

'You know full well what I mean. Rules for their sake, not yours or this place.'

'I am fully aware of your meaning.'

'I won't get into it, Estelle. Not this morning, for God's sake, I'm far too tired already.' Nancy closed her eyes, wishing she could sleep for a week. Grief was an exhausting state to hold for so long.

'It is not grief but anger that keeps you awake, my dear.'

Nancy glowered. With all the energy, she held back the anger. Then, with a deep breath that ended up as a defeated sigh, she wilted back onto the chair. How did Estelle know what she was thinking? Her thoughts were never her own.

'I spoke to the village school last week while I was making plans. They start in two days.' Nancy spoke more to the window than she did to Estelle.

'The school?'

'Yes, after all the crap. After all the upheaval and grief they've had to deal with, they need some normality back.

Hell, I need some normalcy in my life. You know damned well I didn't want to bring them here, so if school is the only slice of a normal life they can have, then...'

'May I ask you something?'

Estelle never asked permission to say anything. Something about being Lady Hardacre or a Hardacre at all gave her the God-given right to say whatever she pleased. Nancy closed her eyes and corrected herself; there was nothing God-given about this forsaken place.

'Go on,' Nancy uttered through a clenched jaw.

'Do you think that will be good for them? I know you mean the best for them—goodness knows I know how that feels— but they are here now. This is where they belong.'

'They are seven going on eight. Of course, it's best. How else are they going to learn? I'm sure as hell not able to home-school in any way. Or do you mean a tutor? I can't afford that.' Nancy's jaw fused, and her teeth ground in her ears.

'Just think about it. That is all I am saying.' Estelle's hand rose between them. 'I just want to help.'

'Do you? Is that all you are saying? Or are you telling me how it will be from now on?' Nancy blurted, her heart rapid and her cheeks flushed.

'Things will change now. The Priory... Things work differently here.'

'Well, the boys aren't your responsibility; they are mine. I have a meeting with their new teacher this afternoon. She said she'd drop by after school—before teatime, I imagine. Mrs Scarfe.'

'Gloria?' Estelle asked with a lighter tone that sung slightly.

'Yes... I think so.'

'Ah, I see. Well, that will be all right.' Estelle eased back in her chair, lifting her cup to her mouth. 'It will allow her.'

Nancy watched Estelle's face as she nodded to the window. Estelle had swiped a thick line beneath her words, ending the conversation.

Nancy spooned the sugar. Estelle was trying, but too much pain lingered on her skin. Like old sunburn, it still flayed if rubbed too hard. This whole place—the lands, the estate—was chafing at her nerves. Maybe she should forgive her. If it soothed a modicum of agony and fear, then perhaps it would be one less pain to haunt her.

They sat at the scrubbed pine table nestled beneath a tall stone window for the next half an hour. The light was intense, but it wasn't enough to warm. Winter lived here, and it had long settled into the cracks.

'I saw him.' Bloody hell, why had she said that? Her mind had wandered and found Andrew. 'Last night.' Her head fell into her hands; tears stung the back of her eyelids. To let them fall now would undo all the hard work of the past few weeks.

'I know. You are not invincible, you know. It is not a weakness to mourn. The lord is witness to the many times I have lamented. What is done is buried. What is here remains.'

'Please don't talk to me about grieving. I've had to do this on my own, Estelle. Not one word from you. Not one. And you don't believe that any more than I do. I know how this works.'

Her anger bubbled and roared as she continually stoked the fires beneath it, but the morning's warm yellow disguise leached under her skin and weakened her resolve. Anger—the only emotion that surged through her veins—was swallowing her whole.

'I'm trying my hardest,' Nancy said. 'He gave me no choice but to make these impossible decisions. I have nothing, Estelle. He left me alone with the boys, with bad memories and no future. I'm trying my hardest to forgive him for that.'

'That is not true. You have Hardacre. The boys are the last. This is their home, and in turn, it is yours. It always has been.'

'This God-forsaken place that breeds only pain? I don't want it. I hate it, and it hates me.'

'When I was young…' Estelle hugged her cold teacup, her long fingers winding through the china handle.

Nancy stared, her back rigid as indignation set her firm against the spindles of the kitchen chair.

'I was young once. Would you believe it to look at me now?'

Estelle pressed her palm to her cheek where her delicate tissue paper skin puckered with the tragedy of her past, a play that had left its leading lady with a continuous curtain call. Her eyes cast down to her hands as she put the cup onto the old pine. It ringed the surface, littered with the stains of mugs and teacups. Evidence of visitors? No, there never were any. No one came and left. Only those who belonged stayed to drink at this table. Only those the house allowed in… or wouldn't allow out.

'I never wanted to come here either,' Estelle declared. 'It was the worst summer of my young life, the upheaval, pain, and sorrow of what I left behind. I was just a child; I had no choice. Neither did my father, in all honesty, just like those boys of yours. The decision was made for us.'

'I didn't want to bring them here.'

'Oh, my dear. I did not refer to my parents choosing for me, just like the situation you find yourself in. It is never a choice we make, you know. It is in our blood. A Hardacre will always come here in the end. You cannot fight it. Even if you travelled to the other side of the world, buried yourself in the deepest, most remote place, the Priory would still find you.'

Nancy didn't reply, nor could she take her eyes from Estelle's face. There was something in this morning light that stripped away the years like layers of filthy cobwebs to reveal the rawness of Estelle's scars.

'However, after the initial turmoil of those first few weeks, there is no denying that part of me relished the adventure. The boys will feel it too. It will help to dampen the turbulence in their bellies.'

The moment was fleeting, yet with blinding clarity that felt fit to stop her heart, Nancy saw Estelle as she had been — young, beautiful, and vibrant. With eyes that sparkled like sapphires and a smile so serene that peace itself sat there. Then, with swift dusty wings, the frantic thrashing of moths swiped that tranquillity away, their filthy wings beating against Estelle's porcelain skin and obscuring her beauty. The impatient flutters finally drifted off into some shadowy corner of the room. They left nothing but grief — the scars of sadness. Loss and sorrow laid bare and wrinkled on Lady Hardacre's face.

Estelle smoothed her cheek with her palm and let it come to rest at her neck, where she lay her hand over her pearls. 'There was a time when we lived here in peace. It was not always so grave and desperate. It took another horror to bring our Hardacre destiny crashing down around us.'

Nancy nodded as much to herself as to Estelle as she allowed the morning sun to touch her eyelids. There was no warmth, but at least it wasn't darkness filling her mind today.

'The war,' Nancy uttered.

'I still feel the irony that it was not the Priory but the transgressions of humanity that took my happiness.' Estelle laughed to herself. 'You can blame the Priory for your pain. We all have at some time or another. Do not mistake the sins of man for the power that lies here.'

Nancy did blame man — that was the problem. She blamed Andrew for all of it.

The night had taken whatever energy she'd had left. She didn't dare think about it too much. To recollect the night's events would only have allowed the Priory's clutch to tighten further. It heard her thoughts — that was how it fed. If she were too careless, she would fall into a deprived slumber.

Nancy jumped at the touch of a clammy hand on her shoulder. Elliot had always had an absurd knack for creeping around without her knowing, whereas she sensed Oliver's movements, heartbeats from another room. Elliot stood behind her as if he had floated in with the dust.

'Mum?'

'What is it? You haven't been bothering your brother, have you?'

His huff ruffled the top of her head. 'No. Oli's asleep. I don't think I could wake him even if I wanted to, and I don't.'

'What have you been doing?'

Elliot stepped back a pace, bashing his grandmother's knee. Nancy spun around in her chair.

'Nothing.' His eyes shot to his hands. His fingers gripped the worn edges of his comic book. 'I was reading, but I'm so bored.'

Estelle placed her arm around his narrow shoulders and tapped her fingers on his arm. Elliot's fierce veneer melted away as he relaxed into her hold.

'It will do me good to have young ones around this place.' She squeezed him. 'There is far too much old age here.'

Stifling the urge to glare daggers at them, Nancy closed her eyes to eradicate the image of Andrew and his mother the day they'd left. The day Nancy had taken him away from his legacy. That was how his mother had deemed it—Nancy had stolen him. Now here was Elliot, quite at ease in Estelle's comforts. Hadn't Nancy known it would be like this? Elliot was every bit a Hardacre.

Estelle eyed him carefully, keeping a hint of softness at the corner of her mouth. 'Listen, if you are good and well behaved, why don't you go and have a wander around the grounds and gardens? The sun is out; it's a good day for a ramble.'

'What's a ramble?' Elliot asked. 'Is that like a rabbit or a hedgehog?'

'No, bless you. It means a roam or a stroll. There is plenty to see—the Priory sits in over nineteen acres. But you must be careful—no going beyond our boundary. No going past the oak into the village or anywhere near the road. You must stay within the Priory and where it can see you.'

Elliot nodded cautiously.

'Most importantly, you must be careful around the Priory ruins.'

'What are they?' he asked, his young brows knitted.

'This...' Estelle swept her hand through the air and came to rest on the window's cold stone. 'This is just the part we live in. The part that once was the gatehouse—an awfully long time ago before it belonged to the Hardacre family—was the entrance to the Priory. It was large and impressive back then.'

'What happened to it? Is it like the abbey ruins in town?'

'Yes, exactly like that. The main Priory was demolished, and the stone was used to build some of the village walls and buildings. So there is not much left, just ruins like the abbey in Bury St Edmunds. But—and this is especially important, so you must listen carefully'—Elliot leant in closer, wide-eyed with eagerness so tangible it almost made the room hum—'You must never walk there. Never. With no exception must you or your brother walk beneath the arches of those ruins.' Elliot started to open his mouth. '*No* exception, do you hear me?'

'Promise?' Nancy added.

Elliot nodded fiercely. His face spoke of adventures that carved themselves between his furrowed brows. A new light shined from inside him. Nancy watched as his face lit up, and when she glanced to Estelle, she saw it there too.

She had lost.

FOURTEEN

Why was Mum always on his back, always so quick to lose her temper? It only made his flare. The fire in Elliot's belly would rise to meet her blaze, no matter how much he tried not to let it. He felt the anger take his hands, making them fists so tight it hurt his fingers.

He would run away. Run down to the village, get on a bus back to town. Stupid. Where would he go? They had nowhere else. He wasn't as foolish as she thought he was. Mum always looked at him like he was thick, explaining things like he was a baby. She never talked to Oli like that.

The terrible pain that blackened the back of his eyes churned in his stomach. It didn't help that he was hungry. He'd eaten breakfast early when Mum had told him to go downstairs and let Oli sleep, but now it had to be nearly eleven. He fancied cake. He'd head back soon, but first, he would go and explore.

The old woman had handed him a twisted walking stick from the rack near the massive front door. 'It is made from the hazel trees in the woods at the far end of our lands,' she had said. 'It is special.'

'The woods?' he had asked.

'Both.' A smile, something extra, glinted in her eye. 'The woods and the walking stick. The hazel tree holds magic, so this is very special.'

Elliot had taken it with an eager grip, felt its smooth polish swirl in his fingers. It felt good just holding it.

'Look after it, mind. It belonged to someone powerful.' She bent closer with those last whispered words. He'd felt her breath on his ear and seen Mum's glare.

'Go be Lord Hardacre for a little while. Roam your grounds.'

Those words had made his heart thump faster, and Mum's eyes crease with anger. She was always angry with him. The blackness in Mum's eyes mirrored the one in the hollow of his belly. Both had become thicker since they'd arrived.

The walking stick struck the ground with deep stabs. Its end dug into the earth. The grass was sparing in patches, small clumps of dull green among the expanse of cold dirt. The lawn, or what had once, lay sprawled in front of him as far as he could see. There wasn't this much space to run in the park—too many footpaths, flowerbeds, and old ruins there. But here, he let the open space fill the void that had been growing inside him for weeks, a cavity that had been rotting away like a bad tooth. He'd tried to fill it with books, burying his head in his comics or drawing pictures with the colouring pencils Dad bought him the last time they went out together. Anything to take the bitter taste from his mouth. The bitter tang of missing his dad.

The memory would have been a mundane throwaway glint in time, but it remained still. It had been a quick trip into town, but the events that followed made the occasion fuse to his thoughts like a sticky toffee to his school jumper.

'Come on, Elliot,' Dad had said. 'Let's get out for a while, just you and me.'

Elliot had leapt at the chance.

They caught the bus into town, wandering the shops, in turn ticking off the items on the shopping list Dad kept in the pocket of his navy corduroy trousers. 'One last shop, then we'll head home if that's okay with you, champ?'

Elliot nodded, not caring how many boring shops they visited or how heavy the string shopping bag was in his little hand. He beamed up at his dad.

A lady stood in the doorway, a young girl by her side, holding the glass door open for them. The memory stuck in his head, the sight of their pale skin and bright red hair. That, and the girl held a giant colouring book and the longest pack of colouring pens Elliot had ever seen. Her large eyes flashed as she smiled.

'This way, up the stairs,' Dad said. 'Think you can make it with that heavy bag?'

With an eager nod, Elliot rushed up the steps as his dad took them two at a time—a game they played every time they found themselves on the white-tiled steps that cornered around to the upper floor of the shop, greeted by the familiar smell of coffee and cakes.

'Fancy a milkshake?'

'And a jam doughnut, Dad?'

'Course. It's not a real milkshake without its partner. Some things just come in pairs, don't they?' Dad ruffled the top of Elliot's head, tousling his mousey hair.

Elliot followed him through the shelves of stationery, notebooks, and brightly coloured packets of pens. His heart halted, bumping straight into the back of his dad, who had stopped dead in the centre of the aisle.

'Dad?'

Elliot grabbed the back of his dad's jacket. He couldn't see what or who stood in front of them, but he knew from somewhere inside his chest that it wasn't good. He buried his face in the soft weave of his dad's jacket, his eyes barely open, seeing nothing but the bright-blue material. Tension stiffened his dad's body vibrating into his, filling him with panic. The heavy silence made his ears hum, his head pound.

Elliot shifted a little, peering around to see a figure. He quickly glanced both sides of the aisle towards the end and the café that awaited them. Shoppers were everywhere, all doing ordinary things.

'Greetings, Andrew.'

Dad gripped Elliot's arm, pushing him behind.

'It is time for you to come home.'

Panic ran Elliot through like a sword, cold, slick, with a strange taste of metal in his mouth. Mum and Oli—was something wrong with them? Did they need to go home?

His dad's grip loosened a touch, followed by a pat. Elliot knew what that meant: *Be quiet. It's okay.*

Between his fingers and the haze of blue material, Elliot peered at the figure. It was a man. But it shifted a touch like a bedsheet Mum had hung on the washing line, gently swaying in folds, there but not there. Though this wasn't white but black. The voice spoke again; the words sounded too distant to make out. Again, Dad didn't answer. This time, the figure pressed its hands together in front of its chest. It had reminded Elliot of school assembly when they sat cross-legged on the floor, their hands together to recite the Lord's prayer.

The hitch in his breath had lingered, burning his chest, still holding the air in his lungs when Dad crouched in front of him, pressed his large hands on either side of his cold cheeks, and kissed the top of his head. 'It's okay, Elliot. Let's go home.'

He shook his head to block out the humming, a deep, swirling sensation about to drown him. 'Make it stop.'

'Deep breaths. Look at me. Keep your eyes on mine. Deep breaths, champ, the feeling will pass, I promise.'

'Who was that?'

'You mustn't worry.'

But he *had* been afraid, and he'd been terrified every day since. Even if Dad hadn't felt the dread that had seeped from the folds of that bedsheet man, Elliot had.

There had been no milkshake that day. The churning sensation had quashed that idea, so too had the thought of the bumpy bus journey home. His dad guided him back to the bright shelves of colouring pencils. Elliot nodded as Dad reached the highest shelf for a large metal tin of colouring pencils and a thick drawing pad.

'This will keep you out of trouble for a while,' Dad said smiling, ruffling Elliot's hair.

They had walked home. It was a short stroll, with every step relished and detested. Elliot concentrated all his efforts on seeing nothing but the staggered lines between the concrete paving slabs.

'Don't stand on the cracks, Dad. That's bad luck.'

He had meant it too. All kids knew that adults couldn't see the truth in such things. Why hadn't Dad listened to him? If he had, he'd still be with them. They'd still be at home, and they'd never have known about the Priory or the old lady with the strange face.

Elliot gripped the walking stick and stabbed it into the grass. The blackness rose in him as he speared the ground over and over. With two white-knuckled hands, his teeth biting into his lower lip, he used the power that rose into his shoulders to plunge the stick into the ground. Again and again, it cut through the earth. Every stab was born of fear and pain. The foundations of the Priory, his ancestors, history, lay within every root and stem, rumbled beneath his feet, and climbed to meet his frustration. The ground shuddered, then ruptured. Generations of heartache bled up through the gouges in the earth until they spilt over the shattered land.

Many minutes passed before he moved. The earth was no longer brown, natural, but red. Spewing out of the broken ground, frothing, and oozing like a school science project. Elliot took a small step back. He should have moved earlier and quicker—his new trainers ruined, stained crimson like blood.

The sight was far too mesmerising.

He should have been afraid, but the notions swirled and tumbled over themselves as they tried to gain a foothold. His keenness was too great, too immense for his curiosity to comprehend. So, he stood knee-deep in the crimson mass, waiting for it to bubble and swallow him whole.

†

'MUM.'

Oliver threw himself down the stairs, tripping over his feet as he stumbled to the tiled floor below. Nancy was already there, staring wide-eyed. Panic quickened, rising in his chest.

'What is it? Are you okay?' Her hands smothered, checking him over for some injury or other.

'Not me,' Oliver shouted.

'Elliot?'

Oliver was at the front door before Nancy had a chance to react. His little hand tugged on the cold iron ring.

Estelle reached over him and freed the handle. 'There you go, but wait for your mum.'

'No time!'

He was out. Thick panic rose in his throat. If he stopped, he'd be sick.

Keep running, keep running.

The grass was hard under his slippers. There'd been no time to dress, so he pounded down the grounds in his flannel pyjamas. He knew where Elliot was, didn't need to see. He'd felt it surge through him and leach around his legs, as real as the wet cold on his feet. The twisted, spiky oak branches pulled him towards it.

Josiah observed from the highest point of the Priory. The stone rose window that glared out as a blind eye had always assured the best view of the grounds. From up here, he had watched many a child play till they were lost. This boy was not the first, though Josiah sincerely hoped from deep inside his hollow chest, he would be the last.

There had been those times in the lost past, in the place where his heart had once beaten, when the child's fate would have filled him with dread. His mind and all he knew to be true had battled with sword and dagger against the mournful loss. Now, however, he did no such thing. History—his and of those who had come since—told him it was a pointless task, a folly to satisfy the feeble.

This Elliot, one half of a whole, was different from the rest. These twins were not like the others. From floor to roof, he heard it being said. The walls were chanting it so.

Josiah had sat within the carved frame in the stone window's arc, his feet and arms crossed and watched as the boys had arrived.

Their mother was a curious thing. He had stood by her bed the first night, watching her. Perhaps it was wrong, though drawn to her, he had found himself there regardless. His brother had told him to never do such a thing in case they felt his presence. To be so bold was a sin.

This mother, though… She was not one of them, and the Priory knew it. It had allowed her in. Josiah recognised her from the past, though it played like yesterday. Where time cast a shadow beneath the eyes of visitors, it was a blink to him. She had been young then— not a child or a lady. The walls had sung her entrance then, too, in a regretful lament for on her departure, she had taken the Last. Yet here she was and with none other than her twins. Perhaps it would play with her a while, just till it grew tired. He had no hold over what deeds the Priory conducted, nor could he stop the terrible darkness from bleeding up from under the foundations. It passed its own judgements for right or wrong.

This evil was gathering at the roots of the oak. Even as Josiah watched, it threatened to swallow the child whole.

FIFTEEN

Oliver couldn't bring himself to look. The truth of it was too real, too terrible. Seeing wouldn't help. So, he squeezed his eyes shut and kept a tight grip on his brother. It wasn't until other hands prized his fingers off one by one that the instinct to look became too great. Finally, he opened them to find his mother kneeling beside them, the earth slick, squelching beneath her legs as she tugged Elliot from the hole.

'What on earth!'

Oliver imagined a swear word to follow her statement. Instead, tears fell down her cheeks, gathering at her chin.

Elliot sat on the ground in front of him, soaked to his waist in sticky mud.

'What were you doing?' Nancy fussed over her son and pulled his feet free of a twisted vine knotted around his ankle.

'Nothing.' Elliot shook his head with the feeble word, but he said no more.

'Bloody hell, you two. This place…' The oak tree loomed overhead. 'This place isn't like a normal house, do you understand?'

Her boys were silent, but there was understanding there; she caught the look that passed between them.

'I wasn't doing anything wrong,' Elliot finally said.

'What were you doing then? Look at the state of the walking stick. What were you doing with it?'

'Just… I don't know. Just…' His eyes fell back to his twin, where the unspoken words were visible.

Oliver sat, his now-empty hands still open, reaching out to his brother. A wild void sat behind Elliot's eyes, staring past him towards the oak tree, the whites of his eyes glistened in the cold sunlight. As quick as a blink, he turned back to Oliver, full awareness on his features, a knowing deep behind his lashes. Elliot nodded. Oliver turned to see.

'It knows,' whispered Elliot.

Oliver jumped to his feet, fretting over the mud that had crusted over his knees. He started to walk back to the Priory, faster and faster until he was in a full sprint.

'Oliver.' He was too far away to hear. 'Oliver, go straight to your room to change.' His mum's words fell in the air.

Nancy bent down, picking Elliot up. He wrapped his soggy legs around her waist; she squeezed as he wound his arms around her shoulders and rested his head on hers. The pain struck her chest with a savage blow as guilt washed over them both. She knew he felt it too. He hugged her tighter.

'I'm sorry, Mummy. I didn't mean to.'

'Me too.' She stroked his hair and trudged back towards the great door. 'It's okay now. You *are* okay? Nothing hurt?'

Elliot shook his head. Tears were strong, and no matter how he tried to brave them, he lost.

'Love, it's okay now, you're safe. What were you doing?'

'It—' he mumbled, barely audible over the sobs.

Nancy stood him on the gravel, straightened his jacket over his shaking shoulders. She pressed her hands to his wet cheeks and stared hard. He was her boy, her firstborn. All the pain of the last months came crashing in as she saw Andrew stare back with those terrified eyes. She hadn't known how to deal with it then. How was she to know now?

'It— That—' Elliot pointed back at where they had come. 'What? The tree?'

Estelle was waiting in the entrance hall. Lizzie held a mop, ready to clean the muddy mess off the hall tiles. Estelle hadn't noticed Nancy step over the threshold, tightly carrying Elliot. Nor had Oliver, who stood at the foot of the staircase, a hand poised on the polished rail, a foot raised to connect with the first rung. No one moved a hair as Nancy trudged new muddy footprints over the black-and-white floor, as Elliot sobbed in her arms.

Elliot stopped crying, the silence deafening to their ears.

'Mummy?' he trembled.

'Love?'

'You won't let me go, will you? Please don't put me down.' He gripped her tighter.

Elliot buried his face in her neck. Tears trickled down her collarbone beneath her jumper. She walked farther in, making her way to the drawing-room entrance.

'Whatever is the ma—' Nancy knew. No one was moving. 'Hello?'

'Greetings, Nancy.' The voice spoke with a soft calmness unfitting for Hardacre Priory. 'And to you again, Elliot.'

Nancy clung to her boy, squeezed him so tight, she might never let him go.

'Hello,' she said. 'Can I help you?'

A glance around the entrance hall made it clear that something was impossibly wrong. But she couldn't quite gather her wits enough to think why Estelle, Lizzie, or even Oliver hadn't noticed the stranger in the drawing-room doorway or why, as another glance clarified, they were motionless. Still.

Elliot yelped and buried his face deeper inside his mother's jumper. Nancy gazed around the space, searching for answers; Elliot caught sight of the stranger.

He squirmed. 'Make him go away, Mummy.'

'It's okay, I have you.' She placed a protective hand on his head. 'What is it you want? Why are you here?'

107

'I fear my visit is long overdue.'

She took a step forward, her foot firm on the floor. A crash from behind her made her swing around to find the mop had fallen from Lizzie's hands. Estelle jumped and scolded Lizzie for making more mess as water slurped over the edge of the bucket. Oliver ran up the stairs like a shot from a gun.

Nancy turned back. The stranger was gone.

'It looks like I may need to mop it again,' Lizzie said. 'Sorry, my lady.'

Estelle said nothing, nodded, and slowly paced towards the drawing-room.

Nancy stood by the fire. Elliot still firmly adhered to her, his arms tight about her neck, bony legs around her waist.

'I didn't see you come in,' Estelle said.

Nancy said nothing, nor did she move. Her eyes were on the swords above the fireplace, then went higher to what lay above, mounted on the wall. Estelle was by her side, gently rubbing Elliot's back as his sobs subsided.

'You seem to have had quite a fright,' Estelle said. 'How are you now?'

Elliot nodded, wiping tears on his cuff.

'How about you follow Lizzie upstairs? She will run you a warm bath and find you some fresh clothes.'

Elliot nodded again. Nancy put him down and gave him one last cuddle before she let him go. He appeared to be the only tangible thing in the room with her. If she let him go, maybe he would evaporate into a dusty corner too.

'He'll be fine, don't worry. Children, boys especially, are more resilient than you think, maybe more than you or I.'

Nancy nodded her mouth a tight line. Any movement might have ended in tears. Estelle reached out her hand, without a sound, Nancy took it.

'That has always been a conundrum,' Estelle said.

'What has?'

'That up there.'

Above the crossed swords, engraved in the dark patina of the wood panelling, was a carving set in an oval frame.

'Is that a coat of arms?' Nancy asked.

'No. This is why it has always held a point of contention with me. I remember arguing, shall we say, with my father. He always dismissed it. I just do not know…' Estelle tilted her head, further observing the object in question.

The shadow of the deep beams cast most of its detail in murky shadow. As Nancy moved just a touch to her left, allowing the midday light to filter in, it became clearer. Mary, with her baby Jesus Christ sat at the centre.

'My boys.' She clutched Estelle's hand, the portrait of a mother and a son so very raw that it jangled her nerves. 'My sons aren't safe here. Please don't tell me that I'm overprotective.'

'Those boys are strong. They are Hardacres.'

'I know the evil here,' Nancy insisted. 'You can deny it as much as you like—that's your prerogative, of course—but me? I'm not a Hardacre. Maybe that's why I can see it, and you can't.'

'I worry that all this concern is far too much for you. Those boys will only suffer if you do not let them settle into their roles.' Estelle was choosing her words far too carefully; Nancy could hear it.

'Neither of my boys will be lord of this god-forsaken place. Over my dead body, Estelle.'

'Neither was my son.'

'Andrew didn't want it,' Nancy spat. 'He saw it for the curse it was; you knew that. You were his mother. You must have seen how suffocated he felt here.'

'I still am his mother,' Estelle said calmly. 'Perhaps he did. Perhaps he was too blind with love to see that he would always find himself here eventually.'

Closing her eyes, Nancy took deep breaths. It was the panic; she knew that. This place had always got under her skin. She'd never understood why no one else felt what she felt, saw what she saw.

'Come.' Estelle guided her to the settee. 'Would you like some tea?'

Nancy shook her head.

'Then we shall sit here for a while, let the events of this morning wash away. I know your pain. I feel it.'

Nancy was still holding Estelle's hand. She didn't want to let go. Somewhere in her normal behaviour, she would have immediately discarded the gesture, but with Elliot and the stranger… it was all just too much. She watched their hands. Hers had warmed a little from the blazing fire. Her fingernails caked in mud from digging her son out of the hole. She wouldn't let her mind linger on it now—there'd be plenty of time for that in the night. As she let her mind settle, she realised this was the first time she and Estelle had ever touched. Lady Hardacre had never been the touchy-feely kind when Nancy had arrived, and Nancy had walled herself into her private prison of grief. Only Oliver made it through. The guilt struck hard once again—the sight of Elliot, the panic on his face. Nancy could still feel the shaking… No, it was Estelle.

She patted the top of Nancy's hand with her other and lay her palm there. She trembled a little, not a shiver or judder but more a vibration that gathered momentum and travelled up her arm. Nancy withdrew, though not entirely—her fingertips still rested in Estelle's palm. She leant a little closer, placing her hand on Estelle's cheek. She pulled away as soon as her fingertips touched the wrinkled flesh. A resemblance to alabaster was all she could summon. Cold.

'Forgive me,' Nancy said. 'Please, I meant nothing by it.'

'My dear, there is nothing to forgive. The sight of me must have conjured many an inquisitive thought over the years.' She folded her fingers over Nancy's hand once again.

Maybe she'd never been close enough to pay attention or even allowed herself to think about it. In truth, Nancy hadn't given it much thought until earlier today. Blind in her determination to have what she wanted, she never looked at those affected by her actions. She shook her head, ashamed.

'Did I ever tell you about the night Andrew was born? No, of course, I have not. We have never been ones to cluck over baby photographs or the family albums, now, have we?' Her mind seemed to wander as she mumbled to herself, 'No, I do not know where they are.' There was a smile at the side of her lips, but her sadness struck Nancy more. It lit her eyes with a clarity that sat at odds with her disfigured face.

'I owe you an apology, Lady Hardacre.'

'Oh, do come on. You have never held with titles, even that day you stepped through the great door. Never had I encountered a will as strong as yours. Neither, it seems, had Andrew.' The smile grew full. 'I am surprised you ever made it up the drive, to be brutally honest. Not once was a soul like yours allowed so close.' Estelle laughed; a sound that hadn't been heard within the Priory's walls for decades.

As the ring of amusement and mirth, no matter how uncertain, left Lady Hardacre's lips, the walls took what they needed, let the unusual sensation reverberate up to the rafters, bleed into the plaster and wood panelling.

However, *it* had heard too. The sound, more than an enticement, fuelled its craving.

The noon sun swept its chill deeper in through the stone casement windows, and the shadows slowly rose to meet it. Unnoticed at first, invisible. Haemorrhaging from the floor in soft wisps, gathering in creepers that twisted and coiled, crawling along the floor to meet its bait. It inspected Lady Hardacre, its gracious host, but it was tired of this game.

It was time.

Confused, Nancy gazed at Estelle, whose laughter still rang in her ears despite the sorrow that sat low on Lady Hardacre's motionless lips. Nancy couldn't unravel the moment, the reasons behind the slowness of her brain.

'I am so deeply sorry, my dear. Shall we get you to your room? A little lie-down will bring some colour back to those cheeks.'

Nancy saw Estelle's lips move, though the voice seemed to come from another time, another place. All energy escaped her. Limp and heavy, her legs crumbled. She wanted to see her boys.

'I shall get Lizzie to make some camomile tea to ease your nerves. What a morning you have had.'

Estelle was no longer beside her. Nancy tried to look around the room, but instead, her head lolled on her shoulders. She found herself being carried from the drawing-room. Heavy as lead, her eyelids shut. She rested her head closer to the figure that held her, felt the rise of every step, one steady after the other in a seamless procession until they reached the gallery landing. Desperation pulled at her eyelids to open but to no avail. So instead, she moved her head slightly, her ears pricked and alert. It would be here. This was the spot by the old, carved chair—she had counted the steps along the landing. Fresh panic set into her chest, she breathed, a musky note filling her lungs that struck her heart with an old arrow.

'Andrew?'

The arm squeezed her a little in reply. '*Rest.*'

SIXTEEN

That sweep of the clock hands when the winter afternoon yawns into twilight. Afore the thickness and concealment of evening and the inevitable nightfall, when the Priory's rooms are dressed in vague light blurred at the edges. Silhouettes hover, and apparitions dance with the dust. Those that hide by light step out of the shadows. Hardacre Priory inhales, filling its chamber lungs and hall veins with the consciousness of its past. The dead rise and the living fall prey... or become hunters.

Josiah sat on the upholstered chair beside Nancy's bed. Watching her lay curled up like a slumbering cat, covered by a thick blanket.

Samuel had warned him not to follow, though Josiah paid no heed. Lizzie had scolded him the last time he had watched Nancy sleep, but he did not want to leave her alone, not now. Not ever. When he gazed at Nancy's sleeping face, something deep inside his hollow chest reminded him — not of someone or something, precisely. Just a memory. Now more than ever did he feel the importance of such things. They had been alone for such a long time. It was easy to forget the softness of another's skin or the warmth of another's breath, what it was like to have your bedclothes tucked in tight. To have someone blow out the candle and say a prayer for his slumber. They had become accustomed to the loneliness and miserable void they occupied.

Nancy's arrival had caused a shift in the Priory's air. It was no longer dormant and stagnant. Josiah and his twin no longer existed *in their own private time, walking the halls and rooms as they had done for more than four hundred years. Now they felt the others.*

Nancy stirred. Josiah had watched her the previous night as she carried Oliver back to bed. It had tried then, had crawled from the shadowy spaces waiting to pounce. It had failed.

Nancy would fight.

History had seen others with such temperament. The Hardacre family tree marked them with short dashes between their years. To fight always appeared heroic in the beginning, but they rarely emerged triumphantly… No. Josiah thought again. None had emerged triumphant. It always won.

Now there was this mother with a ferocious spirit and fighting heart. She would fight for her boys, and she would die for them too; of that, there was little doubt. Perhaps she could do what no other before her had done—win. Nancy was the one thing the others had not been: she was not a Hardacre.

Josiah leant forwards just a touch. The resemblance to a long-lost memory was strong. Even Samuel had not denied it. He, too, sensed the familiarity.

Nancy shifted. A gentle murmur seeped from her lips—words of no consequence, yet they called Josiah forwards a little more till his face was so close. Her breath, her vital essence, a perfume so much like spring flowers that it made him weep.

Carefully, he left the chair to sit on the bed. His small body perfectly nestled between her arm and her pulled-up knees. It was right somehow. He did not want to move, to leave this mother, no matter how much Lizzie admonished him for his reckless actions.

Nancy roused. She pulled her arm up and wrapped it around Josiah, pulling him into a carefree embrace.

'Hmmm,' she whispered. 'Oliver, love, I'll be down soon. I'm just so sleepy.' Her eyelids were as heavy as her slurred words.

He slowly touched her hair. So very soft, like silk thread. He caressed her forehead with his fingertips. 'Hush, sweet mother. Slumber a while longer.'

SEVENTEEN

Through half-open lids, Nancy peered at her wristwatch—a little past six. Her mouth dry, her throat hoarse, she licked her lips as her stomach growled. She pulled herself up and pushed the blanket off, then swung her legs around to sit. Her head felt like she'd been bludgeoned; the dull thump of migraine was settling, the first in weeks. Why she'd thought she would get away without one in this place, she had no idea. This place was the perfect breeding ground for such things. Her nerves were always so tightly wound here. The Priory knew which string to pluck.

She smoothed down her hair and pulled the collar of her jumper straight. With her palms on either side of her, she pushed herself off the bed. A tiny object rolled down the mattress and tumbled into her hand. She wandered to the window. A slender shaft of moonlight glittered down; it was too magical, too enchanting, to hang above the Priory. She pressed her head to the glass and looked over the driveway. A car was heading towards the house—the teacher, Mrs Scarfe. Some normality at last. This was her chance to lay down her own rules within these walls.

With a deep breath, Nancy turned then remembered, pushing her palm open towards the silver light. An acorn. She closed her fingers around it, drove it down into the front pocket of her jeans, and left the room.

There was a decisive shift in the atmosphere as if the Earth had moved on its axis. Nancy made her way down into the large entrance hall as the foreboding sensation crept up the stairs to greet her, causing her to falter a few treads from the bottom. She took a tentative glance back up toward the gallery. There were eyes watching her. Then, gulping down the feeling, she pressed her foot firmly on the tiled floor, cementing her resolve.

Keep it together, even if just for tonight.

She intended to make it to the front door before Dawson. If she could meet the teacher on her terms from the get-go, the outcome would be better. She needed this small win.

'Ah, madam. I see we have a guest.' Dawson was there before she could blink, poised and waiting to serve.

'No, don't worry, I'll get the door. She's here for me.' Nancy twisted the iron ring to open the door.

'As you wish, madam.' With that, he stepped back.

The frigid evening air leapt in like a ferocious beast as the door slid wide open. The hall tiles frosted over. A large silver Jaguar continued to purr until its headlights dimmed and the driver killed the engine. The driver's door opened, a foot stepped onto the gravel, a man emerged, evidently eager to get out of the cold as Nancy was to close the door. Then the passenger and a back door opened, two others stepped out into the dark. All three figures hurried towards the house.

'Ah, Mrs Hardacre, I presume?' The man's genteel manner caught her off guard. 'You are expecting us?'

Nancy nodded, a little off-balance as she stepped aside. A woman and young girl appeared from the darkness.

Nancy turned to the woman. 'Hello. Mrs Scarfe?'

'Gloria, please. And this is my daughter, Josie. Say hello, Josie.'

The girl nodded, her eyes wide as she examined the hallway and sweeping staircase from under a mass of unruly red hair. Her bright eyes narrowed while they lingered on the gallery landing.

'Where are my manners?' The gentleman thrust his hand forwards. 'I'm Mr Beamish from Beamish, Talbot & Fisk.' He nodded again, his narrow eyebrows almost reaching his hairline. 'Mr Beamish Junior, in fact. Mr Beamish was my father and my grandfather before him. We're solicitors to the Hardacre estate.'

Nancy smiled a false, toothy grin she hoped looked more appealing than it felt. 'It's nice to meet you. Please, do come in. It's mighty cold out there tonight.'

Nancy pushed the door to as Josie leapt farther into the hall. Her eyes were still fixed on the upper floor, where now she inspected the walls.

Lizzie appeared, took coats and scarves with a curtsy, then disappearing just as quickly. Mr Beamish headed towards the drawing-room, beckoned by Estelle, who stood within the doorframe.

'Lady Hardacre. A delight to see you as always.' He touched Estelle's hand in a familiar manner. Her fingertips scarcely made contact as her eyes greeted him with geniality.

'Mr Beamish. It has been far too long since your last visit. Please do not stay away for so long.' Estelle moved aside and caught the teacher's eye. 'Gloria, it is a pleasure to see you again. And Josie! My, how she has grown.' Estelle's eyes darted to Nancy, who stood a little dumfounded behind the guests. 'Josie is the same age as the twins,' Estelle added with a nod.

'That's correct,' Gloria declared. 'Josie turns eight just before Christmas. So, I understand that your boys are almost eight too?' She turned to face Nancy straight on, her large wide eyes bright against her pale skin and hair the same blushed red as her offspring's. 'Josie couldn't wait to meet them; hence she came along.' Her face dropped. 'I hope you don't mind me bringing her with me?'

Nancy smiled, this time in earnest. 'Not at all. I think the boys will enjoy meeting someone their own age.'

She looked around for the girl. Gloria followed suit. Panic rushed to Nancy's cheeks; heat found her chest when her eyes travelled to the gallery landing and the old, carved chair. She could just make out a flash of red in the dim light.

'No.' Nancy flew up the staircase as quickly as her heart rate allowed. 'Josie!'

The girl sat deadly still. Her back pressed against the high carved back of the antique chair, her eyes wild and staring. Elliot stood nearby close to the top step, equally static, his hand outstretched behind him to find his mother's.

'I was coming down when I heard—' his voice crackled. 'I heard a cry, and I found her like that. Who is she?'

'She's the daughter of your new teacher.' Cautiously, Nancy lowered, looking the girl in the eyes. 'Josie? Can you hear me, darling?'

There was no answer. Though Nancy felt the shadows move, sense the darkness alter as it flittered along the landing. Then, with all the nerves she could gather, she knelt in front of the old chair and placed her hands on Josie's, which stiffly rested either side of the arms.

'I said *hello*, but she didn't answer me. What's the matter with her?' Elliot went to put his hand on the girl's shoulder but pulled away, clenching a fist to his chest.

Josie flinched. Her eyes flashed and darted around the dim space. 'Where's my mummy?' she cried with a trembling lip; her cheeks streaked wet.

Until she saw Elliot. 'Oh, hello,' she said.

'Ah, hello. I'm Elliot.'

Josie tilted her head to one side and examined him.

Gloria had made it to the top of the staircase, her eyes even wider. 'What were you doing? Please don't ever run off like that.' Her panic charged the air with a familiar scent. 'Remember what I told you.'

Nancy could easily imagine what the girl had been told— this *was* the Priory.

'Come along. No harm done.' Nancy took Elliot by the arm as Josie leapt down from the chair. 'Where is your brother?'

She looked at Elliot as Oliver came bounding down the narrow staircase. Nancy's heart regained its natural beat, and the anxiety in her shoulders eased.

'Mum?' Oliver's eyes found the strangers.

Nancy stepped forward in front of the chair, feeling her skin bristle and her breath hitch.

She took her boy's hands.

'These are my twins, Elliot and Oliver.'

She said nothing more, just stood tightly clutching her twins, longing to run and escape. But, instead, the chair stood between them and the visitors, a possessed carved divide, a barrier to their escape—normality on one side, Hardacres on the other.

†

Mr Beamish stood before the fireplace, the great stone surround framing him. His brown pinstripe suit glowed with a warm orange halo against the flames, but his back was to the room. Nancy knew the moment her foot touched the stone threshold what he was looking at.

'I'm so sorry for dashing off like that, Lady Hardacre. Children.' Gloria expressed; her cheeks flushed.

Nancy wondered if Gloria had even wanted to come tonight, more dragged into the folds of the Priory through obligation or even fear. Her manner was hesitant. She hovered by the settee, looking warily at the tea tray. Nancy's heart sank. The poor woman, Nancy felt every bit of her anxiety.

'Please, Gloria, won't you sit? Let's have some tea.' Nancy placed her hand on Gloria's back as she sat.

The children bundled through the door as Nancy handed them all a biscuit. 'There. Now, why don't you three go and find something to do? Some colouring or a puzzle? Why not show Josie your room—there must be a game you can play.' Nancy felt the stupidity of it all. What visitor in their right mind would want children wandering around the Priory after dark?

'Is that a good idea, Mummy?' Elliot asked, his eyes wide, the whites glistening in the orange glow.

'Yes, let's go and find a game to play. Do you have Operation or Buckeroo?' Josie was already through the drawing-room door.

Nancy glanced at Gloria, who sat on the edge of the cushion, her knee juddering. Estelle said nothing, merely sipped her tea. Oliver followed the girl out into the hallway, but Elliot grabbed his mother's hand.

'I'll look after them, Mummy.' With his other hand to his mouth, he whispered, 'I don't think she should be here.'

Nancy nodded. 'Come get me if anything… if you need anything. But stay in your bedroom.'

'We will.'

The children left the room, taking innocence and the art of conversation with them. Nancy watched Gloria, a woman no older than she and clearly educated with a level of confidence about her. But the woman who had entered the Priory no more than fifteen minutes earlier had altered into a young girl shaking in her own skin.

Nancy reached for the teapot, the best china this time. Pouring Gloria a cup, she glanced back at Mr Beamish, who hadn't moved. His stance was firm, hands static by his side. He seemed to be no more in the moment than one of the ancestral paintings that hung high on the gallery walls.

Gloria rested her teacup with two hands on her knees, the saucer precariously balancing on her blue pleated skirt.

'So, Gloria,' Nancy started. If she could neutralise the atmosphere somehow, she would. 'I thought my boys could start school with you next week, if that suits? I understand I may need to come to the school to sign some forms.'

Nancy sat beside her; her knees turned to face Gloria. She wore a smile, yet it was far from what she felt. Visitors and

Hardacre Priory didn't mix well. It seemed to expel any sense or reason and left guests' mute.

Estelle stood beside Mr Beamish, gracefully holding her cup and saucer before her. 'Oh, I have already explained to Gloria that the boys will not attend the school, my dear. She fully understands the matter of things.'

Gloria nodded, her red hair bobbing too eagerly. Her lips appeared sealed in a tight line just under her thin nose.

'No,' Nancy said. 'I want some routine for them both. They may be Hardacres, but that doesn't mean they are exempt from school.' If the pulse in her temple wasn't pulsating for everyone to see, she would be amazed. 'As I explained this morning, Estelle...' she continued, a touch more grace— fitting for guests, she mused. If she were to play this game, she would do it properly. 'I cannot expect you to pay for private tuition. You have been gracious enough to allow us to stay here.'

'My dear, we do not worry about such things. Gloria has already offered to tutor them for us.'

Mr Beamish turned and faced the room. He stood beside Estelle; his shoulder no higher than hers.

The tea Nancy had sipped made its way back up, the bitter taste of nausea increasing. She rose, hurried to the window, and leant against the stone ledge. The crumbling painted radiator pressed to her legs—cold as usual. Silently as she could, Nancy inhaled, closed her eyes a second, desperate to not be sick. Darkness was thick now. Dismal clouds hid the moon, outside undistinguishable, only the room behind her mirrored on the leaded glass.

Gloria, motionless, her face steady but taut—anxious. Estelle was still sipping her tea, swayed a little in front of the glowing fire. However, it was Mr Beamish who arrested Nancy's full attention that now glued her hands to the stone sill. His eyes flicked to Nancy's reflection, to the carving above the fireplace, and back again. No one said a word.

Josie ran into the room with such speed the air jolted, knocking the silence off-kilter, dragging the room back into the moment. The floor beneath Nancy's feet shuddered; caught off guard, she stumbled a step and turned.

'Mummy, look,' Josie announced, bounding to her mother.

'What have you got there? Oh, now look at that.' Gloria put down her teacup, her face relieved.

Josie held a drawing, animatedly pointing at figures cast in coloured crayons. 'This is me, you, and in there is Daddy. See?'

Nancy's heart settled at the sight of her boys, but they held back a few paces from the girl. As usual, Oliver threw her a glance and smile to check in. It was Elliot, however, his face ashen, who sidled over to his mother. He stood his back to the room and pulled her down to his level. She felt the words waiting to be spoken.

'What is it?' she whispered. 'Everything all right?'

'It's Josie.' Elliot nudged his head towards the girl. 'I don't think she should come here again.' It wasn't just his head that shook; his whole body shuddered.

'Oh.' Gloria stood, gathered her handbag, and looked around. 'It was lovely to meet you, but we must be going.'

Lizzie appeared in the doorway with Gloria's bright-green coat. Nancy could do nothing but watch as the guests hurried towards the door. Elliot still gripped her hand, though Oliver had ambled to his new friend. The crayon drawing lay face down on the settee next to the vacant spot.

'Go on. You go say goodbye, too, with Oliver and your grandmother.' Elliot did as he was told despite the pleading expression that crinkled his brow. 'It's okay.'

'No, Mummy, it's not.'

With a gentle nudge, Elliot shuffled off to say goodbye.

Feeling like there were invisible eyes on her from every corner of the room, Nancy picked up the drawing. As she went to turn it over, she felt a hand on her shoulder.

'Please forgive me, Mrs Hardacre. If I could have one moment of your time.' Mr Beamish eyed her carefully, a hint of concealment in his tone.

'Oh, of course, sorry, Mr Beamish, I thought you had left.'

'I shall, but I need to speak with you.'

'Go on,' Nancy offered.

'No, not here. Would you mind coming down to the office, perhaps tomorrow?'

'Umm, yes, I suppose I can.' Her heart banged against her ribcage. 'Can I ask what this is about?'

'I would rather not discuss it here if you don't mind.' His eyes scanned the room—he felt it too, she knew it. That increasing sense of unease, of knowing something was listening, delving into your thoughts, Nancy could see it in his eyes. 'No appointment needed. Whenever you arrive, I shall be waiting for you. Until then, Mrs Hardacre.' He bowed and left.

EIGHTEEN

Estelle returned to find Nancy, her face more ablaze than the logs that she jabbed and prodded with the iron poker.

'Lady Hardacre,' Nancy announced, turning to face her.

'Nancy.'

Estelle sat in her fireside chair and watched her daughter-in-law gather her thoughts. Always in such pain, such sadness. If only she would embrace the situation she and her boys were in, then the pain would soon disperse into the ether, leaving them all on a far better plane of existence. She didn't want to fight. She never had. However, there were rules at Hardacre that had to be obeyed, or else havoc would reap its harvest—something she didn't intend to allow while she still roamed the Priory's halls.

'Nancy, will you please sit down, dear.'

With no arguments but slow, deliberate steps, Nancy sat hard on the settee. She looked exhausted. Estelle wished that things could have been different, that life hadn't brought them back to the Priory. That Andrew had never met this girl with fire in her belly.

'Before you give me the lecture again that things are done differently here at Hardacre, let me tell you something, please,' Nancy asserted.

She saw no discernible expression on Nancy's face, or maybe that was the expression—closed. 'Go ahead.' Estelle raised her hand with a nod.

Lizzie rushed in with a tray set with two glasses. 'A little something to calm the nerves,' Estelle added, dismissing the maid with a smile.

'No, thank you,' Nancy said. 'I need to get the boys to bed.'

'No need, madam. I have settled them both. They've had baths and are now tucked up in bed.' Lizzie smiled. 'A little supper treat too. I hope you don't mind?'

'No, of course not. Already?' A thick look of defeat washed over Nancy's features as she reached for her glass. 'Sherry?'

'Would you prefer something else, madam?'

'No, no, this is fine. Thank you.' Nancy sipped and rested her head back against the settee. Her hand swept over the cushion beside her. 'Have you seen the picture? Josie left it here.'

'Oh, I threw it away,' Estelle said. 'It was just a silly thing.'

'So, you thought it was necessary to destroy a child's picture?'

'It will be forgotten. Little Josie probably already has.'

'You can't go around doing things like that. It's not right. And there was something about it—I saw the look on Gloria's face. What was it?'

'It is of no matter. What was it you wanted to discuss? The boys' schooling?'

The night was drawing in fast. Estelle felt the floorboards rattle beneath her feet; there had been a shift tonight, the air was charged with change. Along the wooden panelling at the far side of the grandfather clock, Estelle saw the small figure. She smiled, and it shrunk back into the shadow. She knew those twins of the past could feel it. And it seemed so too had the girl, Josie, in her innocence, she had risen to *it*, answered *it*, just as her father had done, and in doing so, there had been a connection. Josie understood what it was, she knew what had happened to her father. Josie opened a door in the divide which could no longer be closed by her or another, cultivating a medium between dark and light. Estelle had been holding it and keeping it at bay for as long as she could remember. Now, however…

She looked directly at Nancy, her face adamant; she had to get through her stubborn barrier, make her listen.

'I know things here at the Priory can seem a little different, even unfair,' Estelle began. 'You must remember that no matter what, I am on your side, my dear. I am under no illusion—I know it was not a choice you wanted to make. Bringing the twins here was the last thing you wanted for them. But—and this you must fully appreciate, or else life here will be a battle in every respect—' Estelle paused a second, took a deep breath, followed by a sip of her sherry. 'It is not a normal life at the Priory, yet it can work. You can all be happy here. It is an existence I had not chosen myself, but I have been happy here.'

'And when you leave us… Let's be honest, Estelle. That's the nature of this discussion.' Nancy tucked her legs under herself on the settee, stuffing a blue cushion behind her neck. 'My boys are here because they are the final heirs to this god-forsaken place.' This wasn't a night for mincing words. It seemed Nancy was keen to abandon all her restraints. 'Let's face it: when you die, all this will be theirs, and Elliot will be the new Lord of Hardacre Priory. Please correct me if I'm wrong.'

'I value your candour. You are correct in many ways, but he will not be Lord Hardacre. Neither will Oliver.' Her eyes didn't leave Nancy's once. She needed to establish the importance of this matter tonight, or she might never get another chance to say it.

'But… If neither of my boys is to be the lord, then why are we here?' Nancy gulped the remains of the sherry in one go. 'You called us here, Estelle. You expected us to leave everything, didn't even say goodbye to your own son. And stupidly, we came. I packed up everything because I thought you needed us. I thought that, even though our relationship has never been one of fondness, we were all you had. *You* are all *we* have. You and this damned place are all I have left of Andrew.'

There was no mistaking the building tears that crackled Nancy's words. Her hard exterior was about to come crumbling down around her ears, leaving her sitting in a mass of rubble—something Estelle had never imagined possible. Estelle rose from her chair and sat next to her daughter-in-law. The settee creaked a little. In the corner of her eye, there was another movement in the shadows. Not the twins of the past this time. She needed to be quick before *it* silenced her words. She took Nancy's hand and put their glasses onto the table.

'Nancy, my dear.' She leant in, her voice no more than a whisper. 'I need you to listen to me very carefully. Do not say a word; just nod if you understand.' Nancy nodded as her mouth opened. 'No words. Just hear what I say. *It* is listening; I must say this before I cannot.'

Nancy squeezed her hand as panic swept over her face.

Darkness spread like the wings of death Nancy had already witnessed. She didn't deserve this. She quickly nodded again, her eyes eager and her mouth tight.

'The end has been a long time coming. I had hoped it would end with Andrew... we all had. Then you came along, bright and breezy with so much beauty. How could he not be devoured by your vibrancy?' Estelle smiled a warm, loving smile that pulled youth out from under the moth wings of grief.

Nancy shifted in her seat, her legs swung to the floor, and looked over her shoulder into the gloom but said nothing. Estelle had heard it too.

'Listen, we must be quick. Andrew was meant to be the last. I was prepared for it to be so, and he knew the task—I made sure of it. Alas, they did not allow it. He fought so hard, but they—*it*—did not listen.'

A deep scratching echoed along the floor. Nancy stood, staring into the shady corner. Estelle gripped her hand and pulled her down to sit.

'Please, ignore it. Just sit down and listen to me.' Estelle pulled her closer. 'The twins are the problem. The boys came after, and Andrew was no longer the last. It has to be the last, you see?'

'No, I don't, I don't see, I don't get any of this.'

Estelle put her fingers to her lips, her eyes saucer-wide. Nancy saw the fire flames reflected there, then something else — a shadow, a silhouette.

'Only the last heir can finish this. It sounds a little dramatic...' Estelle felt the laughter rise and swallowed it. 'Our history reads like a dreadful fairy tale, not reality at all, but it is true. We have been cursed for centuries. I was the last of them. No other branches of the family left. Then, when Andrew arrived... well. And now, as it stands, only those boys can end this misery. It will end before the year is out.'

'And then?' Nancy whispered. Her eyes followed the shifting shadow in the corner of her eye.

'I do not know. Nothing? No one knows.'

'And me, what can I do? The twins are just little boys. They can't do anything. They can't fight if that's what you're saying... can they?' Nancy's voice dropped lower. 'So, it will be me?'

'In a way, yes.' Estelle's voice squealed to a stop like an overwound spring.

Then it snapped.

Estelle's eyes grew vacant, her mouth slack. Nancy's hand fell out of her hold.

The room plunged into silence. Flames no longer danced or crackled in the grate. The whistling wind outside ceased.

'Estelle?' Nancy put her ear to Estelle's face. She wasn't breathing. Nancy pressed her fingertips on Estelle's wrist, feeling for a pulse, then on the cool skin of her neck. Nothing.

'*It is a fruitless task.*'

She froze, her ears pricked. The words came from behind her. A shadow passed the fire, momentarily blocking what light was left, leaving Nancy to reach for Estelle's hand.

'*She is dead, girl.*'

It was playing with her.

'Why don't you get out of my head?'

'*You cannot escape me, Nancy Hardacre.*'

'What do you want? Please, I need to help her.'

'*You should listen to your thoughts. I have heard them. Why do you not listen to them?*'

Nancy could pretend to be brave and brash—anger had kept up that charade these past few months. But she wasn't. She was afraid, and now she felt more alone than she ever had.

'*I find your pretence quite amusing.*'

'Enough. Get out of my way.' With her fists balled by her sides, Nancy faced the fireplace where the shadow covered the embers; although, there was no figure to see, certainly not one to fight.

'*I admire your bravery. Finally, a worthy adversary.*'

Nancy reached forwards through whatever was there for the long iron poker. With fear that coursed through her veins, she swung it. The poker clanked against the marble mantle and rattled the swords above it. Nancy braced herself, inhaled, and flung her arms high with another swipe. She hit the old wooden panelling. The swords clattered to the floor and bounced off the marble hearth, the hilt of one hitting her square in the chest. The force threw her back, knocking the air from her lungs. She landed flat on the floor beside the settee.

Lizzie appeared in the doorway. 'Madam!'

Nancy felt herself pulled to the fireside chair; her head gently pushed back against the wings as a thick blanket covered her knees.

'There, madam. You rest now.' Lizzie put her hand to her forehead. 'All will be well, madam. You'll see.'

Amidst her drowsy vision, Nancy saw Lizzie fuss over Estelle.

'Oh, my lady.' Lizzie held Lady Hardacre's hand and smoothed the hair from her brow. 'Let me get you to your bedchamber. Far too much excitement for this evening.'

Panic rose in Nancy's chest. She should call Mr Beamish, a doctor, anyone, yet no matter how much she tried to move, the blanket held her fast to the chair. Her mind meandered through dark corridors, shadowy hallways and lofty rooms. She called out, she ran, she wept, but above all, she fought. Nancy Hardacre fought hard, but sleep won.

Samuel stood beside Josiah. The twins had witnessed the evil of Hardacre Priory many times. They had faced it themselves, been part of the first and set a precedent for all those centuries to follow. All those who came after, those boys had no choice but to observe while it played out. They had never been equipped to help. For every generation—every heir—the battle was private, but at the severest cost of them all. Over time, there had been a need to concede. Allowing themselves a fondness for the heirs had never ended well.

Samuel had warned his twin not to sit at the mother's bedside. He did not want Josiah to suffer alongside her, yet even he felt that longing. It beat strong where his own heart had once pumped with life. The mother, Nancy Hardacre, was not here because of blood— she was not an heir to this curse, which in itself made her powerful—but Samuel knew it would mean her demise. He heard the whispers that swept the halls at night.

NINETEEN

It was surprisingly bright for a September morning at the Priory. The curtains were flung wide to allow it to drift into each dark corner, banished the shadows. A breakfast tray sat on the table beside Nancy's bed.

Her chest hurt like a lorry had mowed her down.

'Here, madam. Allow me.' Lizzie plumped the pillows. 'There you go, that's better. I took the liberty of bringing you a tray this morning. Rise when you're ready. The boys are up and about. They are lively souls this morning, already playing outside—some adventure, I imagine.'

'The boys are outside after what happened to Elliot yesterday?' Nancy questioned.

'We don't see sunshine like this often and thought it best they make the most of it. It's even quite mild, would you believe it? Best not look a gift horse in the mouth—that's what the mistress always says.' Lizzie stood by the window, quite taken by the sunshine.

'My mistress will meet you in the library when you're ready,' Lizzie said. 'She has something for you.'

'Lady Hardacre?' The image of Estelle, limp and lifeless by the fireplace, darted in front of her eyes. 'She's well?'

'Of course, madam. She has a few minor errands to sort first, so enjoy your breakfast. She also said not to hurry down.' Lizzie bobbed in a quick curtsy and beaming smile.

Nancy reached for her mug as her mind snatched tiny snippets of the day before, hoping tea would aid the task. Possibly some aspirin too. She gulped her tea as the maid vanished, taking her glow with her. She had no appetite—fried eggs and bacon didn't mix well with amnesia. She walked to the window and drained the last drop from her cup. Lizzie had been right—despite the absurdity of it, the day was bright and the sun high. Even a hint of heat seeped through the glass, warmed her face.

There were her twins. The grounds spread as far as she could see, acre upon acre, all the Hardacres. The twins, dressed in shorts and wellies, were running and stopping every so often to twist and turn. Elliot held out the sides of his red anorak like a superhero cape whilst Oliver thrashed the sparse grass with a short stick.

'It won't last, Nance. It can't. We both know that.'

Andrew spread his arm around her shoulders, folding her into him. Nancy eased her head back until it touched his. If she closed her eyes, allowed the sun to warm her eyelids, she could pretend just a short while, forget what truly swept the halls here; time to be the mother of young boys who deserved to be free to run and play in the sunshine. If only it could last just for today.

She sighed. 'I miss you.'

'You don't need to miss me.' He kissed her hair.

'I'm so angry. I keep trying to let go, but I'm afraid I'll give in to all this madness if I do.'

His arms fell from her as the sun dimmed from her eyelids. Nancy opened them to find white clouds had crossed the sun.

'Stupid, foolish grief,' she spat.

'On the contrary, Nancy Hardacre, I am fond of the grief you hold on to so tightly. I do not doubt the strength of that love in your heart. Mind all that harboured anger does not turn it black.'

'Fuck off!' she yelled. 'We're leaving, do you hear me? I'm taking my boys. You won't have them.'

'Do not be so rash.'

She'd had enough. She would pack their belongings and leave this morning… if she could only move… Her feet were stuck, fused to the floor, her bare flesh bonded to the old polish of the floorboards. Her hands spread flat on the glass in front of her, with each long finger spread over the glazed panes, touching the old leading. No matter how she tried, she couldn't budge.

Deep breaths, she thought. *This isn't real.*

Nancy felt it climb. Almost gentle, almost sensual. Thin tendrils found her ankles and coiled up her legs. When they reached her thighs, they pushed her legs apart. She tried to look down, but no matter how much she battled, her efforts were wasted. Opening her lips to speak, she found she was mute. Her cries were silent.

'Why fight it, Nancy Hardacre? Is this not what you want?'

The room sank weighty about her shoulders. Nothing except blackness reflected. She no longer saw the gardens, the grounds, or her boys. The space beyond the glass was a black void, nothing but her wide-eyed reflection. *Close your eyes*, she ordered herself. *I don't want to see.* It was hopeless. Even as she fought, the compulsion to watch rose dark and angry in her gut.

Nancy's hands pressed firmer against the bitter cold glass. Thick frost grew from the sides and headed towards her hands; it closed in on her until it covered her fingers. Tiny, beautiful frost patterns embellished her hands. Mesmerised, she watched, unable to do anything else.

The tendrils coiled and folded around her. With her legs bound and stretched apart, thin finger-like vines snatched her nightgown from her shoulders, it fell to the floor in shreds, leaving her exposed. Her heart froze.

'Do not fight me.'

But she would fight. She would fight so long as air filled her lungs and blood rushed in her veins.

'Oh, you are a delight to behold. Hearing your thoughts only makes you more delectable.'

'I will take my boys away, and you will lose. They are mine.' She sounded strong in her head, bold and determined, though the words never made it to her mouth. No one heard her screams. 'You will not have my boys; do you understand me? Never! I won't allow it.'

'It is not your boys who I want. Not yet.'

Those twisted fronds braced her body, folded, and wrapped thicker, bound over her breasts up to her throat. Moments of oblivion flashed with moments of pure, blinding clarity. The foulness that had encircled her legs now loosened. They were free, but only a little—just enough for what it wanted. Panic. Fear. Nancy clenched her eyes tight. With intense ferocity, it thrust deep inside her, pounding, pulsating, filling her over and over.

She tried not to look, but the pain pulled her back to the now, and her eyes flew open. Nancy stared into the glass. In the dense blackness of the reflection, the shadow coiled into a solid form.

'Something for you, Nancy Hardacre. Consider it my gift.'

Andrew's likeness, as accurate as if it were him, emerged from the fog. The lips that kissed her ear, the tongue that trailed over her neck. The eyes that flashed wicked with lust. Even the smile was faultless.

'I will have you first.'

TWENTY

Wild, carefree, with the sun on their backs and a warm breeze whistling tunes in their ears, the boys skipped and rolled on the grass. They forgot the misery of the past months, how life had tipped upside down, how much they longed to hug their dad, how much they longed to see their mum smile. Today, those were far from thought.

In shorts that skimmed scabby knees, they ran. An adventure of battles, knights on horseback, or cowboys and Indians. Caked in dirt from scrambling around making dens in the sparse undergrowth, they galloped to the lake that swelled from the river even though they knew they'd be rebuked for doing so.

Don't go anywhere near the lake. Water is not a good friend. Lizzie had worn a face of such gravity the boys had frowned at each other, neither sure if she'd meant to say more. Instead, she'd handed them an apple for their pockets and a handkerchief for their cuffs.

They quickly grew tired of the water. The hunt for good skimming stones came up short. Oliver lost interest and headed backwards in the direction of the Priory's ruins that hovered on the horizon with the sun glinting on exposed flints like a beacon.

'No,' Elliot shouted. 'We can't go up there.'

'Why not? Look, they're right there. I'll race you.'

'I mean it. She told me to never go there, to never…' Elliot gathered the conversation, trying to remember. '…to never walk under the arches!'

'What?'

'Nan told me yesterday. Then that thing with the mud happened…' Spiders scurried down his back at the memory. 'It scared me.'

'But you weren't at the ruins, were you? You were nowhere near them,' Oliver declared, shoving his twin's shoulder.

'It doesn't matter. It was a warning, Oli. We're not going there.' Elliot stamped his foot. A flurry of tiny flies hit the air. 'I'm the oldest. So, what I say goes.'

Elliot turned to leave. He stomped through the long, brown grass and watched the creatures that dared to live on the grounds scurry about. Refusing to look over his shoulder, he walked faster and faster to distance himself from the ruins, for in truth, he heard them call him.

They rambled for a while, not a word passing between them. Elliot felt the scorn on Oliver's face, his thoughts shouted in his head, but he wouldn't give in, not now. Making a pathway through the barren land, they tracked back past the Priory. Oliver had overtaken him, running with a stick in his hand, thrashing the grass. Why couldn't they just be the boys they had been?

Elliot couldn't remember the last time he'd watched his favourite TV shows. In front of the telly, Saturday teatime, watching The Incredible Hulk, which had been his time with Dad. Mum and Oli had always been off doing something or other. Elliot had never cared what. He'd buried himself in the living room with his dad by his side. If he were a superhero, he'd have battled and saved Dad.

The twins ran towards the crossroads. Elliot flew on the breeze with his anorak spread wide like a cape. For a moment, he felt light—he'd be a hero now. He'd keep them all safe like Dad should have done.

The great oak loomed overhead, taller and thicker than it had ever seemed. It no longer felt ominous or dangerous.

Lizzie had said to steer clear, to stay well back because it wasn't a good place to play.

Lizzie was wrong. It was the perfect place.

The boys lay on the grass, sprawled out under the great boughs of the oak. The grass appeared a little greener than it had. Perhaps the sunshine made it so. Elliot looked over at Oliver, who lay back with his hands clasped behind his head, resting on a tree root. His eyes closed, comfortable, relaxed; he appeared different. His face was dirty; that seemed wrong somehow, a smudge of what might have been jam around his mouth, now dried with dirt. No matter how Elliot struggled, he couldn't see why it felt dishonest like his brother was an imposter.

Chilling fear churned in his belly. It wasn't the anger and sadness that had consumed him whilst he held the old walking stick but a blacker feeling that made his skin itch with panic. The same feeling he'd had with Dad that day.

'Come on. I'll race you up the tree.' Oliver scrambled to his feet. He laughed as he scuffed the front of his new Wellington boots on the bark.

'Mum's gonna kill you for that,' Elliot said. 'They're brand new.'

'What do I care? Honestly, they're just wellies.' Oliver waved his foot at Elliot's face. 'Look. What does a little scuff matter?'

He climbed the tree. Bony legs dangled from the main branch that reached out farther than any other. Its twiggy fingers extended towards the house, pointing at the stone rose window in the frame of the gable roof. The boys had never ventured up that far. Mum had said the words with a tone like thunder: *never go up there*. They had no idea why. It hadn't been of any interest at the time.

Yet, now, as Oliver stood on the branch looking towards the Priory, that window called to him. It reflected the morning sun, glinting in code like a smoke signal to come and play.

'Shall we go and see what's up there?' Oliver pointed at the window, his thin arm stretched beyond the branch, and squinted with one eye.

'Get down,' Elliot ordered. 'You know we shouldn't climb. We shouldn't even be down this far.'

'You are such a bore sometimes. It's just a tree. What do you think's gonna happen? Is it gonna pick up its roots and walk to the house to get us in the middle of the night?' he laughed. 'Just come up here, will you?'

'No.'

'Because you're scared.'

'I'm not.'

'Yes, you are. You're no fun anymore, Elliot. Come on, have a look from up here.'

'Stop it.'

'Are you gonna make me? You've gotta climb up here to get me first.'

Elliot scrambled to his feet; with a quivering lip, he reached up to the first branch. Before he got any higher, it began. It was slight at first—a minor judder, nothing more. Oliver stood on the vast bough, his arms stretched to a higher branch, the rubber soles of his wellies gripping the bark.

'Look at me. I bet I can walk to the end. You can see the whole house from here. Do you think she's watching us out of her window?'

'Why are you so mean today? This isn't you, Oli.'

The desperate want to shove his brother off the branch fleeted before his eyes, and although Elliot shook it away, it clutched his chest in a vice-like grip.

'The window, it's…' Oliver stopped. 'Look! Can you see them?' He walked along the branch, edging closer to the thin end.

'No, don't do it.' Elliot's heart pounded. It wasn't fear of his twin falling but something else. Something worse. Something deadly. 'Please don't. I'm going home. I don't want to play with you anymore—not when you're like this. It's wrong, and I don't like it.'

Elliot fell back two steps and let go of the low bough, his ankle twisted as he landed. Oliver stood high above on the lumbering limb, his eyes locked, wide, staring.

'Just come down.'

With his hands shielding his eyes against the sun, Elliot gazed up into the tree. An eerie stillness to his brother made his heart gallop.

'Come down, Oli!'

But his brother remained still, static, fixed on the branch, with only his mouth moving.

'What? I can't hear you.'

Oliver let the branch slip from his hands then his arms fell by his side. The only thing in Elliot's head was explaining to their mother that he let Oli fall. What if he died like Dad? Would Mum blame him for it? The blackness churned in the pit of his belly again. He screamed, shouted for Oliver to get down from the branch, to stop being so horrible. Fear gripped his gullet, his voice lost as he silently cried.

Scrambling to stand, Elliot gripped the soles of his new wellies on the huge tree root; catching the bark, he slipped backwards. It appeared to move, rumble under the earth. Then, with a deep breath, he stood looking back up at his brother. The top of the oak was thicker now. It covered the sky, blocking out the sunshine, casing him with leaf-mottled shadows.

He wanted Mum. Needed to run back, get help, tell her that the oak was trying to take Oliver.

'You are going nowhere, young heir.'

A twisted vine unravelled from the tree's thick trunk. Slowly, it looped around Elliot's ankle and squeezed his

Wellington boot to his leg. He screamed and looked up at Oliver. His twin said nothing, did nothing.

It began to tremble, the tree, the roots, the earth beneath his feet. The ground shuddered, softly at first, gradually gaining strength. Every spiky twig, each rough streak in the bark, all the old knots in the great oak convulsed. Ripe acorns pelted down over Elliot, bruising his bare skin as he squirmed to free his foot.

'Hold on, Oli! It's going to make you fall off!' he yelled over and over for Oliver to hold on. 'Please, just come down. Be careful.'

Oliver stood perfectly still, his face vacant and his eyes staring as the whole oak quaked around him. Elliot could do nothing but watch amid the pelting acorns. It was as if his brother had vanished, and there stood someone else entirely.

TWENTY-ONE

With every descending rung, Nancy relived the horror. She could have stayed there, a fallen heap of pain and despair on the bedroom floor. It was not going to get the satisfaction of her defeat, not today. In the bath, she'd gripped the taps as the shower water poured down. But there was nothing to wash off, nothing physical or tangible. She couldn't scrub away the blackness that violated her. It may have won this single battle. But she wouldn't let it win… and if it wanted war, then it would get war.

There was a calmness in every step down the staircase. Nancy had crawled from the bathroom to her bed and sat transfixed by her breakfast tray, a simple sight of normalcy. How was she to reason any of this? It hadn't been Andrew. She understood that. Yet, in a vivid moment of lucidity, her heart had relished the connection, with her body responding as it always had to Andrew's touch. Except, there was no doubt of the vile and deadly motives.

'Ah, Nancy. You are up.' Estelle passed through the hall from the library as Nancy's foot hit the smooth tiles.

There was no escaping the strange air that hovered in the Priory. The usual white-cold light was warm and golden. Even Nancy could have been tricked into thinking that this was an ordinary house. And, maybe, for the sake of her sanity, she would play along with the façade for now.

'Will you join me for a cup of tea in the drawing-room?' Estelle held a large white envelope and waved it a little.

Nancy followed with a quick nod. Not more tea—at some point, she'd have to admit her dislike for the stuff and buy some coffee.

Estelle sat to one side of the settee and adjusted her floral dress over her knees. It was a yellow one today, the colour of daisy middles. There was something else that didn't seem usual—her face was a little smoother, still aged, but the ripple of her moth-wing cheek flashed a touch lighter, silkier. Estelle smiled.

The tall clock with its polished case over by the panelled wall was ticking. Had it always ticked? The sound of its rhythm filled the void of memories that Nancy still couldn't place together. She glanced at the fireplace. Thick logs hissed and crackled in the grate, nothing unusual in that, but... it was different. The room was warm. Sun streamed in through the stone casement windows. She wandered over, gazed out beyond the gravel drive to the gardens where she had seen her twins playing. Her thoughts crept back to the image of Andrew. She wouldn't allow it. Not now. *Go away*, she thought, then turned back to the room and Lady Hardacre, who stared back at her.

'Are you quite well this morning, my dear? You appear a little flushed. Not coming down with something, I hope. I could call the doctor if needs be.' There was genuine concern there; Nancy felt it. It bled like warm honey from Estelle's eyes.

'I'm fine; although, I must ask you something. It's important.' Small puzzle pieces were slotting together. 'Do you mind?'

Nancy hovered beside her, waiting to sit. Estelle patted the seat cushion.

'Last night, you were... What I mean to say is... I'm having trouble piecing together, remembering our conversation. I think you fell ill?' She was reluctant to be blunt; the memory was still unclear.

'As you can see, I am well. I had it that Lizzie got you up to bed after you drifted off to sleep in the chair. Too much sherry, perhaps,' Estelle said with a smile.

'Nothing else? Nothing you would like to tell me?'

'Actually, now you ask… Yes, there is. I was wondering if you would run an errand for me today?' She waved the white envelope again.

'Post office?'

'Oh no. To Mr Beamish, if you would. Something I needed to sign. I forgot to give it to him last evening.'

Nancy remembered then. She recalled it all. Mr Beamish, the odd little man in a brown pinstripe suit. Hesitant Gloria, the teacher and her strange child Josie with her stranger crayon drawing that had made Gloria dart from the Priory with the speed of a bullet.

'Of course. It would be my pleasure.' Nancy reached over to retrieve the envelope. 'I may have a little wander around the shops, too, as it is such a lovely day. I could do with a few things.'

Lizzie appeared with a tray. 'I took the liberty of making you a pot of coffee, madam.' There was that glow again and a smile. 'I also took the liberty of preparing the boys a little picnic for their adventures—just some ham sandwiches and jam sponge roll I made this morning. If there is nothing else, my lady, I shall go find them.' She curtsied.

'I'm heading into the village in a short while. I can give it to them on my way out. Please don't worry, Lizzie. It's very thoughtful of you. Thank you.' Nancy nodded with a natural smile that managed to reach her eyes, but her guts churned. She had *every* intention of finding the boys on her way out of Hardacre.

When Lizzie disappeared back to her chores, Estelle reached for her teacup, with bright eyes again on Nancy.

'Have you had any more thoughts on the boys' schooling?' Estelle asked. 'Gloria is a wonderful teacher. She has agreed to tutor twice a week. In addition, she could regularly bring Josie to play with the boys—they seem to have got along famously.'

'Perhaps you're right. I may see Gloria whilst in the village to make the final arrangements with her. You know, see what I need to sort here, like set up a schoolroom, for instance.' If they were playing a game, Nancy sure as hell wouldn't fall short on the rules.

'Oh, certainly no need for that, my dear,' Estelle declared with a grin, a sight new to Nancy. 'We have a schoolroom. I and so many before and after having been tutored here. Hardacre's have never attended'—a frown wove itself along her thin brows, which Nancy noticed were painted— 'the village school, or any school, after a point.'

'Of course.' Nancy put her coffee mug to her lips, slightly biting the edge of the china.

Stay calm. Stay focussed.

Lizzie handed Nancy a basket as she fastened the last button on her jacket. Nancy slung her leather bag over her shoulder, retrieving the car keys from the front pocket.

'Thank you, Lizzie. I appreciate it.'

Lizzie bobbed. 'Always a pleasure, madam.' She leant a bit closer. 'Always here to help you and those dear boys. You only need to ask.' Her eyes hovered on the drawing-room door. 'I'm on your side.' She let go of the basket handle and placed her hand atop Nancy's.

'Thank you.' Nancy didn't dare say more.

'I mean it, madam. Those boys are dear things.'

'They are.' Nancy eyed her carefully. She appeared a little duller now; the soft glow had gone. It was the tone of anxiety that sat just below Lizzie's skin that caught Nancy.

'Be careful. Remember those gift horses, madam.' Nancy nodded, but Lizzie's hand was going nowhere. She held Nancy's tight and squeezed.

Something dug into at her hip. Nancy pulled her hand away and thrust it into her front pocket. Her fingers gripped the tiny object with the spiky stalk—the acorn. Lizzie fell away, adjusting her apron around her waist and fussing over her collar. Not once did she look at the acorn.

Nancy laughed a little. 'Ah, well, what do you know. I forgot about that.' She rolled the acorn about her palm and rubbed her thumb over the smooth surface. Her eyes met Lizzie's. 'A little gift from Oli.'

Lizzie didn't smile. Her face paper-white, her eyes darted to the top gallery landing and lingered there, stretching from end to end and down the staircase. Nancy's eyes didn't follow. She knew what lay up there now. Instead, she opened the door before Lizzie could look back and quickly closed it behind her.

They had arrived in the Hillman only a few days before, though right now, it seemed like a lifetime. Nancy had entered the Priory with a furious soul, anger in her heart, and her two boys in tow. Yet, as she sat in the driver's seat with the engine purring, she felt defeated.

She put the car into first gear and pulled off. Glancing in the rear-view mirror, she saw the drawing-room window. Estelle stood there, her yellow dress vivid against the room's gloominess. Nancy braked hard, her foot flat to the floor. It wasn't the room that lay in the darkness around Estelle but the darkness itself.

Estelle pressed a hand to the window. Unconsciously, Nancy raised hers to wave, but Estelle didn't wave back, nor did she see. Estelle's eyes glowed opaque white. Her mouth fell open, nothing more than a black gaping hole. The daisy-middle yellow of her tea dress slipped into sepia tones, and her hair gleamed white.

The familiar click of the door locks rang in Nancy's ears. She pulled the driver's door handle, but it was locked. Her clammy hands kept slipping off the window winder. No matter how much she clicked her seatbelt catch, it wouldn't free; she was stuck. Condensation was forming. Nancy wiped her cuff over the rear-view mirror. The air in the car was thick, clammy, suffocating.

Estelle was still there, unmoved.

Please, no.

Shadowy threads licked at Estelle, caressed her arms, and wound around her wrist as her hand rested on the window. Frost formed, fusing her palm to the glass.

It was the moment Nancy feared. It had been inevitable. The shadowy limb embraced Estelle, folded around her thin body, her breast and neck.

'God, no!' The Hillman jogged on its wheels as Nancy pushed and tugged at the door. The engine died. Silence.

She shuddered at the reflected image of her mother-in-law. It only took a few seconds, a blink in time. Lady Hardacre was no longer there. A swarm of fluttering wings, of dusty grey moths, had replaced her.

Nancy couldn't turn away, transfixed by a sight that seemed to play for her benefit. The shadowy limbs swept the air where Estelle had stood, now nothing but wings. The shadows gathered them, folded them in on themselves, consumed them over and over, tumbling until just one lonesome moth remained. It flittered and bashed against the leaded glass, each time more desperate to escape, to find the light. Nancy heard it. She felt its need, sensed its panic in her heart as it thudded against the window, again and again until its last moment. A last long coil of evil swiped at the moth and left it to fall—half withered, half flapping—till it lay dead on the stone windowsill.

The engine purred, the sound scorching Nancy's ears. Without a thought, she thrust the gear stick back into first and pulled off down the drive, spraying grey gravel in her wake. Into second gear, then pushing into third until she was far enough away so as not to see the window while her eyes darted from the driveway to the Priory and back.

It was more intuition than judgment when her boot slammed the brake. The Hillman screeched and skidded sideways to a stop on the verge with a *thud*. Her pulse raced as she pushed the heel of her hands to her temples, her forehead resting against the steering wheel. She shut her eyes in fear of what she'd hit. Banging on the window stole her thoughts. Elliot.

Her fingers quivered as she gripped the handle to wind down the window. Her hands smothered her boy's cheeks, the panic in his eyes echoing her own.

'Oliver?'

He nodded. 'Please, Mummy, make it stop.'

She pulled the handbrake and escaped the car door with a speed that had the heel of her boot caught the rim; and she fell to the ground. Elliot grabbed her arm, tugged her, pulled her free. Her boots thudded hard, every step a marathon and her heart in her mouth.

Not Oliver, please. Please, no.

She felt the oak tree mocking her as soon as she caught sight. It thrashed the warm air. Its longer branches flogged the hard ground. Leaves fluttered like confetti, yet every branch was lush with new ones growing as the last fell. Nothing was still apart from the enormous bough—the one that pointed at the Priory. The one that held her youngest.

Oliver stood high on the branch, much higher than she remembered it ever being. The tree was huge, grown since they'd arrived. It had arrested her wits when she had driven past. She should have reversed down the drive back to normality. Even if it were a life of poverty, they would have been safe.

She saw it now, the evil that seeped in long grey mists from each branch. Every tiny twig emitted it.

'Can you see that, Elliot?'

He looked puzzled. Fresh tears welled, and his voice broke into another sob. 'Make Oli stop, Mummy, please.'

'It isn't him; it's the tree, the evil—all of it. It's this place.'

Nancy grabbed Elliot by the shoulders. 'Now, listen to me clearly. Listening?' He nodded. 'Run as fast as you can. Get in the car. Shut the door and do not open it for anyone. This is important—*no one* but us.' Elliot nodded again. 'Now go.'

'What about you?'

'I'm getting your brother. We're leaving.'

Nancy watched her eldest bolt across the grounds in his wellies, thrashing off the stray leaves with his thin arms. She held her breath as she turned back to the tree.

She barely saw Oliver amidst the flying debris. A cyclone of twigs, leaves, even broken branches whipped the air and thrashed her as she walked closer. Her hands over her head, covering her face with her arms, she gradually paced forwards.

'Oliver?' she yelled as loud as she could before it snatched the air from her lungs. 'Oli—' Nancy fell to her knees, pushed down by the weight of wreckage.

'*You are a determined creature. I admire that.*'

With gritted teeth, she pushed her hands on the ground as each knee crept closer. Slowly, slowly. It wouldn't win. She would be damned if she'd admit defeat.

A giant tree root rippled over the ground like a great snaking serpent. It was in fingertip reach. Just a little farther… If she could just…

'*Not so fast.*'

The root undulated, sending shudders through her hands. Nancy pushed herself up and staggered to her feet. A spray of dirt and debris rose, a muddy dust cloud in her eyes as the root whipped the air and beat her backwards. Gasping and stunned, she lay on the ground. Her chest burned as she choked on the dirt.

'Come on then! You think you can beat me? You will not have another of my family. You want a fight? It's with me!' Nancy sputtered as she coughed up the last of the dirt. She wiped her face, stood, and stamped her boot onto the end of the exposed root. 'Now give me my son!'

'Very well, Nancy Hardacre.'

The end of the root twisted. The sound shattered in her ears. Sharp and caked in mud, it ripped through the air, reached up to the vast bough, and pulled the earth with it, leaving a cavernous trench at Nancy's feet. Over and over, the end of the root flung up to its boughs, battering the boy from his perch.

Nancy grabbed the end as it hit the ground and dug her nails into the muddy tuber. She gripped it as it coiled beneath her. But her arms wound tighter.

Oliver stood unearthly still. Only the toes of his wellies touched the bark. His arms stretched out to each side in a cross. He stood almost suspended, seemingly unscathed by the lashes—silent words forming on his lips. Again and again, he repeated them, though Nancy couldn't make out what they were. She called up to him to answer, but as he spoke with his eyes shut, the turmoil of swirling twigs and acorns fell to the ground with a *thud*. Oliver's mouth closed, and his eyes opened.

'Oli?'

Oliver's rigid arms withered by his sides, his thin legs crumbled beneath his weight as his wide eyes rolled in their sockets, white like milky marbles. Then, just as his eyes shut again, he fell. Nancy caught him, hitting the ground with her back, smashing the lifeless root as it snapped over the gaping furrow. Her son lay in her arms, his head on her chest. Winded, they lay there for a while, too scared to do more.

Nancy looked up to the tallest branches. The sky was blue beyond, the sun glistening on the leafy tops. If she believed hard enough, the terror of reality could evaporate into that bright blue yonder, taking all her cares with it. Could she allow it to take her? Would it take all the pain with it?

'Mummy?'

It was a muffled word but enough to ignite her instincts. Dazed, they gripped each other as Nancy scrambled from the muddy hole.

'Quick. We need to leave right now.'

Nancy squeezed Oliver in her arms and ran. Had the car been this far away? The ground seemed to go on forever as she determinedly staggered over the gardens. She had barely left the Priory behind, her green Hillman still parked on the sparse gravel and its front wheels wedged on the grass where she'd left it.

'Elliot?' she shouted as loud as she could.

His hesitant head popped up from the back. He peered between the front seats, his face ashen. Nancy bundled Oliver into the back next to his twin.

The keys jingled in the ignition. No matter how she tried, she couldn't move. Her back pressed hard against the seat, her head on the rest, staring in the rear-view mirror. Her boys were there. They were safe, all she had left in the world.

Move, Nancy. Start the bloody car and move your arse.

'Who are they?' Elliot was on his knee, his forehead pressed against the back window. He pointed.

Nancy's view was limited. 'Is it your grandmother?' The vision of that weak, lone moth behind her eyes, Nancy swallowed and attempted to move her head. 'It's okay; we're leaving.' The car roared to life.

'It's not Nan,' Elliot said. 'I'm not sure who they are. There are lots of them.'

The car sped down the drive.

'Elliot, sit back down. Don't look at them.'

'Are we coming back? They frighten me, Mummy.'

'Over my dead body.'

Nancy peered at them both. Elliot's face was white and panicked as he gripped Oliver's arm. His twin, on the other hand, was still, hadn't moved since she'd bundled him inside. His eyes were open, but her heart sank at the vagueness in them. Where was he?

Nancy pulled up along the quiet stretch of county road heading back to the village. The crossroads, the entrance to Hardacre Priory, far enough behind that she couldn't see it or the oak tree. There were no cars or walkers while they sat there. If anyone had enquired, what would she have said? But they wouldn't have stopped. This was an unassuming village; she wasn't known here, wasn't a local.

Lost in her scattered thoughts, Nancy hadn't noticed that the boys were no longer confused or worried; the panic still running through her seemed to have left them. Elliot was tucking into a sandwich, Oliver a green apple.

Nancy flung around in her seat. She reached behind and slapped the basket lid shut. 'What are you doing? We can't trust anything or anyone.'

Two puzzled faces looked at each other, then at her.

'Mum, it's just the picnic,' Oliver said. 'Did Lizzie make it for us? It has cake and everything,' he beamed.

'What?'

'I'm hungry.' Oliver took a bite.

'After what just happened?' she spat, then swallowed slowly. *Keep it together.*

'Lizzie said she'd bring us lunch and sent us out to play.'

'They are all…' How could she explain it to them? 'We're leaving, and we're never going back.'

Oliver closed his mouth. His lip quivered.

'Okay.' Her eyes focused on the road ahead, Nancy revved the Hillman back to life.

TWENTY-TWO

Raynham was sunny and utterly oblivious to the horrors that sat just outside the village. Nancy drove slowly without direction, her heart lodged somewhere near her throat and threatening to lurch. The car came to a natural stop in the high street as a double-decker bus pulled away in front. Her chest was tight, restricted. She had to decide where to go. They couldn't sit here all day.

Nancy glanced behind her to see the boys still eating. A pang of guilt stung her at the memory of Lizzie as she'd left. Lizzie knew what evil was there, knew the danger they were in. *Bloody hell, Nancy, of course, she does. She's one of them. Get yourself together.* Her head fell into her hands, her elbows on the steering wheel. Tears were forming, but she wouldn't—couldn't—allow them to fall. She'd be damned if she would let the Priory break her.

'Look, there's Josie.' Oliver banged his hand on the car window. Josie beamed. 'Let's go say hello. Please, Mummy? I like Josie.'

'Oli, sit still.'

Could she trust Gloria? She had morphed into a terrified mouse perched on the drawing-room settee and had disappeared into the night as if fleeing a crime scene.

Nancy leant over the seat to open the window, keeping her eyes on the twins, her lips a thin line in a look of *do not say anything.* Gloria and her equally rosy daughter stood by Nancy's passenger window and waved.

'Hello there, Nancy.' Gloria leant in a little and rested her hand on the open window. Josie waved to the boys.

'Hello…' she replied, finding nothing else to add.

'You off to see Mr Beamish? He said you might pop into the village today. I passed him a message to ask you, but, well… you are here now and so am I, so I shall ask you myself. Would you all like to come over for a while? After you've seen Mr Beamish, of course. For some tea, or coffee.' She chuckled, blushing. 'I thought the children could play for a while. Josie doesn't get to see many friends outside of school. It's a lovely day; they could play in the garden.' Gloria turned to the twins. 'What do you think?'

Nancy stared at her boys, defying them to speak. They didn't. Instead, they nodded with equal enthusiasm. Josie jumped on the spot and tugged at her mother's dress. To refuse now would have been a mistake. Whether Gloria was an ally or foe, what did Nancy have to lose? Apart from her sanity and her twins. Hell, she had forgotten about the solicitor. He was another oddity Nancy wasn't sure she had the stomach or stamina to confront today.

'Ah, yes, Mr Beamish.' Nancy nodded, trying to buy herself some time. 'I, um…'

'He said he has something important for you.' Gloria's face fell from its joyful mount to Nancy's level of torment. The memory of the last evening at the Priory had possibly returned.

Gloria's face tensed as she scanned the small high street and let her eyes rest on the solicitors' office. Nancy hadn't realised how close she'd parked. Perhaps it had been subliminal. Beamish, Talbot & Fisk Solicitors was nestled into the row of ancient buildings, its metal sign lightly swinging on its bracket.

Nancy turned back to the boys. 'As you see, I have the boys, so I'll just call in quickly to arrange another time.'

There wouldn't be another day. Nancy Hardacre was planning the moment she'd turn the key and start her Hillman.

'Oh no, Nancy, you can't do that. Mr Beamish is expecting you.'

Her eyes weren't on Nancy but the window across the road. Nancy's eyes followed, but the black glass only reflected the street. She turned back to Gloria, who nodded, a worried expression on her pale face.

'Very well.' Nancy had no choice but to concede. Something in Gloria's expression made the guilt of running impossible to overcome. She'd make it quick. She could trust the boys to sit quietly for ten minutes, fifteen if they had to. Surely it wouldn't take too long. Something regarding Andrew and the estate, she imagined.

Oh, the letter.

Nancy dug her hand into the depths of her handbag and pulled the crisp envelope out, its pure whiteness glaring.

'I do have something for Mr Beamish.'

'Ah. Well, that's settled then. Why don't I take the boys to my cottage to play? I can get the tea ready, and you can come over when you've finished. I don't mind.'

The plea in Gloria's eyes pulled on every string. This woman had a way of digging into her heart.

'My cottage is over there.' She pointed towards a turning just off the high street. 'I live just there—Lavender End. It's the thatched cottage with the lavender hedge.' She smiled. 'Obviously.'

'I'm not sure. I can take them with me.' Nancy regarded the twins, who looked pleadingly at her.

'Please, Mummy.' Oliver's face was more earnest than his brother's. 'We'll be good, we promise.'

'Fine. Okay.' *You win*, she wanted to say.

Nancy pulled the keys from the ignition and closed the door behind her once her boys safely stood on the footpath, holding hands.

'Don't worry, Nancy.' Gloria nodded. 'They'll be okay. I'll look after them.'

There was more to that line than there should have been, a declaration or oath rather than a quick I-will-watch-how-they-play remark. It struck Nancy's heart with a swift blow and almost bowled her over.

She nodded to Gloria and her boys, who looked far too caught up in the ecstatic dance of seven-year-olds. *As it should be,* the thought stung. They were just children; they shouldn't have been party to any of this death, this horror.

You won't win this war, Hardacre Priory.

'Are you quite sure of that, Nancy Hardacre?'

Nancy watched them go until they disappeared around the corner at the end of the high street. Her heart was empty, her chest hollow like someone were digging it out with a dull knife. She still stood in the road, her back to the car, and watched the solicitors' sign sway. Life in this sleepy, rural Suffolk village looked so mundane.

'You need to do this, Nance.'

'Fuck off, Andrew.'

'Why are you so hesitant? You know you have no choice.'

'Get out of my head. You're not real; you're dead. You left me in this god-forsaken hell hole, so fuck the hell off.'

A man with hair the colour of coal and a moustache to match halted mid-step. 'You all right there?'

Nancy nodded. She pulled her jacket close and swung her bag over her shoulder. 'Fine, thanks.' She tried to smile—the muscles in her cheeks twitched; evidently, she'd forgotten how.

'So long as you're sure.' He continued down the street but stopped when he got to the pub. He glanced back and went inside.

'They'll think you are some crazy woman speaking to yourself if you don't just go inside. Nance, honestly, love, you have no choice. You must see this through. Haven't you realised that you can't run from this?'

She didn't rise to the voice in her head.

The solicitor's office was cooler inside and more oppressive than she'd hoped. Deep down, she'd known that it would be. Everything was connected.

'Ah, Mrs Hardacre.' Mr Beamish stood in the doorway leading to the back of the building. Light filtered around him. It looked a touch more inviting than the gloom of the front entrance. A young woman sat at a corner desk to the left. Nancy hadn't noticed her until she moved, causing a little dust to scatter in the air. Nancy jumped.

'Shall I arrange some refreshments?' No older than her early twenties, the woman with a mass of peroxide curls and pink lip gloss stood up from a desk and headed towards a door next to Beamish.

'Thank you, Suzette. That'll be great. Please, Mrs Hardacre, do come through into my office.' He stepped aside with a flourish of his arm, and Nancy followed. 'I'm so pleased you came. There was a niggle of doubt that you might not, I must confess.'

Nancy said nothing until the door closed behind them. The room was welcomingly light.

She exhaled. 'I almost didn't.'

'Well, you are here, and I can't begin to tell you how grateful I am.' He pointed at a leather chair, coaxing her to sit. Then sat in his chair opposite.

Nancy took a moment to gather her surroundings. The room wasn't large by any means, but it had an air of peace about it. An odd observation, she thought, as it swamped over her like a soft cloud. It almost felt safe. Mr Beamish aired the same quality. It hadn't seemed that way the evening before when they'd stood in the drawing-room. Perhaps the Priory swallowed such attributes at the door.

Suzette, in a swift blonde haze, arrived with a large tray of refreshments. 'Will that be all?' She didn't wait for a reply and left.

'Now, before we get down to business, Mrs Hardacre...'

'Call me Nancy. *Mrs Hardacre* makes me sound—' She didn't finish. How could she say that she hated sharing the name of that damned place? 'Nancy will be fine.'

'Very well, Nancy it is.' He smiled with a warmth that made her heart plunge heavy into her gut; she gulped, trying to hold the tears back. 'I think you may have something for me, a document? And please, if it suits you, call me Peter.'

'Yes, I do. Here.' Nancy lifted the flap on her bag, reached in and placed the white envelope on the desk between them. 'Estelle—'

The room filled with moths, grey, dusty, and erratic. Nancy covered her face, closed her eyes as her hands shooed them away from her ears. They flapped their filthy wings around her head and caught in her hair. They wanted in. They were trying to break into her head. She wouldn't let them.

'Are you quite well, Nancy? Whatever is it?' Peter asked as he stood quickly.

How could she tell him? She had to contain herself. The moths were in her imagination, even if they felt real, even if she felt their wings on her skin. It was Estelle—Nancy knew what she'd seen. She understood the absurdity of it, how ridiculous it would sound if she explained it to the solicitor or anyone.

Slowly, Nancy lowered her hands and opened her eyes to find the room as it had been. The solicitor observed her, his hands clasped in front of him.

'You poor, dear woman.' He handed her a box of tissues. 'Can I get you anything? Some water?'

'No.' Nancy took a tissue and pressed it to her eyes. There were tears. There was a pained sound, too, which came from her chest. 'Oh, forgive me. I'm so sorry, Mr Beamish. I don't know what's come over me.'

He sat back down, his clutched hands on the desk.

'I feel it's I who should apologise,' he began, then waited for her to settle herself. 'I fully understand what you've been through of late, what the whole family has had to endure.' He eased back in his chair a little to allow his arms to stretch, though his hands remained on the desk, his fingers pressed together. 'They are just boys, after all. It's a great travesty to lose a parent at such a young age.'

Nancy hated the scrutiny. He was watching her. A question on his face hovered between them.

'Mr B— Peter. I wonder...' She held her breath a moment until it stung. 'Can I trust you?'

He looked admonished but smiled, nevertheless. 'I fear there's more to that question. Am I correct?'

Nancy nodded. Her hand went to her hair, her eyes scanning the room again.

'You are safe here, Nancy.' He leant forwards and poured them coffee from the pot. 'Maybe this will help.'

The small office lay in silence except for the sound of cups and saucers and the gentle slosh of coffee against china. Nancy swept her hand around her head. Every so often, the sound of moth wings thrashed madly at her ear. Peter watched.

'Can I be candid with you?' he asked as he sipped his coffee. 'I'm not one for riddles, tales that leave nothing but an enigma to solve. I've found that most situations call for frankness. Looking at you, I wonder if honesty would serve us both today.'

His words broke the theatre of moths and snapped her out of their spell.

'I would appreciate that,' she breathed, trying to steady her voice. 'I've found nothing but the contrary since I arrived in the village.'

'I imagined it was so.' Peter lay his cup and saucer back down and steepled his fingers at his mouth. 'There are some who would respond with disbelief at what we both know to be the truth of Hardacre Priory.' He blinked slowly. His face mellowed even more, taking on an expression of such calmness it slowed Nancy's erratic heart. 'I think we both understand the matter, don't we?'

'The truth? What I've seen and felt doesn't fit the word truth. To be honest, Peter, that's a word that sits at odds with what I've seen today alone.' Nancy shuddered.

'These things you've seen—have they seemed real to you?'

Nancy bobbed her head. 'They have.' Her hand shook as she struggled to grip her cup.

'And if I asked you to tell me of these things, would you tell me the truth?'

It felt a little too cryptic, everything they'd agreed they didn't want.

'Peter…'

'Forgive me. What I'm trying to gauge is… No, let me try to rephrase it. What I need to know is this: are you fully open to speaking the truth? Can we agree that only truth will be spoken here?' He spread his hands around the room. 'This office is a safe place, a sacred place, certainly to me. The truth can be spoken without the fear of mockery or…'

'I understand, and I'm grateful. It's not that I'm afraid to speak the truth or that you might not believe me—to be honest after today, thought crazy is the least of my worries.' Her jaw ached, but she couldn't shift the tension that made her teeth grind, and her hands shake.

'Then what is it that concerns you? I want to help.'

Nancy laughed. The thought that this man in his navy pinstriped suit and matching floral tie could help was farcical.

'I worry that it would be time pointlessly spent.' Nancy shook her head. 'You can't help me.'

'I see,' he replied slowly, all the while looking directly at her.

Mr Beamish poured more coffee into his cup. He offered sugar and milk while Nancy watched the vein in his temple pulse. She was wasting time. The morning was ticking by, but she had no idea what time it was; she'd forgotten her wristwatch, it still lay on the table in her bedroom. Nancy shivered, scanning the room for a clock, but there was little besides a desk, a wall of cupboards—nothing else.

Apart from one thing.

On the far wall behind Mr Beamish, where the wall was painted white, hung a small picture. No, not a picture—a carving. It looked familiar. She began to drift back to the Priory.

'Nancy?'

She jumped at her name. 'Yes?'

'I was wondering if I could give you a little history, take you back to the beginning as much as we know it.'

'Family history?'

'In a way, yes, and again no. More the history of the Priory before the family. Before the Hardacres set foot through its doors.'

'When it was just a Priory?' Nancy sat forwards, trying to retake her cup, it clunked on its sauce, and she gave up. 'Do you mind?' She stood and walked around the desk to the other end of the room. 'I've seen this before.'

'I believe you may have. It has a twin,' Peter replied.

'A carving much the same hangs in the drawing-room, doesn't it?' Nancy's voice was low, her words slow as she studied it. 'So, you know what this is?'

'Of course. It's a carving of the seal matrix.'

'Like a crest or coat of arms?'

'In essence, my dear.' Peter stood beside her. He traced the carved image of a seated Mary, her son Jesus Christ in her arms. 'In a way, the story starts here. This is the seal—the crest of St Augustine—for the Priory as it once was.'

'Before the dissolution of the monasteries,' Nancy added.

'Quite so, my dear, quite so. It was once a place of faith where only goodness lived.'

'No bloody goodness there now…' Nancy nodded more to herself than to her companion. 'What happened there?' she asked as she turned to face him. 'Monasteries, abbeys, priories all over the country suffered the same fate. I know the history, Peter. So why is that place any different from others?'

'Some evil spans beyond time or reason. What lies beneath the earth of those grounds is evil at its purest.'

'The devil himself…' Nancy laughed and felt the shadowy limbs around her shoulders as they had been that morning. She closed her eyes, willing the sensation to vanish, but Andrew lingered.

'It may feel that God has forsaken Hardacre Priory,' Peter said softly.

'Forgive me, I'm not sure I understand. To be honest, I don't go in for all that stuff. God and the Devil, heaven and hell.'

'Ah, no, my dear. We're not talking about the devil. He himself was once an angel— fallen, yes, but of heaven. This is nothing of heaven and hell.'

'I'm not religious, Peter.' Nancy crossed her arms. 'If you are about to tell me how that hell has risen, or quote verses from the bible… Well, as I say, I'm not religious. I don't believe in any of it. Forgive me, but I find it all nonsense.' Nancy gulped down a choking lump. *No*, she *wasn't* religious. So why was the darkness of hell in the pit of her stomach, whispering inside her head, touching her skin, plaguing her thoughts. She shuddered.

'As I said…' Peter paused. 'This doesn't have its origins within the pages of the bible. It's something ancient that walks those halls.'

Nancy concentrated on the carving. 'Do you mind?' She raised her hand, the tip of her forefinger inches away.

Peter nodded and gave a satisfied sigh. 'If the need is there, then you must.'

Nancy took a tiny step closer. A bright sunbeam struck her cheek as she did. Bringing her nose in touching distance to Mary, she closed her eyes and pressed her hand to the wood. It warmed beneath her palm as a wave of something potent, something tangible, washed over her. Nancy pulled her hand away and stepped back from the carving.

'I've never been to church. Would you believe that?' She laughed. 'What I mean is, I've only been to weddings and funerals…' Andrew was there again. 'My Sundays are for ironing, not praying.' Her laugh turned to tears. She didn't know why she was crying; she didn't have faith. She certainly didn't have faith in anything good at the Priory. She blinked away her tears and took a deep breath. 'My only relationship with God is in my vocabulary—*for God's sake*…' she laughed again.

Peter nodded, smiled, and took her elbow. He guided Nancy back to her chair. 'I have always seen the matter of faith in another way. I feel it as a matter between the individual and God.' He sat, his hands laid out between them and his palms open. 'Do you believe?'

Nancy stared at Peter's hands. He really was an odd man, but not in the way she had imagined. He possessed a quality that demanded attention though she didn't understand why.

'Do I believe in God? I have already said I don't.'

'Yes.' He smiled. 'Then, let me rephrase it. Do you have faith?' He lifted his palms a little higher, so the light touched his fingertips. 'Look at my hands. They are open, but what do you see?'

Nancy shuffled in her seat. She carefully eyed the solicitor, then looked at his palms. 'I'm not sure what you want me to say. They are empty.'

'Physically, yes. I hold nothing solid in my palms, but are my hands empty?'

She shook her head, her eyes narrowed.

'They hold faith, Nancy. I hold it in my hands and my heart. You felt it.'

'Did I?' She felt a stab of annoyance.

'I think so. You may not think it is faith in God,' he added.

Nancy smoothed her hands over her legs, noting mud smears on her thighs, and was flooded by a thought that her time was swiftly running out. 'Then what is faith if not in God,' she stated, crossing her arms.

'In something other than evil. Faith that something bad can be defeated by goodness.' Peter looked around the room. 'I feel it here even though we're not in a church, just in my office that has nothing sacred about it. There is no altar, stained glass or steeple.' His eyes fixed on hers. 'Now, do you understand?'

She nodded, thinking, then she unfolded her arms and stared down at her hands. 'I'm not sure if God believes in me.' It was a strange thing to say; she had no idea why she had. Had she been thinking it?

'I believe that answers your question.' Peter threw his arm towards the carving of Mary. 'A mother will do all she can to protect her son... or sons. I feel that God sits by your side, Nancy. But...'

'...evil stands on the other?' she said sarcastically.

'I know the truth, as do you. There's no doubt that evil resides at Hardacre Priory. One that sits at its foundations that runs through every acre of land. This is why I asked you here today.' Peter eased forward toward her, marking every line of scepticism on her face. 'It must end. It has lain there unchallenged for far too long...' he hesitated. 'No, it hasn't gone unchallenged. We've never found the one who can face it head-on.'

'Me?' she snapped incredulously.

'You are special, Nancy. It's time. It has challenged you, hasn't it? You have seen what it can do. I know you have.'

She laughed. It had done more than challenge her. She bit back the tears and balled her fists in her lap.

Peter stood and gave her a quick nod. 'I have something for you.'

He headed to one of the cupboards along the wall. He reached inside, almost lost from view, and reappeared holding a black bag. He placed it on the desk and pulled out a small leather object.

Nancy frowned at it, then back up to the carving.

'I'm not sure how much time we have.' He held the object in both hands, following her eyes to the carving. 'This once belonged to the Priory. It's an item of the greatest importance—I must stress that.'

'Then why give it to me? Why doesn't Estelle have it?'

'It's too late for Lady Hardacre.' His face was matter-of-fact. 'I shall not mince my words: Lady Hardacre has been dead many, many years.'

Deep down in the pit of her stomach, Nancy knew it was true. She'd seen it. But to hear it spoken by someone who had been in their company the evening before, how could she respond? Her hand flew to her mouth as she tried to swallow nausea, but it sat a choking lump in her throat.

'I saw her. I mean, I have seen her like… that. Today.' She buried her face in her palms. 'We've never been friends, I'm sure she would agree, but…'

'It has begun.' Peter closed his fingers. Tight fists rested on the desk. 'All who reside in Hardacre Priory are long gone, my dear, long gone, some much longer than others.'

'My boys?' Nancy whispered, her hand on her chest. 'I need to get my boys.'

'They are safe; none there will hurt them. Estelle loves them dearly.'

'No, that's not what I meant. They're not there. They are with Gloria.' Panic skittered down her arms. The sensation of those terrible moth wings played again on her skin.

'I must go. We must leave.' Nancy went to stand.

Peter reached his hand out to her, resting it on the desk between them. 'You must get your boys and return to the Priory. They need to be there with you.'

'That doesn't make any sense. It wants my boys, whatever it is.'

'Only you can defeat this, Nancy, but you must stand together.'

'What the hell can I do? It wants me dead.'

'That's precisely why you are the one, don't you see?'

'I never wanted any of it. I don't want any of it now. I just want to take my boys and leave this bloody village behind.'

Nancy stood and gathered her bag.

'Please, Nancy. It has to be you.'

'I'm not even a damned Hardacre. Not really.'

'That's why you might just succeed.' Peter held out the leather object, eager for her to take it. 'Please?'

'No, I won't.' She had her hand on the door handle.

'Please, for the sake of your boys?'

Against all instincts, she took the object. It lay in her hands—a small thing, really—wrapped and bound in an ancient piece of leather with a wax seal like the carving. 'No,' Nancy declared and shoved it back into Peter's hand, though her eyes were on Mary and her tiny son. Nancy felt all that love—a mother's love for her children.

She would die for her boys.

TWENTY-THREE

Nancy's hands shook as she struggled with the key, but it wouldn't fit in the lock. For the life of her, why couldn't she get it in? She thumped the car roof, cursing; her heart thudded against her ribs. She needed to escape. Finally, she managed to open the car door then slammed it shut behind her. She flicked down her door lock; no one was getting in. The sensation of being followed, watched, wouldn't shake free. It wouldn't have surprised her to find someone in the backseat. She glanced in the rear-view mirror.

She had to get her boys. Her shaking hands gripped the key and turned it. The engine revved to life, the Hillman Avenger roared up the road and down the right-hand turn where Gloria and the children had walked. A little more than few feet along the road was a thatched pink cottage surrounded by a wide lavender hedge. Nancy parked behind a blue Morris Minor. Breathing deeply, she waited for her heart to settle.

Laughter reached her as she walked towards a white-painted gate.

'*Children playing. What could be more satisfying?*'

Nancy ignored the voice. The words were nothing more than poison to tease and tempt her. Instead, she painted a smile on her face and knocked on the door.

'Around the back,' Gloria called from the side. 'Nancy? We're in the garden. Just follow the path around.'

Nancy followed it, a jiggled array of grey paving that led her to an open garden with the greenest grass. She had almost forgotten what natural, thriving grass looked like. The smell, too—it enlivened her senses with an abundance of lavender, rose bushes, and a large peony shrub. It had no blooms—the flowers of this year were long dead like so much, but all Nancy Hardacre saw was her own peony in full flower, large heads of the deepest crimson.

The memories of all her losses snatched away whatever last shreds of composure she'd been holding on to. She crumbled to her knees, her hands pressed onto the grass and her legs nestled in the thickness of nature. Her heart broke. Her spirit drained. Vast, salty tears puddled by her hands as she sobbed.

'Oh, Nancy.' Gloria knelt by her side. 'Children, go inside, please. Josie, find your colouring things. Why don't you all draw some lovely pictures?'

The children nodded and ran upstairs with thudding steps, leaving nothing but the sound of heartbreak, raw and desperate. It blocked out the bird song, the cars on the street beyond. Nothing existed but her deepest despair.

Gloria stayed, her hand resting on Nancy's shoulder. She said nothing. It was what she didn't say that spoke the loudest.

Eventually, when the tears subsided, Gloria ushered her inside the cottage, closed the bathroom door behind Nancy, and then went to the kitchen. The tiny room was beamed with a crooked door shut with a bar latch. Nancy wanted to stay in there, locked safe in the orange room in the ordinary house, away from all those things that were the contrary. Nancy didn't dare look in the mirror. She heard the kettle whistle— Gloria was making coffee.

'Here you go.' Gloria handed Nancy a coffee. The two women wandered around the garden, holding their mugs close like talismans to ward off their grief.

'You have a beautiful garden.' *I miss mine*, Nancy wanted to add. 'It's larger than I expected it to be.'

'It was the one thing that made us buy it. The cottage needed a lot of work, but the gardens… We saw the magic here.'

Gloria sipped her coffee and stopped close to a length of tall, thick boxwood hedging, running her hands over the small foliage, the leaves flittered between her fingers.

'Nancy,' she whispered. 'Can I trust you?'

The question Nancy had asked no more than an hour before shocked her. What reason did Gloria have to ask? Nancy nodded and put her hand on the woman's sleeve.

'Yes, of course.' Nancy hoped she wouldn't regret it.

'Are you one of them?'

'One of what?'

'Those.' There was no need to elaborate. Gloria's eyes said more, and Nancy read them loud and clear.

'I'm not. I'm not even a Hardacre, am I?'

'No, but those boys are.' Gloria nodded as much to herself as to Nancy. 'That will never change, no matter what. That place…'

'Well, we're not going back there,' she sighed. 'I've left. We'll go back to town or another town, or another county. I don't care. Anywhere but there.'

'Oh, but you can't do that.'

'Whyever not? You know what that place is like. You saw last night; I know you did. You know what lives there.'

'There's something I want to show you.' She stopped, her eyes wide, 'You need to see this.'

'Honestly, if it's another thing like what Beamish gave me, then I'm not interested.' Nancy stood firm. The heels of her leather boots slowly sank into the soft lawn.

'What did he give you?' Gloria shook her head to rid the curiosity from her thoughts. 'Whatever it was, he'd have a good reason for it.'

'I didn't take it. Something about its history. It's not my task—as I said, I'm not even one of them.'

'All I know is, that place takes and takes, and it never gives. It's been the same for generations and…' The pause stretched between them until it snapped. 'Even if you are leaving, you need to know what happened. It affects you too.'

'Is it about my boys?'

'No.' Gloria shook her head and narrowed her eyes. 'In part. It's more about Andrew.' His name sparked those hot tears again. Gloria gripped her shoulder, her eyes mirroring the emotion. 'My husband was Allan.'

Nancy had heard the name but placing it was far beyond her capabilities; the Priory had tainted her ability to think straight. She shrugged.

'Allan got a telephone call late one night.' Gloria stopped, her hand on her throat as if to prevent the words from spilling over. 'At first, we tried to ignore it, but it kept ringing, after three times of trying to get there before they hung up. Allan sat in his pyjamas on the stairs, watching the telephone. I told him to come back to bed, that they would call back in the morning if it was important, but it was like he knew who it was.'

Nancy didn't have the heart to interrupt. It was a memory Gloria wanted to hold on to or perhaps needed to relive. Nancy understood. There were those mundane snippets of life that her mind replayed over and over simply to feel Andrew again.

'They did finally call back.' Gloria gulped. 'Allan had the receiver to his ear before the second ring. I watched from the landing. I saw the look in his eyes. The colour drained from his face.' Gloria stared as the vein in Nancy's temple throbbed, and her jaw stiffened. 'The call was from someone he'd known when he was a boy.'

Nancy watched her, still none the wiser.

'It was Andrew.'

'What?' Nancy tried to think. Memories mingled and bashed into one another. 'When was this?'

'It was in the early hours.'

She pondered, weaved together the tiny threads of information. Nancy froze until it struck her and knocked the air from her lungs.

She nodded. 'I remember.'

'Yes. The day Andrew died.'

'How do you know that?'

'Because it was the same day Allan...'

'I'm sorry, but I don't get it.' Sweat trickled down between her shoulder blades. She realised how warm it was and tugged at her collar, slipping her arms from her jacket. 'Sorry, Gloria, I feel faint.'

The recall of that night brought Nancy to her knees. Andrew had paced the bedroom, the early moon peering through the window. He had refused to get into bed, his eyes on his hands as he'd constantly run a finger over his palm. She had tried to look at it, see what was bothering him, but he had thrown her a cautious look that warned her off, soon after Nancy had fallen asleep. She'd cursed herself for it every moment since. She had awoken to Oliver shouting and run downstairs with the contents of her stomach in her mouth. The phone receiver had lain discarded on the hall carpet.

Nancy's hands grew clammy. The mug slipped from her fingers, splashing lukewarm coffee over the hem of her jeans. Gloria helped Nancy out of her jacket and folded it to lay it on the grass.

'I'll get you a cloth for that coffee stain.'

Nancy wiped the tears away.

Gloria returned moments later with two folding deckchairs and placed one close to Nancy. 'Here, sit.' She did the same with the other chair beside her. 'And here, this will help.' She handed Nancy a cloth.

'No, please. It doesn't matter. They are already filthy.' But she took it and mopped up most of the spilt coffee. 'Thanks.'

Nancy plunged her hands into her front pockets, trying to get comfortable on the deckchair. Her mind still swirled with thoughts of Andrew and late-night phone calls.

'Come on, Nance. It wouldn't normally take you this long to catch on.'

'Can I get you anything else?' Gloria asked. 'You look quite pale.'

'No, honestly, it's just been a…' She couldn't finish the words, but Gloria knew; she could see she was scarcely holding herself together. 'Tell me about Allan. I'm struggling to make the connection.'

'He was a gardener.' Gloria closed her eyes a moment and reached down to the grass as if to feel his presence beneath it. 'He and Andrew were at school together, best friends for many years.' She leant in, her hand shielding her mouth. 'That's the only reason I'm allowed into the Priory.' She nodded like it made sense of everything.

Nancy returned the gesture, accompanied by an odd realisation as she pulled her hand from her pocket.

The sun squinted out from behind a grey cloud to reveal a fractured beam that glinted between a thinning weave of the boxwood hedge. A flash caught Nancy. Gloria saw it, too, though she went to great lengths to pretend she had not.

Gloria swept her arm across the manicured lawns and up to the house. 'Gardens, plants, trees… they were his life. He fed off nature, and in his hands, nature thrived,' she sighed. 'He loved his garden.'

'Andrew was a carpenter.'

'Two sides of the same, or just the other end of its natural life. Turning what was once glorious by nature to something functional or attractive.' Gloria nodded. 'Allan always saw the beauty in that.'

'Have nothing in your house that you don't know to be useful or believe to be beautiful,' Nancy said with a faint smile.

'Yes, William Morris had it right. No need for the surplus or the ugly.' Gloria's eyes shot to where the sun had taken Nancy. This time, there was no denying it as it flashed again.

'What is it?' Nancy asked.

'Something that came home with him earlier that day. It has sat by the shed ever since.' Gloria wrung her hands in her lap several times until she rubbed her palms on her knees, smoothing out the folds in her green plaid dress. 'I don't like it. I don't want it.'

Nancy had no clue to what she was referring, but the expression on her friend's face denoted no desire to explain, either.

'Then can't you get someone to take it away?' Nancy asked. 'What is it?'

'I want to show you…' Gloria moved her feet as if to stand. 'Again, Nancy, I know you're not one of them, but you must promise me something. Can I trust you to do that?'

Nancy wanted to reply with certainty. She was trustworthy, a good person, yet the fear that this request held more to it petrified her.

'What is it? Show me what it is.'

Gloria stood and crossed the grass to the hedge. Nancy noticed an opening; a tall wooden archway burrowed inside the foliage, mostly covered by leaves.

'Come on,' Gloria said. 'It's a piece of the Priory.'

Nancy followed her through the arch but froze when she saw what stood on the other side. A dark-stained wooden shed that still smelled vaguely of creosote and a lean-to porch along one side, in whole no bigger than Gloria's orange bathroom. Clearly, this had been Allan's domain. A selection of gardening tools was visible through the window. A tall rake with a painted green handle rested against the padlocked door. Gloria stepped aside to allow Nancy closer and pointed to *it*.

Propped against the other side of the shed was an object that looked so out of place it may as well have been a door to Narnia. A mirror, tall, wide, with a deeply carved decorative frame; fragments of its gilt finish rubbed and peeled.

Nancy had seen it before, a long time ago.

'Allan brought it home with him. I have no idea why. I only know it came from the Priory.' Gloria stood behind Nancy, as far away from the mirror as she could get. Her face turned away, her arms wrapped around herself. 'I can't bring myself to look at it, let alone into it.'

'Did he explain why?' Nancy's skin crawled. The Priory's wispy shadows skulked around her ankles. 'Nothing good can ever come of a thing that belongs to that place. It would sooner be at home in hell.'

Gloria flinched. 'You may be right. I, too, know the evil of that place. It must stay where it is. To move it now, well…'

Gloria turned away. She headed back into the bright garden, leaving the Priory's shadows behind her. Nancy dug her hands deep in her pockets, wondering what the hell this had to do with Andrew, apart from how everything was connected to the Priory. She pulled her hands out, the acorn rolled around her palm.

Then something else caught her attention. It was small and almost hidden by the mirror.

'Honestly, Nance, what are you going to do with that?'

She bent down to retrieve it. 'No idea yet,' she whispered.

Gloria paid no attention to Nancy as she grabbed her folded jacket. Instead, Gloria's eyes fixed to the top window nestled below the thick thatch. Josie gazed out; one of the boys, too. There was no need to follow their eyes—she knew very well where Josie was looking. She wore the same expression she'd had the evening before on the gallery landing.

Josie saw the evil.

TWENTY-FOUR

Josie's bedroom was pink and yellow. The twins had followed up the narrow staircase, which wound around and opened onto a square landing. They now stood in the low doorway as Josie flung herself towards a toy chest. Her enthusiasm was palpable, bouncing off the floral-papered walls. A brightly patterned carpet butted up to the yellow flowers. The boys gawped at each other, shrugged. They'd never seen a girl's bedroom before. It was different—fuzzy

Josie propped open the lid of a large trunk. 'Look at this.' She leant right into it; her long, white socks and black shoes were all the boys saw. 'Come in then. Don't just stand at the door. Look what I have.'

She was a strange girl. Elliot wasn't sure if he liked her or if it even mattered. Something about her made his neck prickle. Dad had always told him to trust things like that.

Oliver was the first to take a step in. Elliot hesitantly followed. They sat on the floor atop a round, pink rug. The room was bigger than it had first seemed. An alcove to one side fitted with painted cupboards and the headboard of a thickly dressed bed. The rest of the room lay open for playing.

Josie pulled out several colouring books, pads full of coloured paper, and the longest pack of coloured pens Elliot had ever seen. Only, he had seen those pens before. The large, shiny copper finally dropped, clunking like the last penny in a seaside amusement machine. He'd seen Josie before. Dad popped back into his mind. He didn't want him here today. Not now. The thought of Dad only brought sadness and anger. Today, all he wanted to do was play, forget. He looked at Oliver, who eagerly flicked through a book for a picture to colour. Why did he look so calm? But he hadn't been there that day; he wouldn't have recognised Josie, hadn't seen what he had.

Oliver nudged him. 'Which book do you want?'

Elliot didn't want any of them. All he could think about was his dad and the strange bedsheet man. It hurt his head. The memories kept surging in like seafoam at the beach until he choked and suffocated. Something felt wrong. He tried to catch a stray thought, yet it swam back out to sea every time.

'Here you go, Elliot,' Josie said. 'You can use my special book if you like,' she grinned, with two missing front teeth. 'I haven't used it yet. Look, it's new.' She fanned the pages, all pristine white. 'Here.'

Even her smile irritated him.

Elliot took the book. A hint of a smile sat at the side of his mouth for politeness, but inside, he was screaming. He picked up a pencil and pressed the graphite nib to the paper until it snapped. The lead flicked across the room. Looking back to the mass of white paper, he wanted to stab it. With a deep breath, he grabbed another pencil and gently set the nib onto the page.

'Oh, are you drawing a picture?' Josie asked. 'What is it going to be? I love drawing.'

Oliver looked over at him, knowing he wouldn't answer her—when Elliot had a pencil in his hand, he never spoke. He wouldn't be drawing; he would be writing.

Josie threw Oliver a confused look. He replied with a quick shake of his head and walked to the window. 'What's that?'

The back garden looked pretty—it reminded Oliver of home—but there at the back, something didn't fit. On tiptoes, Josie stood beside him. He pointed towards the other end of the garden, behind a wall of shrubbery, there was a glint, something shiny.

'Oh, at the back?' Josie pointed, her fingertip pressing against the glass. Oliver nodded. 'I don't know. Mum said I'm not allowed down there. She said that was Dad's stuff and we should leave it alone. But I did go down there.'

The words came out so factual that they made Oliver shudder. Where was Josie's Dad? He'd never given it much thought that it was only him, Elliot, and Mum now. To think of anyone else having a dad when they didn't made him feel sick in his stomach, a pain that kept rising to his throat.

'Your dad?' Oliver asked.

'Yes, he's dead. Your dad is dead, too, isn't he?' Josie didn't smile, but there didn't seem to be any sadness either. That worried Oliver. 'Mummy said he died like mine, but I don't think my dad died.'

'He's still alive?'

'I think he got lost.'

'Where did he go to get lost? Was he an explorer?'

Josie gawped, then giggled. 'No, don't be silly. He used to drive a van with gardening stuff. One day, he came home with some odd things.' Her eyes flashed to the garden. 'I went to school, and then he was gone.' She was winding her red hair around her finger; the end of it turned blue as a bruise. 'Mummy said he died. She cried a lot.' Oliver felt the tears she was holding in but said nothing. 'But he never had a funeral. Did your dad have one?'

Her eyes drilled through his skin. Oliver nodded.

'Were you allowed to go? I wasn't. Mummy said it was no place for a child, but I don't think there was a funeral. She wore black for a long while.'

'How couldn't there be one if your dad died?' Elliot questioned, his voice loud across the room.

Oliver jumped. Josie smiled and wandered over, leaving Oliver by the window. The sun sent shards of glinting light up to him, signalling him like a secret message.

Elliot sat with his back to the wooden trunk, the pad resting on his knees with an open page full of writing, his pencil mid-word. He looked at Josie. 'We didn't go to our dad's funeral, either, but he did have one. Lots of people dressed in black came to our house afterwards. Mr Beardsmore's daughter made sandwiches and cakes.'

'Oh,' she replied. 'That sounds nice.

'Well, it wasn't!' Elliot snapped.

'So, what are you writing?' she asked. 'A story?'

The urge to stab and scream rumbled him again, just as it had with the walking stick. Maybe he'd stab the pencil in Josie's eyes—that would shut up her stupid face. Elliot closed his eyes, wishing the urge and Josie would disappear.

'You're strange,' she said. 'You write funny too.'

'What? No, I don't!'

'Yes, you do. Your paper is round the wrong way, and your pencil is in the wrong hand. My mummy is a teacher; she taught me how to write properly.'

Oliver joined them on the carpet, his nerve endings on fire, sensing his brother like a rash.

'Elliot is a lefty,' he said. 'I'm a righty.'

Josie looked from one to the other.

Oliver grabbed a pencil and pretended to write. 'See? I use my right hand, Elliot uses his left. Mum says we're a mirror image of each other, two halves of a whole.' He smiled, hoping it would rub off and put an end to it.

She nodded thoughtfully. 'Perhaps it doesn't make you strange then. Maybe it makes you special.' She smiled to herself.

They sat in silence, with just the scratch of pencil nibs and brush of pens. Elliot eyed Josie over his dark lashes. He didn't like her.

TWENTY-FIVE

It hadn't lingered long in their absence. The desire to lay pretence at the feet of its long-serving residents had passed. In ritual, the sun was overwhelmed by peremptory clouds, colourless, unmoving, and unyielding. The warmer climes of yesteryear lost to the plummeting temperatures that cultivated the perpetual winter of the Priory—a fitting gesture for the boys of winter.

Lady Hardacre had watched Nancy's departure until she could bear it no more. Swiftly, less torturous than it had once been, the Priory took her for its own. She could reflect on the pain, the injustice of her lot, though it wasn't a pain she desired to heal; to be free of it would mean her surrender, and that she wouldn't do. The Priory would not see the utter demise of Lady Hardacre this year no more than it had in her own time.

Ghosts of war flittered across her vision as the vista beyond the window whitened. The uniforms had descended upon the Priory in a time of need: a country at war. Those poor souls had had no idea they'd entered a new battleground. They were simply casualties. There had been little triumph for the last few left within the walls of Hardacre. It had seen to that. Then, just as it had on so many occasions, it had fed on those hearts fuelled by fear, hatred, and greed. Its true desire was nothing so meagre as a tender heart.

Estelle sat at her desk, a great expanse of leather-topped mahogany which had once belonged to her father. The room overlooked the rear of the grounds, an equally barren landscape as the rest. Though here, the ruins dominated the view—the Priory that had once sat high on the horizon, vast stone arches were all that remained. Now, as the warm charade had been swiped away, there were crows, dozens of them. The sky was murderous with their black shapes against the now bleak white palette.

Lady Hardacre reached for the telephone and placed her forefinger in the round of the first digit. She pressed the handset to her ear and dialled the number three, followed by the next four numbers. Each time, the dial returned to its starting point—a point at the start, she mused. A moment in time when whatever evil lay at the foundations had begun its devouring hunger. She looked to the ruins. These grounds had once known peace, faith. God had sat here.

The call connected and shook her from her thoughts. 'Hello,' she said. 'Mr Beamish?'

'Lady Hardacre! I was about to call you.'

'Is it done?'

'Not quite, I'm saddened to say.'

'She did not take it?'

'No. But all is not lost.'

He paused. She understood his hesitations. It was a delicate matter, to fail now would cost them all dearly.

'There was an… incident,' he said. 'It gives me hope.'

'An incident?'

'Mrs Hardacre found, let us say, a connection. She was quite overwhelmed by it.'

'So, I was correct to hope then?'

'There's no doubt in my mind that there's a special quality to her.'

'So, I take it you have opened the envelope I sent you? Nancy gave it to you?'

'She handed it to me as soon as she arrived. I'm afraid something has caused her a great reluctance. May I ask what happened this morning?'

'I fear she understands the truth of it as we stand Mr Beamish... or as *I* do.'

'I realise that, but I worry it's getting to her, that the Priory is taking hold. If we wait any longer, we may be too late for her.'

'I share your fears, Mr Beamish. Tonight, then.'

'Tonight.'

'Oh, before you go, my grandsons—did they give you any cause for concern?' She pushed the handset to her other ear and stood to face the Priory ruins straight on. They appeared larger, taller, more imposing today. As it should be. 'I thought they would have returned by this hour. There has been no word.'

'The boys weren't with Mrs Hardacre. She left them in Gloria's care for a playdate with young Josie. It'll do them good today as the sun is shining.'

There were only the black birds against white through Estelle's window, but she imagined how it would be in Raynham; there would be sunshine. There were memories there—a childhood with friends; visits to the village shop, the library for a new book, or the post office to run errands—but those memories were often lost behind the plasterwork.

'Gloria, you say?'

'That's right. Is there something wrong?' Mr Beamish hovered on his last word.

Estelle felt every one of his thoughts as if he sat across the desk from her.

'Do you think Gloria will... Never mind. Forgive my unnecessary concerns. In the circumstances, I take it you will do as my letter outlines?'

'You can rely on me.'

'Thank you, Mr Beamish.' She replaced the receiver on its cradle, ending the call with a clunk.

Her eyes cast to the large expanse of wallpaper opposite her—a place where the colours and tones were richer, more vibrant than the rest, which had faded with age.

With temptation too great, she walked over, ran her hand where the mirror had once hung. Remnants of its energy were fading, though its connection lingered. She feared that would never be broken. It had been forged with greed and vanity, and those were too solid emotions for evil to allow to dwindle. It was in the very atmosphere. The mirror had needed to go, to have it here when they'd arrived would have been a travesty. Too many had fallen waste to it. Little had she known, it had only accelerated their arrival and at the cost of her son. She cursed herself for having allowed it, even if she'd had no choice.

Andrew had feigned surprise when he answered, his voice slightly higher and shaking a little down the telephone line, though she knew he had expected her call. He would never have been able to deny the connection. She'd seen it in the mirror. Estelle had pressed the receiver closer to her cheek, perhaps hoping to feel him down the line. The years had grown long for him, though for her, it was merely yesterday. Andrew Hardacre, the last heir, had left the Priory grounds, passed the great oak, the outside world as tempting as the girl on his arm. The door had closed itself in his wake. Yet, within the walls, the plasterwork, the polished floors, there had been a settling. Estelle had felt it for days as his absence was absorbed. What infested the foundations had whispered its glee—yet another of hers lost. It had marked it as the final triumph.

'Hello? Mum?'

She had twitched a little at the word, the relaxed way her title had dwindled. She was his mother. Nancy would be *mum*, wouldn't she? Of course, she would. A mum full of love and blessings, where Estelle had missed hers.

'Andrew,' she had swallowed hard. 'I need your help.'

She had never asked anything from him, thinking she and all his history had evaporated from his thoughts, just forgotten memories. She had been wrong.

'Yes, of course. What is it?'

Estelle had kept the details brief. The Priory knew her thoughts; her words would solidify within the woodgrain. 'You will need a van.' They had been the only words spoken before the receiver was replaced.

If only she hadn't called him. Would it have changed the outcome?

She glared at the vacant spot on the wall.

'My lady, do you desire anything this afternoon? Some tea?' Lizzie paused on the threshold, an unusual dullness about her. 'They haven't returned.'

'No, thank you. I am not in the mood for such routines this afternoon.' The need to say she felt defeated was strong, but she resisted. 'Thank you, Lizzie.' The maid nodded, but not once did Estelle's eyes move from the empty wall. 'I am sure they will be home soon,' she said.

'I'm sure you're right. I will bake some scones. The boys will like those.'

There was no mistaking the fondness in Lizzie's tone. But it was a foolhardy emotion for those cursed in a never-ending circle of nothingness. There had been enough wallowing in grief today. Nancy would return with the boys; Estelle was adamant about that. The Priory wouldn't allow her to wander too far before it called her back.

Her concern now was Gloria. If the teacher could hold herself together, hold her tongue just a little longer, they had a chance, and all could be saved. Estelle had felt her grief as soon as she'd entered yesterday evening. The room had been palpable with it, and it had echoed Nancy's. She'd seen the picture young Josie had drawn too. The Priory already had its grip on that poor child. There was no denying why, either—

she wasn't a Hardacre, but it had allowed her to cross its boundary, and because of that, she was cursed.

Estelle had known the afternoon the van had pulled up on the drive with Andrew in the passenger seat. She had recognised the other man; saw the boy he'd been; the Priory had allowed his admittance then, and it was no different that day. Andrew had known the same. As a child, Andrew had invited others, boys who had faltered at the crossroads. Not once had their shoes been allowed to step past the oak. They had all run home with an inexplicable feeling that they had forgotten something, unable to recall why they'd been on Priory grounds in the first instance.

But not Allan Scarfe.

Estelle had stepped aside as they entered.

'Hello, Allan. It is good to see you.' She had lied, knowing the necessity of it. 'I am extremely grateful for your help today, Andrew.'

The desire to hold her son close was so overwhelming, she pressed her hand to the doorframe, her eyes closed a moment.

'Mum?'

She dismissed his questioning tone and pointed towards the library.

'That's lovely,' Allan said. 'What an enormous mirror! Where are we taking it? Auction house?' He stepped closer then, framed within the mirror's gilding.

'No, it is a little trickier than that. I shall let Andrew explain on your journey back. But, please, don't stand so close to it.' Estelle turned to her son. 'I trust you can deal with it?'

Andrew nodded, knowing better than to delve into the matter any further. 'It shall be done.'

'You will need a blanket to cover it.' She nodded. 'Do not touch it until it is completely covered.' Her brows knitted as she looked at Allan, who still wore the same open expression. He had always been an obliging boy. Perhaps that was why the Priory had admitted him. She worried if his openness would be his ruin.

They covered the mirror in thick blankets, tightly wrapped and bound when Allan and Andrew took it off the wall. Then propped it against the wallpaper to drink the cups of tea Lizzie appeared with. Estelle heard the murmurs, the whispers. The Priory felt her treachery.

Andrew put his empty mug on the desk, eyeing the mirror, had bent down and pulled the blanket over the bottom edge. As he pulled the thick cover across the surface, his finger snagged the worn gilt frame. It splintered, leaving a small, fractured part of itself in his hand; he cursed as his blood smeared the glass.

'Let me look.' Estelle bent down to see the long shard of splintered wood embedded deep in Andrew's palm. '*No.*' She fell back on her heels, her hand on Andrew's shoulder.

'It's nothing,' he'd said. 'I'll get Nancy to look at it later.'

They carried the wrapped mirror from the room into the great hallway before Estelle had made it to her feet.

'*I will take these small victories, Lady Hardacre.*'

She cried when the van pulled away. There had been no saving Andrew from this; what would be would and she knew all too well, she held no power to interject. The evidence of what was possible, of what could be from such a small thing, still walked the Priory's halls—lost, blurred memories of what they had once been.

Estelle turned her back on the wall. She wouldn't give it any more of her sorrow today. Instead, she opened the library's glass doors, which led out into the cold, white landscape. Her feet took her in the direction of the ruins. With a swift flap of wings, the crows fled, leaving one lone bird circling above. She gave it no heed, swiping her hand across the sky indifferently. With a curious eye, it cawed, swooping low overhead then flew off.

This was a moment for faith.

With slow, resolute steps, Lady Hardacre followed those who'd walked before her. They were here today. They had been pacing the grounds, summoned through her faith and that of Mr Beamish. With them here, they had hope.

She paused behind one of the brothers. He turned, his black robe grazing the frozen tops of sparse grass.

'Lady Hardacre.' He bowed his head and allowed his eyes to meet hers. 'We feel your faith today. It is strong...' He smiled, and her heart almost beat. 'As is the child's.'

'The child?'

'Your grandson, the little lord.'

'May I ask which one it is?'

'The eldest. He has a fierce heart. There is no doubt of the darkness that sits in his thoughts; although, it is only to be expected. The children have witnessed a terrible fate.' The brother lowered his head, his hands pressed together. 'This child does not shy away from the truth, unlike his younger sibling. That one, I am afraid, may be susceptible to what lays beneath. It may already have him within its grip.' He planted his foot hard on the frozen ground, his mouth a firm line of disgust.

'But the eldest? Elliot?'

'His faith is strong, my lady. Enough to see what is truly here. Enough to see us.'

'I fear the faith of both my grandsons will need to be strong tonight. It will try us all.'

The brother pondered a trice. 'We feel your urgency. We feel its presence close by, and we are praying for all our souls.' His golden-brown eyes closed, silent words on his lips.

She lowered her head to mirror his gesture. When she opened her eyes, his bored into her, his manner questioning.

'What is it?' she asked.

'If we fail...'

'Do not speak of it. We cannot fail.'

'But, if we do, I shall take the matter into my own hands. I shall make it my duty to fulfil this task, or I shall not rest.'

'Nor shall any of us…' she interjected.

The brother nodded. He took her hands into his and squeezed them oh so gently. 'Then we shall not fail. I, with my brothers, have wandered these grounds for more than four hundred years.' He swept his gaze across the whiteness. 'Once, it was lush and abundant, but most of all, it was alive.'

'We *all* were alive once,' she mused. 'Though, I admit, it is not life that I miss.'

'Nor I. It is goodness. It will be here again. You must keep your faith.'

Lady Hardacre lowered her head in prayer, but also to keep her bitter tears hidden. 'Thank you for your council, Brother Nicholas.'

Since the sun rose, chasing the night shadows, dispersing them into the light, the twins of the past watched and waited. Though time itself meant very little, anything other than winter was a gift to be relished. The sunshine took them to the rose window, which held physical memories of their childhood. A place where they had hidden from their father, both for play and out of fear of punishment. While he had been a good man and a good father, he had deprived them of the nurture they craved. They were young, after all—no greater in living years than the boys of winter. Mother had left them behind with their fates in the hands of God. Or had it been in the hands of the evil that lay at the root of it all?

It had wanted them.

Josiah and Samuel had been the first Hardacre Twins. With the Priory's cruel endeavours, they still reigned as such. They had lingered in the halls and corners where the whispering evil lay hidden for more than four centuries. Generations had come and gone. Some had passed on, some had not. Those poor, wretched souls remained in a perpetual hell, concealed from the rest and alone in their torment. The twins had regarded them all, bearing witness to their last mortal ticks of the clock until the hands struck death.

However, not every Hardacre had fallen prey to what had risen. Some had escaped its clutches, perhaps through chance as much as their virtue. It hadn't always been the cruel, the greedy, and lustful heirs that had suffered this fate, though it had always been the foulest of natures that fell prey. Some more pitiful souls had been mere victims to their mortal events.

Lady Hardacre had been one of those.

The boys had found her as a girl, lost and lonely. She had not belonged at the Priory then any more than she did now. Her spirit had been bright, luring them to her like moths to a flame. Both boys had been cautious at first, wary of her generation. Many with an appetite for greed had gone before her. Those, they had shunned. They had been good boys in life, and death had not cast another side to their nature. Estelle had been the same. Gradually, light found the grounds. Nature gained a gentle foothold on what had lain barren for generations.

Then another kind of evil brought others into the walls; men other than Hardacres walked its floors and lived within its rooms for the first time in centuries. The Priory and its lands had been nudged, a crack across the earth, a shift in the very atmosphere. War, Estelle had told them. They had understood what that meant, if only with vague aptitude. She had become a woman by then, and the boys had loved her, looked to her as a mother.

Those visitors had been of hostile heart, their minds full of warfare. Love and kindness had been the only weapons to win the true war, and so, it had taken what it wanted and given grief as its offering. The Priory took and took, granting nothing but emptiness. It had been inevitable.

The twins mourned Estelle's loss. With her kindness and compassion, she had kept them safe within the Priory; strong faith had swept away the evil for a while. Grief itself had swept it back in, filtering in under the door and whispering through the passageways until the house reeked of nothing else.

Samuel had lain by her bed, his cool hand holding her warmth until hers chilled his. He had seen grief take before, but it had been superstition, fear and ignorance that sat at the root of their story.

He had pined for her through the night hours until the sun rose through the drapes and revealed the dry crusts and husks of a thousand dead moths.

Josiah had pulled him away, back into the shadows.

'She will return to us,' Samuel had said.

And she had. Lady Hardacre was still the residing heir of Hardacre. She had no choice—the life of her son kept her here. Evil would reign again. It would be free to wander the longest passages, to seep through every lock until it wrapped like creepers around the very rafters.

Today, the house was cold again, fearful, and weary. The sun had gone. Nancy and her boys had taken it with them.

Josiah sat close to Lady Hardacre for most of the day in silent thought and with a watchful eye. Samuel took comfort in the kitchen with Lizzie, who reminded him of life... but only after he had returned from the gardens.

Samuel had watched as the oak held Oliver captive. That old sensation had woven its way across his chest and gripped his heart. He knew what he had done was wrong. He had broken his vow, which had been made when their forms were new and shook and quivered.

You must never take another's form by will or by force.

What if there is no other choice?

Even then, for it is a terrible thing to do.

But... not even to save them?

Never.

Samuel would stand by his decision when the reprimand came, and he would make the same choice again.

He had to save Oliver. There was kinship.

The oak, the evil, all those that whispered awful thoughts had done so to Oliver. It would have killed him.

Samuel had watched them play. Oliver had changed. Samuel had witnessed it for himself, seen each look, each slight alteration in his character. It had been swift and shrewd. His manner had become short with a temperament to match. Consequently, the oak found its way in, using power over him.

His brother Elliot would not be able to save him, so Samuel had to. He had felt himself high on the branch, his once solid form standing firm on the great bough. He remembered how the bark sat beneath his feet. The horror of that night so long ago still raged raw when he came too close to the tree, but today, a desperate need had overwhelmed that horror.

Oliver had not known or felt when Samuel had rushed beneath his skin and into his thoughts. He would not remember, either. Elliot, on the other hand... Samuel could not guarantee his memory if he had seen the difference in Oliver.

Nor could he guarantee Nancy's. She had battled the tree with such force. Samuel's soul had swelled with pride at her determination. If only their mother had fought with such vigorous obligation.

Samuel and Josiah stood in the open doors of the library and watched the wintry sun fall over the old Priory ruins.

TWENTY-SIX

Nancy bundled the boys into the car. Having grabbed the item from outside Gloria's shed, there was no way she could stay. Looking at Gloria would have unravelled her resolve. She'd never stolen anything in her life.

There'd been little argument from the boys. Tension had followed them down the narrow staircase. Josie had worn her usual smile, yet the twins had a look that spoke more of drudgery than play. Elliot had stood by the backdoor a moment and cautiously stared at Josie. He'd gripped a folded piece of paper and tucked it into his shorts pocket along with a pencil. Oliver ambled behind him with his hands in his pockets, casting an eye at Josie over his shoulder every other moment.

'Time to go, you two. It's getting late.' Nancy's voice had been uncommonly high and far too chipper. Fortunately, no one had noticed or at least said nothing to the contrary.

The boys had nodded. Elliot had hurried to escape though Oliver had hovered a while to say goodbye to Josie.

'I hope you both come to play again,' she'd sung. Her red hair bobbing as she jumped off the last stair.

Oliver had nodded. 'We would like that. See ya.' He followed Elliot out.

'You can keep my pencil if you want,' she'd called as the boys disappeared around the doorframe.

The twins waved at Mrs Scarfe and Josie as they stood at the painted gate. They looked safe there, tucked away in their little cottage, pretty and thriving even with the sky deepening

190

by the second. They'd be snuggled in their cosy home for the rest of the evening, unaware of the inevitable horrors like the one that stood propped against the garden shed. Nancy knew that one day, it would bring it all crashing down around Gloria, her pretty cottage, and her smiley daughter. Gloria knew it too. Sympathy came in a wave as Nancy slammed the car into first gear and drove off. Her twins may envy Josie now, but she knew the Scarfes had nothing to be jealous of.

The road curved around the back of the house and emerged at the bottom of the high street. She'd have to drive past the solicitor's office—she didn't know another way. The dread of seeing Mr Beamish's disappointed stare from the front door made her heart sink.

'Mum, can we stop at the shop for some sweets?' Oliver's pink cheeks glowed in her rear-view mirror. 'Please?'

She couldn't stop, not today. If she pulled over now, she might never start the engine again. All the determination pumping through her veins would fizzle and go out like a spent birthday candle.

She shook her head. 'Sorry, love. Not right now.' She saw the defeat. 'Look, if you promise to do exactly as I ask today, I promise you, tomorrow you can have sweets, cakes, chocolate, a new toy—whatever you want. Understand?' Her foot was on the brake, her heart in her mouth, she watched her boys in the mirror.

'Okay,' Oliver said. He nudged Elliot, who merely nodded.

'What's the matter, Elliot?'

His expression looked alien on his young face. It made her heart hurt. Elliot's bottom lip quivered, and those big, dark eyes glistened. He was different. She examined his features, saw something she hadn't seen before, and cursed herself for it. The Priory had changed him. Everything had. Despite herself, she pulled over on the high street in front of a row of red-brick houses with carved date plaques over the doors.

'Elliot, what is it? Talk to me.' She quickly wiped her eyes.

'He doesn't like Josie,' Oliver said. 'She was making fun of him.'

'I don't care about her,' Elliot snapped.

Nancy saw the look on his face; this had nothing to do with Josie. She unclipped her belt, turned, and held out her hand.

'Now, whatever it is, no matter how small or big, I'm your mum. You can tell me anything.' She couldn't think of anything else to say. It all sounded lame in the circumstances. 'I love you both. You are my world, and I will always be here for you.'

'And when you're not?' Elliot asked.

'Don't be silly. I'll always be here for you.'

'Dad said that—'

Nancy gripped his hand. 'No matter what, I'm not going anywhere. I'm not leaving either of you.'

'Then the bedsheet man came and took him away.'

Oliver's lips curled, screwing up his nose. 'What?'

Nancy gave her boys a slight shake of her head, her lips tight. She couldn't cry. To lose it all now wasn't an option.

She nodded, painting a faint smile on her lips. 'Lots of treats tomorrow then.'

The boys returned the nod. Elliot blinked the tears away.

With a roar, the Hillman pulled away.

The afternoon had dwindled, and it would be dark within the hour. The high street was quieter, deserted; everyone had begun tucking themselves away, locking doors, everyday lives behind small squares of orange glow.

Elliot jumped in his seat. 'Mum!'

Nancy slammed on the brakes; the Hillman Avenger stopped, screeched to a swift halt in the middle of the high street. A tall man stood in the centre of the road. He faced away from her, in the direction she would go if only the moron would move.

Bloody tourist, she thought.

'Get out of the road! Idiot. He's going to get himself killed doing stupid things like that.' Nancy hit the horn. He was still. 'What the hell?' She beeped again, and again, longer this time.

He slowly turned, looking stunned, he raised his hand in apology. Nancy's heart dropped into her lap as the familiarity struck her.

'Who is that?' Elliot pointed straight out the windscreen. 'He looks just like—'

'Back in your seat, Elliot.'

Nancy tapped the steering wheel, while her eyes never left the man. His dark eyes flashed as the setting sun hit his white hair. He mouthed his remorse as he stepped back up onto the footpath, his hand over his heart. There was sincerity there. There was something else too. His eyes spoke of the same feeling that swept through her. She knew him, and he knew her.

He stood in the doorway of the solicitor's office. Mr Beamish wasn't there. She thanked God, or whoever, for that small mercy, but guilt still ran rife, flushing her cheeks.

Slowly, Nancy pulled away, trying not to look back. She made it as far as the pub, but as she went to turn the corner, curiosity got the better of her. The boys waved and smiled at the man. He waved back.

Deep, heavy defeat was beginning to set in.

'Keep it together, Nance. You can do this.'

Nancy turned off the village road at the crossroads. The entrance to the Priory lay open before her. The damned oak tree loomed overhead as she pulled on the handbrake.

'Okay.' She turned in her seat to face her twins. 'You need to listen to me very carefully.'

They eyed her cautiously.

'What's the matter, Mummy?' Oliver asked.

'After what happened this morning, you must promise me that neither of you will ever go near that tree again. Do you promise?'

'What?' Oliver looked at Elliot. 'What happened?'

Elliot shook his head, his eyes wide. His mouth folded in on itself when he glanced at his mother, fear deep in his eyes, he shrugged a nod.

'The bloody tree,' Nancy said. 'You up in the tree, all the leaves and that huge bloody root trying to kill—'

Oliver's face dropped. He had no memory of it.

'It's okay,' she said. 'Don't worry. Just remember—that tree is out of bounds.'

Elliot gripped his brother's arm, his fingers a little too eager. Oliver flinched, looking shocked. The oak tree rustled in the growing wind, and storm clouds swept overhead.

'It's going to rain, and there'll be a storm.' Nancy looked up through the windscreen. 'Of course, there will. Why wouldn't there be?'

Her eyes were on the tree as it dwindled in the rear-view mirror. It finally disappeared when she headed over the brow of the hill and met the Priory's austere exterior.

'Why does it always have to stare at me like that?' The words had been to herself, but Elliot shuffled in the back.

As she parked, he put his arms around her shoulders. 'It will all be okay, Mummy. You have me.' He squeezed her and pressed his lips to her cheek. 'I remember what happened,' he whispered. 'I saw it. I saw all those people too.'

The engine died, plunging them into ear-buzzing silence. Nancy looked at Oliver, who sat unnaturally straight in his seat. His eyes bored straight through the windscreen to the great door. It was open. She grabbed Elliot's hand, and Nancy felt the tightness as Elliot's face screwed up. She turned towards the house.

Lizzie stood on the stone porch, her hands clutched in front of her. Nancy had never noticed it before. Did Lizzie always look like that? Dawson walked up behind her, his hand on her shoulder. Nancy hadn't paid much attention to him — he was never there for long before he was off doing whatever he did — but Lizzie... Nancy had spent time with her in the kitchen, the drawing-room, had brought breakfast to her room that morning. Nancy shoved the memory, held it back enough not to revisit it.

Lizzie wasn't of this time — that was the only way to put it. Nancy's mind rolled over the thought, trying to give it form and meaning. Why had she never realised it before?

Lizzie wore a brown gown that skimmed the floor, thick and laced, with an apron and a white cap on her head. She carried a lantern.

Nancy pulled the keys out of the ignition and raised her hand to wave as Lizzie scanned the grounds, but she didn't see her. She hadn't even noticed they had arrived.

'Okay,' Nancy mumbled. 'Best go in.'

The sky had fallen over the Priory like a frozen curtain. Lizzie's lamp grew brighter against the freezing air. Nancy kept her eye on the maid as she locked the car door. Elliot gripped her hand, squeezing, draining the blood from her fingers.

'Hey, it's okay, I promise,' she soothed, casting them both a smile and nod. 'Let's go inside.' She sighed and shoved the car keys into her jeans pocket. There it was again. She pulled the acorn free, rolled it in her hands as it caught the lantern's light.

'I still have it, Oliver. It's been in my pocket all day.'

'What's that, Mummy?'

'The little acorn you left me. I found it when I woke up.' As the words left her lips, she knew it hadn't been Oliver or Elliot. She hadn't let herself unravel it until now. She looked back to Lizzie, who had been joined by a boy. He was small, no bigger than her boys, with soft mousey hair. His face spoke of sorrow and loss. His eyes fell on Nancy, pinning her to the spot, and she knew. His pain hit her heart.

'Mummy?' Shaking, Elliot grappled with the edge of her jacket. 'I think we should go inside, now. Please.'

Oliver took the acorn from her palm. 'This was a gift from Josiah.' He pointed to the boy, his finger eagerly waving before them.

'Who?'

'The boy, Mummy. One of the boys.'

Her attention didn't linger on Oliver's words for long before Elliot began to cry. He pushed her forwards, his hand on her back.

'Now, Mummy, please.' He grabbed her hand. 'I won't let them take you.'

'Who, love?'

'Them.' Elliot was stiff, his face a mask of terror.

Although her eyes dashed about, searching, Nancy saw nothing. She took their hands and flew to the door. When her foot touched the worn stone step, Lizzie turned and looked directly into her eyes.

'Oh, there you are, madam. I've been so worried and fraying my wits, wondering what time you would return. Thank the lord you are all here, home safe and sound.' Her hand went to her heart, then to her throat. 'Thank goodness.'

They stood inside the entrance hall—lanterns littered around the area. Dawson's shadowy silhouette stood to one side, he nodded, bowing slightly, as he carried a bundle of wood and kindling in his arms, then turned towards the drawing-room.

The place was cold, it always was, although tonight, it was more than a natural chill that shivered through Nancy. She tightened her grip on her boys. The air hung around their shoulders, leaving a white, milky residue. Oliver pulled to be released, but no matter what, she gripped harder. Why did it feel different?

'Where is Est— Lady Hardacre?' Nancy couldn't deny the ache in her heart as she asked. 'Is she…'

'She is waiting for you in the library, madam. Shall I take the boys for you?' Lizzie reached for them, so they skipped over to her and slipped their fingers into hers. 'I'm so pleased you're home. Did you enjoy the cake I made?' Her eyes glistened; her voice was soft and tender.

The twins nodded.

'Yes, thank you, Lizzie.' Nancy conceded. 'They are probably hungry again.' She allowed her heart to loosen its grip just a touch as Lizzie accepted the mantle.

The twins followed her into the kitchen, leaving Nancy on the cold hall floor. She cast her eyes down, expecting to see the familiar Victorian tiles, but they were gone. Instead, she stood on cold flagstones. Her stomach leapt when a cool hand slipped into hers. She heard her boys' excited squeals and giggles from the kitchen. The hand tightened as tiny fingers closed around hers. Nancy looked down as Josiah stood by her side, his other arm wound tightly around hers.

'Mother.'

TWENTY-SEVEN

Josiah held his mother tight. Where once his beating heart had ached, it now skipped. His arms wound around her neck, his weary head resting on her shoulder; he pulled himself so close her presence nearly consumed him. He would not let go, not tonight and never again. With him in her arms, she wandered towards the great room where a fire roared. Dawson placed another thick log in the grate and poked the flames. Josiah felt warmth if he imagined it hard enough—he would have believed anything at this moment.

Samuel stood in the shadows and watched.

She sat on the carved oak chair, its acorn carvings glistening in the firelight. Josiah snuggled onto her lap as she fussed over his hair.

'I have missed you, my dear heart,' she lulled and pulled him into her firm embrace. The scent of her hair and skin stirred images of flowers and woodland in him. 'Where is your brother? I haven't seen him.'

Josiah felt his twin's eyes bore into the back of his head from his dusty corner, but he didn't move an inch. Josiah paid no mind to his hesitance. He wouldn't allow Samuel's apprehensions to fizzle the moment.

Josiah eased from her hold enough to look into her eyes, they were the warm embers that kindled his heart.

'I won't leave you again, my child. How could I have left you before?'

He wanted to answer, to recall those despairing moments that lingered beneath his skin, but he feared them. His lips remained sealed, keeping them secret. Instead, he kissed her cheek. She returned the smile, patted his hand, and opened her fingers to reveal the acorn that rolled in her open palm.

Samuel watched from the shadows, hidden in the darkness behind the firelight. A prickle travelled down his back and plummeted to his feet, where the wisps wove around his ankles. He couldn't escape them now any more than he had in his own time. They were here for him again—another time, another boy, but for him, nevertheless.

He shared his twin's desires. A fire had sparked in him just as it had in Josiah, and he couldn't pretend otherwise. How many times had he warned Josiah to be wary? It was a dangerous game to play. They wouldn't win. They were just boys—how could they fight this? Unlike Josiah, Samuel saw through the deceit, these lies they were being fed.

No matter how strong his brother's resolve was, it was a foolhardy wish. The acorn would only hold the spell for so long. Beyond that, beyond nightfall, she would awake, and all would be lost again.

†

Lizzie guided the twins into the kitchen, hearing their hunger rise as their bellies growled.

'A hot bowl of mutton stew—that'll warm you both up.' She glanced to the window. 'There's a storm coming.' She pointed to the deep sink at the back of the room. 'You two wash those hands and pop yourselves up at the table.'

The boys glanced at each other. It was swift, but it sparked.

'Come along. Eat it while it's hot.' She placed a large bowl in front of them.

They sat opposite each other on the wooden chairs with the high stone window to their side. Lizzie examined their reflections in the dark glass. Two halves of one whole. So similar, yet so unalike, and both changed.

The kitchen fell into a calm silence.

Elliot watched as Oliver glanced up as his spoon reached his lips. There were unspoken words between them. Only to be expected, though Lizzie had sensed the shift in them that morning.

'You two go out and play,' she had said.

Oliver had grabbed his boots and coat without so much as a twitch, his hand already on the door, but Elliot had stared at her. His face blank, as if other thoughts, other voices, vied for his attention.

'Elliot.' He looked at her and smiled. There was no mistaking what else she'd felt. 'What's this?' she asked, pointing to the object hidden beneath his jumper.

'Nothing.' He was adamant not to show her. 'It's nothing. We found it.'

Its shape and the dark sensation struck her fingers as she touched it.

Lizzie knelt before him. 'There are some things that shouldn't be found. This is one of them.' She knew he wouldn't give it to her—she had learnt that lesson a long time ago. 'Why not put it back in your room? It may get lost or broken if you take it out to play.'

It had worked. Elliot ran upstairs. Lizzie watched whilst his feet hovered a moment too long on the gallery landing before the carved oak chair. 'Quickly, child,' she chanted under her breath with her hand over her heart. No good came of lingering there.

Elliot looked back. Her heart had ached at his smallness, that young face painted with fright that she, too, felt.

Quickly, she thought.

Lizzie had urged the clock hands to tick faster as she waited. By her side, Oliver was none the wiser. When Elliot returned to the gallery, she felt the terror in his racing heart. He had crept slowly with his back to the balustrade, his face away from sight, but Lizzie knew his eyes fixed on the chair.

Elliot halted; his hand reached out. But the temptation had been too great for such a child. Boys of that age were far too curious for their own good. He ran his fingers over the polished seat and traced the acorns deep etch on the carved back. The comparison had struck him—it was all connected. *They* were all connected.

'Come on, Elliot. You'll miss the sunshine.' She stood at the bottom of the stairs, her hand on the carved finial. 'Please.'

It had been swifter than a blink, though it created a tremor that sent a hot poker through her ribcage. It lashed the air, whipped the boy's ankles. She rushed to his side and pushed him behind her.

'Go downstairs, Elliot. Stand with your brother, please.'

His footsteps had been a skittering vibration that sent another lash through the air. Shadows deepened.

'Leave them alone,' she scorned.

'I won't allow it. Not again.' Lizzie moved backwards to the top step, her hands gripping the bannister before she turned her back on it.

The boys stood on the stone porch. The light had flooded the hall, the ring handle still in Oliver's fingers.

'I'll bring you a treat later,' she said. 'Some cake.'

Now this evening, as Lizzie almost melted into the surrounding kitchen, she watched Elliot's eyes dart from his brother into the hallway and to the grounds beyond the darkness.

Lady Hardacre paced the library carpet, tracing the pattern with every step. This wasn't a night for deliberations. Moments for doubt were long gone. Now, there was nothing but to stand firm, resolute.

The telephone rang.

'Hello? Mr Beamish?'

'Hello. Sorry, no, it's Gloria Scarfe. Sorry to disturb you.'

'Not at all. Please, what can I do for you? Nothing urgent, I hope. I am waiting for a telephone call, you see.'

'Oh, I understand. That's why I'm calling you.'

'Go on.'

Gloria's hesitance held a tangible quality that seeped through the receiver and stiffened Estelle's nerves. She sat at the desk, facing her reflection in the black glass doors. She had no time for Gloria tonight. The blank wall of bright wallpaper tapped her shoulder, and she quickly turned around. It was a reminder: Gloria still had a part to play.

'I wondered if it would serve you better if the boys came to stay with me for the night,' Gloria said. 'I—'

'Oh?'

'I was wondering if it might help,' Gloria quickly added.

'I do understand your motives, but I can assure you— no, I must be adamant that there is no need for that.'

'But surely—'

'Gloria.'

'I understand, Lady Hardacre. But, of course,' Gloria paused, her breathing heavy. 'My Allan…'

'Look, there are no words to express the sadness I feel at your loss. I, too, understand that. Of course, I do. We all do.'

'But sacrifices must be made. Is that it?' Gloria spat.

Silence followed.

'If I had known,' Estelle said, 'I would never have asked. You must know that.'

'*Casualties of war*—isn't that the term?'

'Perhaps,' Estelle conceded.

'So, those innocent twins are more casualties?' Gloria asked. 'Is that what you're saying? Because if it is, then I can't sit around and let it happen.'

'Now, please hear me, Gloria…' Estelle steadied her voice. 'Those boys are my grandchildren, the only living connection I have left to this world. You understand the situation, I take it? You know the truth as much as I do. I love those boys.'

'So be it.' Gloria disconnected the call.

Estelle let the receiver fall into her lap and stared at her reflection. *Enough of this*. She looked at the carriage clock on her desk. It was almost time. She left the room, closing the door behind her with a thud.

'Nancy,' she called as he reached the drawing-room.

Estelle watched from the threshold. She had been there long enough to realise what had transpired. They had been warned. Nancy lay asleep in the fireside chair, her head to one side towards the crackle of the logs. The light danced on her cheeks, casting her in a content glow.

'Nancy.'

There was no reply, Estelle hadn't expected one, though she had hoped. She had trusted Josiah to keep his distance today. It had been too much to ask the child—his draw to Nancy was far too strong. She understood, but it didn't stem the fury.

'Josiah, leave us. Now.'

He jumped at her words, leaving his mother's lap in a single bound. He slid into the shadows beside his twin.

'What were you thinking? Darling...' she softened, and the boy sidled up to her. He pressed his head into her hands and leant hard against her. 'I understand, I truly do, but look at me.' She pulled Josiah's face towards her, her finger under his chin. 'Did you give Nancy a gift?'

He nodded through tears. 'I've been sleeping beside her at night. I miss her,' he sobbed.

Samuel inched from the shadows, a face of regret and contempt. 'I told him so. She isn't Mother. I warned him, just as Lizzie did.'

'She is!' Josiah spat. 'Don't say such a thing. I know it. I feel it. And so do you.'

'You two must listen to me very carefully,' Estelle calmed. 'Nancy is not your mother. You both know who she is.' She pressed her finger towards Josiah when he went to respond.

'I understand our history, but what is done is in the past. You cannot bring your mother back, even if she is...' Estelle sighed. 'Nancy. She doesn't know; she doesn't remember.'

'But I do.' Nancy sat forwards with her head in her hands.

'When?' Estelle asked. 'For how long?'

'Maybe for a long time, maybe just tonight. There've always been small things, snatched moments I couldn't place.' She pushed her open hand towards the twins. 'This was from you, wasn't it?' Nancy ran her thumb over an acorn. Josiah nodded.

'Madam? My lady?' Lizzie's ashen face appeared in the doorway. 'It's the twins—I can't find them. I've looked all over...'

'What?' Nancy jumped out of the chair. *No, not now, please God, for once will you be kind, please?*

Nancy tore from the room, flinging the front door wide.

Lizzie stood behind her. 'How will you find them in this weather? There's a storm coming. Perhaps they are still in the house?'

'Have you looked?'

'Yes, all over, but... wait till we can get help, madam.'

'From whom?' Nancy shouted. 'You know as well as I do that there is no help in this place.' Her eyes flew to Estelle, who watched from the window.

'But madam, please.' Lizzie wept.

'Everyone here is just waiting for us to die,' she spat.

Nancy fought with the key in the lock, finally flung open the car door and reached over to the passenger's seat. She pulled away her jacket to see the item she'd taken from Gloria's shed. She grabbed it and marched down the garden.

TWENTY-EIGHT

Peter Beamish shoved the leather-bound object into his jacket, patting the navy pinstripe pocket several times to make sure. The high street was dim as he turned the key in the ignition.

Could he make it to the Priory before the ironic coming storm and hell broke loose? The Jaguar purred under his feet as he pulled away, his eyes on the blackening skies overhead. The residents of Raynham had felt the mood change—the village was deserted, all curtains were drawn against the night, all windows were closed, and doors bolted. If he got through tonight, then tomorrow would bring a brighter forecast.

The Jaguar stopped at the crossroads. He pulled into the drive, and the engine died, sputtering as it did. Peter turned the key again. Nothing. His hand hung there while he deliberated his next move. He looked at his watch; a few minutes early, not that it mattered. Then, taking a moment to gather himself, he tried the engine again. Dead. He'd have to walk.

A wild rush of wind and a rustle from above marked his arrival.

Very well, he mouthed.

He locked the car behind him and faced the lane that led to the house. It would have been safer to drive. The thought of walking the Priory grounds at night had never been a welcome one. To witness what was to come, whatever it was... if it could have been done from afar, it would have been better, but here he was, about to be in the thick of it all.

The oak creaked overhead, its boughs and branches twisted, and a shower of leaves scattered over Peter's head. He ignored the gesture and walked farther up the drive.

Over the brow of the hill, the Priory's silhouette rose against the thunderous sky. Its windows were dimly lit, though the great door was open. The impulse to run towards it gripped his chest. He turned up the collar of his jacket and patted his pocket again. The object began to hum, sending vibrations through his palm up to his arm and into his ear. But it was more than a hum. It was a voice.

Peter stopped. He pulled the object from his pocket and put it to his ear. The voices didn't come from it but from everywhere. They filled the space he stood in, the very air he breathed. They urged him on.

He began to run.

The sky split with a shockwave of thunderous roars. A fierce strike of blinding lightning pierced the ground before him, then another and another. It threw him backwards, and he fell onto his back as the object flew from his grasp. Peter scrambled about, feeling his way forwards. Lightning struck twice more, each closer than the last. Bolts of fire scorched the grass, pushed him back as he desperately searched the ground. Finally, he staggered to his feet and examined the horizon for some movement, for help.

The Priory door was still wide, though the light was fainter now. In the distance, he could just make out a figure running towards him. A crackle of lightning lit the skies and cast brightness over the whole of Hardacre Priory. The figure stopped mid-step. Nancy stood in the distance; her eyes wide with fear as she pointed towards him. Peter's mind went blank, nodded, then shrugged as he looked back to the ground.

I dropped it, he mouthed.

Nancy shook her head, her eyes wild with fear. 'Run!'

A long, twisted root ripped from the soil, echoing the thunder as it thrashed onto the ground and sent torturous thuds through the earth to his feet. It tossed him backwards through the air, showering down wet mud. Peter landed a dozen or so feet at the foot of the oak tree.

†

Elliot had sneaked past Lizzie up the stairs. Oliver followed, in instinct, but he hadn't known why. When they reached the gallery, the air altered, thick, suffocating.

'We need to get out of here, Oli. Right now.'

'What do you mean? We can't.'

There was no time to explain. They made it to their bedroom. Elliot quickly shut the door and flicked on the light.

Oliver wandered over to the window and stared into the night. 'We can't leave. Mum will kill us if we leave the house. Look, Elliot—it's dark.'

Elliot stared at his twin. He knew it would kill them all if they stayed, but he didn't say it. If Oli didn't remember what happened with the oak tree earlier, he wouldn't listen now.

'We need to get Mum.' Elliot rummaged under his bed.

'What are you doing? What's that?' Oliver scowled as Elliot pulled something out from under the bed. 'You took it.'

'I needed to. We need it.' He stepped his bare feet into his wellies. 'Best take those slippers off.'

There was a low knock; a slow creak opened the door ajar. The boys jumped, scrambled in panic, and sat on their beds. Elliot put his finger to his lips, signalling his twin and his eyes fierce under his scowl. Oliver nodded, playing with the cuffs of his jumper sleeves.

Lizzie peered through the crack. 'There you are! You gave me a fright. Please don't run off like that again.' She smiled, but Elliot saw the worry at the corner of her mouth and in her downcast eyes. 'Why not get yourselves into your nightclothes? It's almost time for bed.'

207

They both nodded as Oliver pulled off his jumper.

'Good boys.'

She carefully closed the door. Elliot sat tight-lipped until her footsteps fell out of earshot.

Oliver was already in his pyjamas—knights on horseback. He fastened the last button, stood ready and pushed his feet into his blue slippers. Elliot just stared.

'What are you doing? We can't leave in our pyjamas?'

Oliver shrugged. 'I'm not leaving.'

Elliot huffed, then shrugged, and looked around for his own. He couldn't find them.

'I need to borrow some of yours.' Elliot tugged open the drawers. 'Why can't I find my Hulks?' he growled. He pulled out a pair with cowboys and Indians and scowled and grumbled as he changed, his fingers fumbling with the buttons.

'I think they look nice.' Oliver sat crossed-legged on the end of his bed.

'Don't just sit there. We need to go.'

'Now?'

'Yes.'

There was no plan. Elliot had no idea where they were going, they just needed to find Mum and leave. And now they both stood in stupid pyjamas. Pulling a cardigan over his nightclothes Elliot grabbed the mirror, stuffed it under his top and folded his arms over it. He then nodded towards the door as Oliver carefully opened it.

'Don't look at the chair,' Elliot said.

Oliver stared at him.

Elliot shook his head. 'Just hurry and don't look at it.'

They needed to stay calm long enough to get outside. Maybe they could make it to the village road without anyone seeing them.

The boys both gripped the balustrade at the top of the staircase. The great hall was empty, just a vague glow coming up from the kitchen, but the only true light came from the drawing-room. They'd be in there.

Elliot nudged his twin and nodded towards the muffled voices. 'We need to be quiet,' he whispered.

Something was different tonight, and his brother felt it, he saw how Oliver's eyes lingered on the open door of the drawing-room.

Not now, Elliot mouthed and grabbed Oliver's hand.

They made it to the hallway. Oliver seized the iron ring with both hands and yanked it round. The door gave a low moan as his mother's voice came from the room.

Elliot shoved his twin outside and pulled the door to. They ran into the night, darting the bolts of lightning as they stabbed the ground ahead of them.

Oliver squeezed his hand. 'Who is that?'

Elliot froze. The bedsheet figure flittered for attention. He swiped his hand over his eyes.

'Come on, Elliot. They could help.' Oliver pulled him towards the grounds.

'No. No one can help us now. We have to do it.' His breath was short with panic. 'We need to get to the village, get help.'

'Mrs Scarfe?' Oliver thought of Josie and her big eyes. 'She's Mum's friend, isn't she?'

'Okay, but we can't go near the driveway, or they'll find us. So, we'll have to find our way around.' He looked about the grounds. 'We can go around the side—I think there's another gate or something down there.' He pointed across the bare gardens as the view evaporated into the darkness. 'Somewhere over there.' But he didn't really know.

'What if we get lost?' Oliver moaned.

'We'll have to make sure we don't.' Elliot thrust his foot forwards, gripping the mirror with his arm.

They ran towards the lake, around the side down to the bottom trees. Elliot knew there must be another way out, somewhere. If they had to climb over a wall or dig themselves out under a hedge or fence, they would. They had to.

'Elliot?' Oliver's voice was faint, lost somewhere in the air.

'Where are you?' Elliot stopped, his wellies slipping on the sodden grass as he spun around.

He leapt forward and saw Oliver lose his footing at the water's edge. Dropping the mirror, Elliot flung himself forwards and grabbed his brother's wrists as his body slipped under the dark water.

Elliot's chest burned. 'Hold on!' he cried.

With his elbows dug firm into the sodden mud, he heaved until he felt some movement. But Oliver kept falling back from his grip. Something or someone was tugging his twin out of his grasp.

'No. You won't die like Dad.'

Elliot scrambled to get a hold with his knees. He wedged them behind his hands, with his toes deep in the sticky, slick bank, he tugged. A hand rested on his shoulder, solid and calm. Without turning, he closed his eyes and pulled harder, stronger, more assertive. The joints in his arms strained, his shoulders about to pop from their sockets.

Something gave way and propelled Elliot back, banging his head on the wet ground. Finally, Oliver's head emerged from the depths, and his limp body lurched forwards. They both lay slumped on the bank, unmoving at the shallow dark water's edge.

The round oak mirror lay close by, wedged in the mud.

The moon peaked through the storm clouds with a glint on its surface. A swirl of something dark, something sinister and predatory, hovered within its glass. One side reflected the darkness towards Hardacre Priory; the other side reflected the boys of winter.

It was raining, every drop the size and velocity of biblical proportions—just what Nancy needed. So bloody ironic. Propelling herself onwards, dodging the lightning strikes, she pressed on with no other thought than the need to find her boys.

Peter Beamish was there, and that bloody oak tree was at it again. She pressed her hand to her hip as a painful stitch twitched her sides. She didn't have time for this.

'Oh, for God's sake!' she cried. 'What else are you going to throw at me?'

Peter lay unmoving, his arm unnaturally twisted beneath him.

'Can you hear me? Please, can you hear me!' She tapped his cheek and checked for a pulse. He was alive, that was enough for now. 'Peter, please, if you can hear me, I promise I'll get help.' She pressed her hand to his cheek.

Nancy clambered to her feet and headed towards the oak, that damned, blasted tree. She stamped her boots, creating her own tremors.

'Where are my boys!'

A lone lightning strike lit the ground before her, casting the tree in an eerie glow. The land at its roots rumbled, and thunder shook her core. She could barely see through the rain. Every drop stung her skin.

'I said, where are my boys? You won't have them. Not again.'

'*Such a fierce heart.*'

'Don't play with me.' Her throat was hoarse and raw. 'Go to hell. I'm not playing your games anymore.'

She stamped her foot repeatedly, her hands balled into fists. Anger bubbled up, she screamed. Her boot hit something and sent it flying to the exposed tree root.

The leather object.

Nancy dropped to her knees. She ran her hands around the muddy earth and wiped her jacket sleeve over her face to see.

Her long hair stuck in wet lashes over her cheeks as she dug her fingers into the mud.

'Where are you? If there's a god, please, will you please help me?' She thrust her hands into the gaping hole by the thrashing tree root. 'Please.' She rummaged in the thick mud, which oozed between her fingers. It was there. She gripped it, but her feet struggled to gain a hold on the slippery ground.

'Not so fast, Nancy Hardacre.'

She turned towards the Priory. With the leather-bound item in her hand, she marched against the wild wind and raging storm. Droning thunder pressed in on her ears. The wind spun her, stopped her in her tracks, and slowly brought her to a halt.

'Such determination should not go unrewarded. You may choose one this time.'

'Go to hell or wherever you came from. Leave my family and me alone. Now, give me my boys.'

Slick with mud, the long, tuberous root gathered itself up from the ground. It wound in the air like a whip. Nancy held her breath, there was no time to brace herself.

'Very well.'

TWENTY-NINE

Gloria tugged on her coat as she closed the car door behind Josie. The moment she pushed the key into the ignition of her Morris Minor, she knew there was no turning back. The little car roared up the road and turned onto the high street, all the while squinting as the windscreen wipers fought against the onslaught of rain. Thunder bellowed. Josie clutched the collar of her coat to her mouth, her eyes tight. Gloria switched her gaze from Josie to the road; the panic she would feel knowing her child was in danger would be too agonizing.

'Nancy would do the same for me,' she chanted as she pushed her way up the gears.

The village was deserted. It knew. They all knew, had always known the terror that lay at Hardacre. She wouldn't let this happen again. She had lost Allan to that place. No one else. She had a duty, didn't she? As a teacher, she had a responsibility to care for those boys.

She was out of the village. Here, the night was thick and heavy. She turned off the main road and into the crossroads. A flash of light illuminated something in front of her. Beamish's car. Gloria slammed her foot on the brakes, swerved on slick mud as a high screech of metallic griding brought her car to a halt.

'Are you all right?'

Josie nodded and pulled the door open. 'Mummy?'

'It's all right, darling. Not sure I can say the same for the cars. But no time, we need to find the twins, okay?'

With their coats pulled tight around them, the raging storm dragged them into Hardacre.

'Look!' Josie shouted.

'Oh, dear god.'

Peter Beamish was sprawled on the mud, his limbs twisted at odd angles. Gloria bent down to check for a pulse, and he gently murmured.

'Oh, thank goodness. Can you hear me?' Gloria smoothed the rain from his face. 'The boys—whatever happened?'

'Nancy…' he wheezed. 'You must find her.'

'Mummy, I shall go get some help.' Josie started up the drive, heading towards the Priory.

'No!' Gloria screamed. 'Don't go anywhere near there without me.'

Peter squinted against the rain. 'Let her go.'

'It's all right, Mummy.' Josie ran like a determined tornado against the elements. Nimble and eager, she wound between the gusts, darting out of sight.

'Okay but go straight inside and don't—' Gloria didn't know what else to say. The Priory was the place of nightmares, and she was sending her daughter into its mouth.

'Where's Nancy?' Gloria knelt on the wet mud; her ear close to Peter's mouth. 'What do I do?' she pleaded.

He was unconscious. Gloria pulled off her coat, laid it over him, placed her hand on his chest, and looked up at the tortuous sky.

'We'll get help, Peter,' she said softly.

Gloria stood in the shadow of the oak tree. It loomed over her thin stature, taunting her. As the rain eased, she felt a jolt under her feet. For a moment, the world fell silent, still.

The wild winds, which had flogged all of nature into a frenzied twister, ceased. Gloria stood in the eye of the storm, nothing but her and the oak tree and a static sheet of glaring electricity that lit the sky.

The ground was broken. Gashes scored the mud, unnatural cavernous channels where roots had once been buried. But this was Hardacre Priory; nothing was natural; she swore under her breath. Evil erupted at the roots of the oak, a weak point in the earth. Maybe faith had always been at its most vulnerable here. She knew her history. This was the crossroads where ley lines met, crossed, it held power. Moreover, centuries ago, the oak had once been a hanging tree. What lay beneath had fed on the sadness, the ager, all the evil and cruel deeds

She took a step closer to the trunk but lost her footing and fell ankle deep into a hole. Something caught the heel of her shoe—a small, leather-bound item. She pulled it out and wiped the mud away. Before she had a chance to plunge it into her cardigan pocket, a thin vine swept around her wrist. It twisted and coiled in the lightning's bright, electric glare and dragged her closer to the tree.

The sky flickered, plunging the grounds back into darkness. She reached the oak, and with one hand, slapped the trunk in anger, the other folded around the wet leather. She shuffled over holes and trenches around the trunk to gain a stronger foothold. Her toe hit a large, knotted root as a lightning bolt struck the ground inches from her with a crackle and sizzled the wet grass. It was swift but bright enough to see what glinted half-buried at the base.

Gloria tugged the vine at her wrist, her nails digging it away as it tightened. She bent forwards and pushed the leather-bound thing into her pocket. Pulling as far as she could, desperate to reach for what was half-buried. The taut vine's thin truss bit into her wrist. She screamed as it cut through and a stream of blood dripped down her arm. The pain was too much. She closed her eyes and collapsed to her knees. The trunk of the vast oak pressed against her chest— breathing, pulsated—its heartbeat.

She dug her fingers into the vine, picking it from her gashed skin.

'I won't let you do this,' she swore through gritted teeth as tears ran down her face.

The vine crept away. Tree wreckage whipped around her head in a thrashing frenzy then fell to the ground, pelting her with acorns and branches. Gloria hurled herself forwards, dug away at the mud until she found it. An axe—Allan's.

'Nancy?' she yelled. 'Nancy!'

With the smooth wooden handle in her grip, Gloria struck the axe at the bark. It swung back, knocking her to the ground. Biting her lip, she got to her feet and swung it again. With every swing, her breath hitched in her burning chest, driving her forward with more determination.

'This is for Allan,' she screamed.

The axe split the bark. Again, the blade bit through the tree, then again, until she fell to the ground. Her heart throbbed. Her short breath wheezed in her chest.

Gloria got to her feet and aimed the axe high. Its final blow hurled her backwards. Staggering, she left the tree, moving away into the grounds. Amidst the continued onslaught of thrashing branches, Gloria looked up; something sticky dripped onto her face. She wiped her forehead with the sleeve of her cardigan. It wasn't the rain.

With her arms wrapped over her head, she peered into the heights of the oak. Up high within the twisted boughs, barely visible, was an outline, a silhouette. The oak shuddered as the highest branch broke. What had lain within its hold fell through the tree mass until it stopped with a swift jerk just above Gloria's head.

It was a figure, arms outstretched and bound tight. The thinnest and sharpest twigs thread through the body.

Nancy Hardacre had been crucified.

Elliot lay in the mud. His chest burned as his vision finally cleared. He realised then. He didn't remember why or how, only that all the darkness that had been festering inside him had spilt over.

His hand reached out, patting the ground next to him. 'Oliver? Oli?' His arms swept through the mud, making a sticky mud angel.

He strained to sit up, but the mud held him fast, tried to calm his breathing to stop the panic from swallowing him, but it already had. Tears fell. A scream ripped from his lungs filling the air, his chest heavy with pain, he pushed his hand over his heart and hit something hard—the mirror. He dragged his legs up and pulled himself free of the muddy bank, and swung them over, pushing on his elbows.

A loud crack lit the sky like day, a great sheet of lightning over the Hardacre grounds. He whipped his head around, but he was alone. He remembered the figure on the driveway, remembered the fear that had taken hold, the need to run. It had made him think of Dad and the bedsheet man.

Elliot trudged through the slick grounds. Every other step slipped in the deep muddy patches. Standing on the brow of the hill, he glanced behind him towards the Priory. They hadn't got far.

Had they come looking for him and Oli yet?

Did they know they were missing?

Beyond was the silhouette of the oak tree.

Panic made his feet move, and he began to run. He had to find his twin. The mirror hummed, a sensation he'd felt before—it was like the energy he'd found in the walking stick, the power that had purged his body when…

He shook the thought away. None of it was real. It had burrowed inside his head, made him feel and think awful things. He hated Hardacre Priory, and it hated him.

Elliot ran. *I must get out. Get help.*

There was a movement by the oak. Elliot skidded to a stop, and his wellies sank to the ground. He fiercely gripped the mirror to his chest. *Don't let go. I must not let it go.*

Someone was at the tree.

He pulled his boot from the mud and took a cautious step closer. With speed, the sticky sludge took him. Elliot fell onto the slippery slope and slid into a knotted root a dozen feet from the oak, hitting his head. Dazed, he rubbed his temple. The sky had darkened again. Sharp flashes and forks of lightning mixed with rumbling thunder.

Elliot pushed his hand to the ground, and it squelched into a pile of fallen leaves. The stalk of an acorn pierced his hand. As he pulled it free, a bead of blood swelled on his palm and fell, seeping into the earth.

'*Oh, now what do we have here?*'

Elliot froze.

It wasn't real.

He clambered to his feet, desperate to steady his legs, and willed his boots to move.

'*Not so fast, young heir.*'

The sound rang through the atmosphere like a siren. The long, voluminous root crackled up from the earth, shaking off wet soil. It twisted, coiled high into the air and lingered above him for a moment. Taunting him, freezing him to the spot, unable to move. He stood rigid, his eyes wide and knowing while he could do nothing but wait.

It whipped.

The thick tail of the root thrashed him about the head, then with another lash, propelled him through the air until he landed at the foot of the oak.

Elliot lay winded, panic-stricken.

'*Your mother could not choose. It seems you chose for her.*'

Gloria had not taken her eyes off Nancy. Deep rumbling rang in her ears as the earth quaked underfoot and took her legs out from under her. Thunder roared in her ears as sharp bolts hit the ground. A few feet away, a cloud of dirt churned through the air, then a loud thump.

Gloria crawled over.

A boy lay twisted over the base of the trunk—one of the twins, though which one?

Gloria pushed her fingers to his neck, her ear to his mouth.

He was alive.

She pulled off her cardigan and wrapped it around him. He was wet through to the bone, dressed in only his pyjamas and wellies. She looked at his small face. Even though he was unconscious, she saw terror painted there. Then, tentatively, she looked back at her friend's body.

Gloria patted his cheek, carefully running her hands over his arms and body to check him over. He seemed okay.

'Are you okay, darling? Can you hear me?'

'Mummy?' the boy murmured. '…what's happened to my mum?'

'Oh, you poor darling…' Gloria hugged him close. For this poor child to witness such a horrific sight… oh God.

Gloria patted his arm, bringing his face up to meet hers. 'Look at me, darling. Don't look anywhere else, just look at me—' She gulped down a sharp tang of bile. 'Are you hurt? I don't think anything's broken.' She chastised herself as the words left her lips. What did it matter? His bones would mend. A few bruises were nothing to witnessing the sight of his mother. That would never heal.

He shook his head.

Gloria stared at him, straining to think which twin he was. 'Darling, where is your brother? Are you Elliot or Oliver?'

The boy mumbled something vague and breathy. His hand scrambled over the ground, frantically fumbling in the grass.

'What have you lost?'

He found it and pulled it to his chest as he moved off the root. Gradually, he shuffled away from the tree. Not once did he look at her.

Gloria studied him as he trembled.

'Oliver,' he slowly muttered, then fell back to the ground, gripping the mirror to his chest. 'Mummy?'

Gloria hushed him. 'I know, darling. I know. I'm so sorry. I couldn't—' She wiped the tears from her face and tried to stay calm, then patted his shoulder, smoothed the hair from his forehead. 'Where is Elliot?'

He stared, his eyes full of fear, then they flicked to the mirror and back to the oak tree. He shook his head sobbing, opened his mouth to speak and closed it again.

'My brother is lost, and it's all my fault.'

The rain stopped. The storm eased.

On the sodden ground in the oak's shadow, Gloria cradled the boy in her arms. She didn't dare look up. She had been too late to help her friend; she wouldn't fail this poor child.

PART THREE

THE PRESENT

THIRTY

They say your life flashes before your eyes when you die. What they don't tell you, and for good reason, is that it does something else too. We'd like to imagine that we see those we have loved and all the attached memories when in truth, it's nothing except fear and guilt.

Shame brought me to my knees. The last forty years had been a lie. I wasn't sure if I'd known, but I was an imposter. I'd been living the life of my brother. I couldn't remember whether I'd meant to correct Mrs Scarfe that night or I'd intentionally allowed her to think that I was, in fact, my twin. As every day had grown into the next, the memory of that night had dissipated like a ghost. I was now Oliver. The recollection of what lay in my past had died with my mother in that storm.

The agony wrenched my heart in two. Sobbing, I sat on the stone porch of the Priory. No man likes to admit defeat in such a manner. My companion knelt by my side. As the tears subsided, my pain curdled into anger, and I realised that Gloria had wanted to tell me how she knew my dirty little secret. If that was the case, so had Vera and Bob.

I was a murderer.

I looked at Fisk. Anger locked my jaw while my teeth ground hard in my ears.

'How long have you known?' I asked.

Fisk took my hand, helping me to stand. With my back pressed against the open door, I heard the whispers from inside. They weren't finished with me.

Fisk patted my shoulder. 'You need to end this.'

'What?' I eased my jaw. 'What am I supposed to do? This…' I pulled the leather object from my pocket. 'We don't even know what it is.'

Fisk grabbed my wrist and pulled my hand and the object closer. 'This belongs at the Priory. Where they failed, you cannot.'

'Or what, it'll kill me like my mother?' I spat.

Fisk shook his head. 'No, Oliver. It'll do much worse.'

'Worse than death?' I shut up, knowing there was something far worse than simply being dead.

My days at the Priory had been short, but I'd lived with them all my life. Ghosts had a way of finding me. I was never free of them. In the night, they whispered their secrets and filled my head with their memories. It hadn't been the Priory that had caused it—I also remembered that day with Dad, the ghost, the bedsheet figure. So many ghosts of the past. So much pain. So many unanswered questions.

I closed my eyes, nodded, and turned my back to Fisk. 'Okay,' I said.

He grabbed my arm. 'Are you sure?'

'I guess we left the point of no return by the roadside.'

He nodded solemnly.

If the Priory required this from me, then it will have to give me something in return. I wanted answers.

The hallway was dark and empty, but with every step, it gave away more secrets. I remembered my mother, the sight of her hanging from the oak. Those snippets from 1979 started to settle into my bones. I smelled her perfume and felt the softness of her skin.

Guilt swamped me again. I'd let her down, and my brother's death was on my hands.

I turned back to face Fisk. He still stood within the frosty stone arch of the porch.

'Are you coming with me?' I asked. 'If I'm to do this... Honestly, I need your help.'

'If I step over this threshold'—he flourished his hands through the frosty air— 'there's something you need to know.'

'More?' I laughed, then my face fell serious again at the sight of his. 'What is it?'

'You must understand my motives are true and only are ones of faith.'

'Okay...' My finger began to throb. I gripped the carved finial at the bottom of the staircase. Looking down, I realised I'd already taken two steps up. What sat on the gallery landing above seized my eyes. It was too dark to see, but I felt it. I knew it was there. That childhood sensation crept down the stairs to greet me.

'Oliver.'

I turned back to Fisk. 'Go on. I've come this far.' I glanced again up the stairs, then back to the door. 'How bad can it be?' Laughter rumbled in my chest.

'Very well, Elliot Hardacre.'

My head fused to my shoulders, hearing my name, my true name, struck lightning brighter than it had been that night.

Behind Fisk, the grounds were whiter than I could ever describe. A brightness that should have burned my retinas glowed stronger by the second. I walked back to the door, looked farther over the grounds. Every frost pattern, every twiglet tree on the horizon clarified as if I zoomed in on them, my mind swam—dizzy. I steadied myself, resting my hand on Fisk's arm. He bowed his head, and in that second, I saw them all.

I slowly paced backwards down the hall while caution kept my eyes on his. The black-and-white tiles beneath my soles froze as winter followed me. On the frozen grounds stood those I had seen in my childhood, those who had stopped my heart with icy fear. Those I had run from.

Words were lost in the mire of battling memories. My adult mind knew what I saw, but to shake my childhood fear was impossible. It was too entrenched in my history.

This had been a place of God and faith. The Augustinian friars of the Priory had gathered here. Fisk bowed his head to me as he stepped into the great hall. Where his suit trousers met his shoes, they dissolved and were replaced with the long, black robe that I recognised.

'Hello, Elliot.' He bowed again. 'We have work to do.'

'Fisk?'

'Brother Nicholas,' he said softly.

He walked in farther, his eyes never leaving mine. My feet took me backwards. I felt myself tumbling into the past with every step. Those childhood fears lifted every hair on my neck, stunned, shaken to my core.

'We've met before,' I said.

'Many times. Not once did I mean to cause you fear or concern.'

I sank onto the stairs with my head in my hand, the other closed around the object. Every time we'd met replayed in my head like a film — nostalgic, tinged brown — only to burn black at the edges.

Nicholas took another step. His black bedsheet robe billowed. The friars outside took a step closer too.

'Now, you all just hold on a minute,' I asserted.

'There are many questions to be answered,' Nicholas said. 'I hear them in your heart. *It* knows you are back. *It* invited you. We both felt it. There will be enough time later. But, for now, we must act fast before it is too late.'

I hadn't blinked or moved a muscle, but he was by my side, his hand firmly on my shoulder.

The leather item hummed in my hand until it burned my palm. I let go, swearing at the pain as I rubbed my hand over my leg. It tumbled to the wooden stairs and bounced off the last step onto the tiled floor. As I watched with my stomach in my gullet, the black-and-white tiles vanished. The grand hallway was paved with large flagstones, the walls awash with flickering lamplight. Gone was all reference to the interior I remembered.

Under the aged leather, the frost melted and left the stone dry and lightly polished from wear. Stunned and wordless, I watched. The wax seal snapped like chocolate, and the thin leather binding unravelled, revealing its content.

Nicholas reached down and closed his fingers around the small amber-like article.

'What is it?' I asked.

'Many centuries ago, when the king held our faith hostage to his whims, our kind were shunned. Our monasteries, abbeys, priories were demolished, taken.'

'Henry VIII and the Reformation,' I said, nodding, maybe a little too impatiently.

'Yes,' he concurred.

'Forgive me, Nicholas.'

'There's nothing to forgive. It is history. Though to us...' He looked at his brothers, who stood in the doorway and beyond out on the grounds. 'It is our time. We live within these moments. We relive them. Although we are conscious of the here and now. Your grandmother was a conscious one too.'

'Nan?' The memory of the old lady hovered on the threshold of the drawing-room when I glanced over. 'A conscious one?'

'When you arrived with your mother, Lady Hardacre was already gone.' He bowed his head. 'You were children, and for the most part, children see what is in front of them without question; however, she had been dead for many years.'

'I didn't see it.'

'And now?' Nicholas rolled the item in his fingers and rubbed his thumb over the surface.

'As the years passed, I knew the truth. They visit me. I've told their stories. It's only mine I'm unable—' All those ghosts of the past. Were Oliver and I not part of them? 'Why couldn't I remember my part in it all?'

'I wish I had that answer for you. You and your brother were the last of them. The moment your mother brought you here, your fate was sealed.'

'What fate? Look at me, Nicholas. I've lived a lie, and my mum and dad…' I swallowed that hard lump, staring at him. 'What happened to my father that night? I remembered when I first saw you.' The pain rose, my face hot with the memory.

'Andrew knew his destiny. He had waited for it, but when the time came…'

Darkness rose. My legs pulled me up, although I had no control over my actions.

'Was it because of you? My father died soon after that day.'

'I am just the custodian. I have no say. I cannot change the way of it no matter how much I have wanted to. I still want to, especially now,' he said softly. 'And I hear your thoughts and fears, Elliot. You did not kill your twin. Your brother's fate was not by your hand.'

'I allowed it to happen. It's the same thing.'

'You were children, just little boys.'

'I promised my parents I'd look after him.'

'Always so angry. Although, it has never been *your* anger. It comes from another place. Look around you.'

My fists were tight, my legs rigid. I walked down the great hall, watching my shoes move on the flagstones. They appeared genuine, but I knew the trickery, all those games the Priory liked to play.

'It is not Hardacre Priory. It is the evil at its roots.'

Nicholas held out his hand.

'What is it?' I looked closer.

The object rolled in his hand. There was something inside the amber-like casing.

'The final day of the Priory, when the lands were surrendered to the crown, the seal matrix was used to wax-stamp our surrender. The document. It was used for the last time to bind this. The seal was to remain intact until it was in the hands of the last heir.' Nicholas proffered the item to me. 'What you hold is sacred, Elliot. It is our holy relic of St Augustine. We removed it from the altar for safety.'

'A holy relic?' It looked far too underwhelming to hold such a title.

'You hold St Augustine's forefinger, and with it, you hold the faith that kept these lands pure for centuries.' Nicholas shook his head and closed his eyes in prayer. When they opened, they were wet. 'It was placed in my care. My sole mission was to safeguard it with my life, and after, in death, until the moment came when I lived again. And here we are, it is in the hands of the last heir.'

'Me?'

'Yes. I'm sad to say your father did not have the…' There was hesitation in his pause as he searched for the right word. 'I wonder if your father did not have the faith to fulfil the task. He knew his destiny, had known since he was a boy, but he left the Priory.' He smiled. 'Though your mother… There was courage and strength of heart I have not witnessed in many a century. We failed her. I will not let that happen again.'

'So, what now? What am I supposed to do with that?' I looked about. 'Nothing has changed. I still feel it here just as you do.' I looked up to the gallery. The movement had caught my attention at the mention of my mother. Whatever it was that lived here stirred at the thought of her too.

'It needs to be returned to its place,' Nicholas said.

'In the Priory?'

'The altar.'

THIRTY-ONE

Josie shut the car door on her mum and sat in the driver's seat. Her hand shaking a little as she fastened the seatbelt and started the car. Her mum stared, a desperate look of apology in her eye.

'I didn't know, Josie. Not until after.'

'It's been a long time, Mum.'

'He needs to know. I should have told him long before now.' Her mum pressed her hand to her chest. 'I've lived with this guilt for so long.'

Josie turned the key and pulled out of the pub's car park. The sky was thick and heavy, Nick had been right about the storm, but there was no sign of rain. It just hung overhead like a dark memory, or a new beast.

She remembered that night. She relived it every time she closed her eyes. For years afterwards, she'd felt the dim call of the past through the Priory's open door. Could still feel the single round eye of Hardacre drill into her back and breathe down her neck when thunder roared.

The locals knew to never wander too close and to avoid the crossroads at all cost. But it had been different, harder, for Josie to keep her distance because Hardacre hadn't held its. It had stayed close. For forty years, it had remained a part of her. Even now, hidden and overgrown with creepers, the mirror stood. Her mother avoided the subject and left the room when it rose like a demon in conversations. So, it was Josie who remembered, and her father.

She had left Raynham for a while, tried to put it behind her. She had been sent to stay with her grandfather in Devon for the winter; Mum had visited that Christmas. The dreams had ceased a little, dampened by the brisk sea air, she had swallowed them like a bitter taste. Though, when she returned in January, nothing had changed.

Apart from poor Peter Beamish.

Josie had visited him once. Curiosity had got the better of her, and her teen years had given her an extra boost. The sun had shone, the village seemed cheery. She had wandered with a friend to get sweets after school, stood in the short queue and gazed out of the shop window. But then, movement from the solicitors' window opposite had snatched her eyes. She should have gone straight home, but she had thought of that night, of poor Mr Beamish lying twisted on the ground as the rain poured.

The solicitors' office had been silent, the room empty, when she closed the door behind her. Mr Beamish had appeared in the end doorway, fidgeting with his tie and his eyes flittering about the place, a walking stick in the crook of his arm. She hadn't stayed long. He had asked after her mum and how she got on at school. They had skittered around the subject of that night until it crept up on Josie and burst through the pleasantries. She'd cursed herself for it after, but at that moment, she had to know.

'What happened to Oliver?' Her mind had wandered back to the day they'd stood at her bedroom window and stared at the mirror through the hedge. 'What really happened? The truth.'

'Come sit.' He'd pulled a chair out from the desk by the window and waved her to continue

She sat. Her eyes hadn't left his, which held something distant, forlorn, and forgotten. He'd looked different—less sure, less like Mr Beamish. More of a shell.

'Mum won't talk about it, but I need to know. Please?'

'How old are you now, Josie?'

'I'm thirteen. Fourteen soon.'

He leant on his walking stick. 'You were the same age.' The answer was there, etched into every line on his face. 'Oliver… That poor child.'

'What happened?' she'd repeated.

'You know where he went. He's with your aunt in Yorkshire.'

She thought about playing along; it was easier for the adults. It was always simpler to play their games.

'I think you know what I mean,' Josie said. 'I've always known. I think you do too.' Josie leant back with an air of defiance. She would have her answers.

'I'm sorry, Josie, I'm not sure what you mean. Oliver is with your aunt. Is he okay?'

'Elliot lives with my aunty, not that I've seen him. Mum thinks the sight of us might bring back those awful memories, that he's better off living a new life. Or a *lie*.'

'Oh…'

'He doesn't remember, you see. Wouldn't you want to know? Wouldn't you want to find your twin?'

'Sorry, Josie, I don't quite follow.' He swayed a little as he shifted his weight from foot to foot. 'Elliot?'

'Yes, and I think you know that too. I want to know what happened to the other twin. What happened to Oliver?'

He sat. His walking stick crashed onto the polished floor; his face whiter than his shirt.

'Elliot,' he'd said again, more to himself.

Maybe he hadn't known after all.

'Is Oliver one of them now?'

He hadn't answered her.

Josie drove out of the village. Every other second, she glanced at her mum. The guilt of that day with Mr Beamish would sit heavy in her heart forever. He'd looked at her with glazed eyes as he'd clutched at his chest and pulled his tie loose. As soon as she had realised, she grabbed the telephone on the desk and dialled for an ambulance, but they hadn't made it in time.

Mr Beamish had lain on the floor, Josie by his side, as his heart surrendered to the attack. The ambulance driver had said it had been quick and as painless as could be hoped for. But Josie knew better. Had seen the agony in his eyes, desperate and pleading. There *had* been pain. It had sliced through him along with the lie.

'Then Oliver is lost,' Mr Beamish said, clutching his chest. 'Like your dad, Josie.'

She'd seen the dark shadow slither back in the obscure corner of the solicitors' office. *It* had lain by the door at the far end, lingered as she tried to focus on it. It knew she wasn't afraid. She'd faced it on the gallery landing.

Josie pulled up at the crossroads and parked next to Fisk's car.

'Well, they're definitely here then. Part of me hoped he got on a train.' Her mum unclipped her belt. 'I suppose it's best this way.'

'He had no choice,' Josie said. 'We were all there this morning. You saw it as well as I did. If he came back to Suffolk but not here, it would never let him leave.'

'Will it let him leave anyway?' Her mum closed the door behind her and stood with her back to the car. She looked up at the oak. 'In all these years, I haven't looked at this tree since—'

'It's okay, Mum. I know.'

'She was my friend, and I couldn't help her. The image of her up there has haunted me all these years. And seeing Oli—Elliot this morning has unearthed everything.' Gloria sighed, pressing her hand on her chest.

'That night has haunted us all.' Josie stared at the oak tree, then at the frosty lane beyond. 'Do you know how many times I've wanted to change the pub's name?' She laughed.

'Every time I did, I thought, *no*, I won't give *it* the satisfaction of winning. This day was always going to come. But now that Elliot and we are here, I don't know what we're supposed to do, Mum.'

'Neither do I, but I know he'll need us one way or another, this side or the other. I let him down before. I won't do it again.' Her mum pulled her coat closer and headed onto the frosty lane.

The Priory's door was wide open. Gathered on the frozen gravel was a group of friars Josie had seen before. Her mum snatched her arm and pulled her back when they reached them. Her eyes flicked from Josie to them.

'It's okay, mum.' Josie patted her hand. 'They are from the Priory, the real one; they're here to help.'

Josie bowed her head as they dispersed, allowing them to enter. They stood just inside the stone porch, the great hall open in front of them, but nothing fitted. It was as it had been that night during the storm so long ago. Josie, stunned by the feel of the stone under her shoes, the light that filtered from the lanterns. But mostly, it was the change in the very essence of the space, which hovered thickly in the air—ancient.

'Where is he? Not here, either of them.' Josie searched the rooms that spurred from the great hall while her mum stood within the stone porch.

'*You will find them at the Priory,*' the voice softly echoed.

Josie walked towards her mother and looked past her to one of the friars. A single figure stepped forward a pace, solidifying with clarity. He pointed towards the grounds beyond the house.

'Brother Nicholas has taken the lord to the Priory.' He stepped back into the mix of hazy black robes.

'Come on, we need to find them.' Josie pulled her mum outside.

The black vapour dispersed as they channelled through. Her mum looked over her shoulder to find them gone, nothing but a soft glow in their stead.

The grounds beyond the house were barren, maybe more so than the gardens. There were no trees or shrub boundaries here, just acres of bare, frosty lands. As they walked, the Priory rose from the horizon with massive stone arches.

Her mum stopped, her hand on her throat. 'I can't, Josie. I just can't do it.'

'You don't need to do anything, I promise. We're here to help the boys. They need us if only for… I don't know, moral support,' said shrugged.

'What good is that? I couldn't save Nancy.'

'No, but I have known since that night that this day would come. I'm doing it for Elliot and Oliver and… for Dad,' she nodded. 'Mum, I know.'

'Know what?' Her mum held her breath.

'I know what happened to Dad, even though you didn't talk about it.'

'He died.'

'No, he *didn't*. You can tell yourself that if you like—you've done it for forty years—but I know it's not true. For Christ's sake, he didn't even have a funeral, did he?'

Her mum shook her head.

'I saw him that night,' Josie said.

'No, you didn't. You were asleep. You were in bed.'

'I saw him *here*. That's why I'm here now. This place has a lot to answer for, I'm here for those answers. We've waited long enough. Now, are you coming or not?' Josie stood with her hands on her hips. 'I'm not a little girl anymore.'

'You saw your dad?'

Josie held her mum tight. 'He's lost. They both are—Oliver and Dad. I don't know how; I just know it. I felt Dad that night in Elliot's hands.'

'I don't understand a word you're saying.'

'I sat in the back of the car with Elliot that night, remember. I was with him when you took him away from here. I saw the look on his face. I knew it was him and not Oliver. I could always tell them apart.'

'Darling, Dad was already gone by then.'

'Do you remember what Elliot held that night?'

Her mum shook her head. 'A small thing. Something he wouldn't let go of.'

'And did he say anything at all when you found him?'

'Only *Oliver.*'

'Yes, because he was talking about him. He was gripping a mirror—a round wooden mirror. I watched him the whole journey. He wouldn't look at me because he didn't take his eyes off that bloody mirror. So, I grabbed it and asked him what was so important.' Josie closed her eyes to recall the moment. 'I don't know how, but Oliver was in the mirror.'

'Just his reflection, Josie. You were… It was a terrible night. You were exhausted and—'

'I was holding the mirror mum, if it were a reflection I saw, it would have been *me.* The mirror came from the Priory, just like that thing that has sat by Dad's shed all these years—I know it is still there. And we both know that if it belongs to Hardacre bloody Priory, it's as creepy as the rest of it. Oliver is lost somewhere in Hardacre,' Josie urged and swept her hand around the air, letting it rest at her throat. 'Just like Dad.'

They both looked back towards the house. The brothers gathered again and slowly became visible.

Josie pointed to the ruins. 'We need to get there. Look.'

They hadn't walked another step though the horizon had grown. The view had developed before them. The Priory was no longer ruins but a vast stone edifice of tall arches.

Josie clutched her mum's hand. 'We need to be quick.'

We stood beneath a great stone arch, metres above our heads, towering to the sky beyond. I held the relic in my open palms, wondering what the hell I was to do with this thing. I glanced at Nicholas with unspoken questions, too afraid to open my mouth. He slowly nodded before us. I turned to look in disbelief as from the ground grew an enormous altar. In the centre of its surface was a deep gash, surrounded by splintered, fractured wood.

'This is where I broke it free,' Nicholas whispered. 'It was here for centuries. Encased in its seal, set into the wood of the altar. Sacred.' He inclined his head.

The grey storm clouds split above us, letting a bright shaft of light fall in. I clenched my eyes against its glare. In my ears, the sky roared with the tremendous clash of stones and rocks. The tumbling of rubble and stone, the crackle and chink of glass, was awash with the splintering of wood. Tentatively, I opened one eye to see the impossible. It was building, constructing around us—the Priory, which had once stood yard upon yard high and covered acres of this barren land, was tall and solid. The ground was no longer frozen dirt but hard stone beneath our feet.

'You've returned the relic,' Nicholas said, casting his eyes around the grand stone edifice in which we now stood. 'You have restored the Priory. And, in turn, we have the power to expel what has wreaked havoc on your ancestral lands.'

'But these were your lands long before they belonged to a Hardacre.'

'The loss of faith here was not always so easy. Your first ancestor here was a good man who held his faith firm. It was those who came after him whose grip was not so tight. They were easily enticed by the evil that lay here. It has fed on the sins of man, their greed, their hatred. It feeds on weakness. You know your history as well as I do.'

'They have visited me for as long as I can remember. But where is my family now? If those who are long gone can pester me, then why is my family lost?'

'I wish with all my faith that you will find the answer.'

'I lost my brother that night. It was my fault.'

'I do not believe that. He has been with you these past forty years. You know that much.' Nicholas pressed his hand to my shoulder. 'Who brought you here? Think about the letter.'

I didn't answer him. The relic was scorching my palm. I realised the roaring of stone upon stone was starting to ease.

'We are now gathered. It is time, Brother Nicholas. We have visitors.' One of the friars stepped forwards from the gathering around us in robes of watercolour black, not solid or transparent, but fluid and hypnotic. Their existence was strong. I could feel every heartbeat drumming through my skull. Beyond them, I saw a flash of red hair.

Josie ran over. She dispersed the gathering as she flung her arms around my neck.

'What the heck are you doing?' Hesitantly, I hugged her.

'We couldn't let you do this alone.' She turned to point at Gloria, who faltered behind her. 'We'll do this together.'

'I don't know what to say. I don't think you should be here, either of you.'

'Oliver…' Gloria paused. 'Elliot, I failed your mum that night. I'm sorry.' Tears collected in her eyes. 'She was my friend, and I couldn't help her.'

I said nothing but nodded.

'Where's Mr Fisk?' Josie looked around. Her eyes met Nicholas, who bowed his head in return. She gripped my sleeve, her eyes wide.

'It's okay.' I stepped a little closer and took her hand.

The ground trembled. A split travelled along the open stone floor in a long, jagged crack. I fell to my hands and knees. The relic rolled along the ground and tumbled into a crevice.

'Quickly. It knows we are here.' Nicholas jumped forwards, his arms elbow deep in the crevice, and seized the relic from the hole. 'It must be now, Elliot.' He threw it to me.

I reached forward, taking one step, then another. With a deep breath and trembling fingers, I plunged the relic into the altar, pushing it into the hole, pressing my hand over it. Growing hot on my palm, it melted into place. The amber resin casing settled as every splinter fitted into its gouge. The altar and relic of Saint Augustine became one as if they had never been apart.

The air shook around my shoulders. My ears filled with earth-shattering judders, which bought me to my knees. 'Please, God, I prayed. Please. If there is a god, help me.'

We were in the centre of what I imagined a bomb explosion felt like. Not only debris flew around the air—an onslaught of emotions and sensations swirled with every spiralling stone splinter. Voices—words and chants—filled the air and grew into agonising screams. I didn't know any of them, but all were familiar—generations of Hardacres, their pleading cries rang through me. Lost souls caught up in a whirlwind, which shook the Priory's ancient stone walls.

I covered my eyes but caught a glimpse of Josie and Gloria huddled together on their knees. I crouched into a ball, my arms about my head. The deafening *thud* of the earth rumbled under the stone floor. If the priory fell again, we'd be lost, dead, beneath a massive pile of rubble.

'We need to get out,' I shouted.

Squinting, I peered through a half-opened eye against the stone dust and wiped my face with the back of my sleeve.

I found nothing.

They weren't there.

I was no longer there.

THIRTY-TWO

'Elliot.'

I turned at the sound of my name. Rain was pouring, the sky thick and angry. Thunder roared; I pressed my hands over my ears to think, what had just happened. I no longer saw the stone walls or arches of the priory.

'Over here.'

I spun to find the voice but lost my footing and fell to my knees. My hands sank into the wet mud. I tried to push myself up. I knew something wasn't quite right as I brought my sticky palms up to my face, then stared down at my legs.

'Down here.'

I forced myself to stand, my legs shaky, my mind confused. I shielded my face from the hammering rain with my arm and looked beyond. The oak tree: I could see it on the hill's incline.

I ran, my feet tripping over themselves as the momentum carried me off. Jolted when my foot caught something hard, I propelled forward, smashing to the ground. My hands scrambled over the wet grass, fumbled through the mud. I dug my fingers down to grab the object. Weighty and slick, it slid easily into my hands. I gripped it and pulled the thing up, wiping the dirt off with my sleeve. In the flash of sheet lightning, I saw its shiny surface. The harsh, sudden light cast the landscape into daylight, bright and vividly white. I was holding the round mirror from my childhood. I lifted it to my face. Saw the boy I had been.

'Here!'

Oliver stood in the tree's shadow, the enormous leafy boughs low, dripping heavy from the rain. His pyjamas soaked through, his hair stuck to his brow, he pointed to the ground, insistent, his face pleading. I stepped closer to something small, half-hidden in the earth. I reached down, dug my fingers, found a handle, gripped it, and pulled it free. An axe. I held it up in front of me.

Oliver nodded.

I shook my head. 'We can't chop it down. Not with this.'

'Not only with the axe, champ. With faith, too,' said another voice, soft and deep. I felt his hand on my shoulder long before I could think, wonder, or even reason.

'You can do it,' Oliver said. 'We can do it together.'

With Oli at my side, I gripped the axe, not once looking behind us. If I did, I feared the spell would break.

I glared straight up into the thick boughs, rain dripping from the sodden foliage. The skies continued to roar. I swung the axe high over my shoulder, my arm shaking with adrenaline. Allowing momentum to take it, I brought the axe down hard on the trunk with a loud *thwack*. It split. I raised it again. This time, lightning struck the highest branch when the blade hit the tree. There was a flash, a sizzle as it kindled— another axe blow, followed by a firebolt that lanced the tree's centre and flamed the core. Over and over, I raised the axe and brought it down harder than the previous strike. My chest burned. My hands channelled forty years of grief, anger, hatred into every fierce blow.

The tree sputtered, hissed as flames gradually took grip, smouldering the wet bark and twigs. Leaves burned, and acorns burst and pop. The growing flames engulfed it all. From inside the trunk, a deep growl reverberated over the ground, and from under our feet, the roots shook. The tree split, a cavernous gash in the bark that splintered the whole oak in half. Roots ripped from their beds, shredded the earth around as the two halves of the tree fell to the ground in opposite directions, awash with flames and sparks.

I looked at Oli, his face small and fragile, just as I remembered him. He smiled with trembling lips.

'That's enough.' Dad's large hands pulled us both back, and Oliver pushed his hand in mine, squeezing it tight.

'My boys, look at you two. You did it.'

It was over the moment I accepted the Priory's invitation. I'd never be allowed to leave Hardacre. I had escaped once, but not again. It was a small price to pay after so many had paid the same before me.

We live in perpetual summer now. Winter has left Hardacre, though I still feel the frost gather beneath my feet if I remember that winter for too long. Those are the moments I stand my ground. I make fists and feel the young boy in me stamp his feet and wield that axe.

I stand at the great door, flung wide open, and look out over the gardens lush with the season. The grass is abundant with daisies today, bright white with yellow middles. The colour feels familiar, like a soft mantle around my shoulders.

Some memories come and go, like the ghosts that stand on the drawing-room's threshold every so often. I wait for them to come in, invite them to sit with me by the fire. Not all of them are conscious like my grandmother. Those others have staggered around in their own misery for centuries, and now the Priory has settled from floor to rafter, the time boundaries have shifted.

They may trust me in time. Their stories are full of history, theirs, and mine. They are all Hardacres.

After all that's been said, after all I've seen, maybe this is just a good old-fashioned ghost story.

This one was mine. Perhaps it's time to tell theirs.

EPILOGUE

No one knows what happened that day—apart from us, of course. Only mum and I are left to remember. But I'm no storyteller. Not like Elliot.

We never told a soul. Who's there really to tell? Stories about that place have been passed through generations in Raynham, but I doubt many believe them to be true.

The last clear memory I have is parking the car, then mum and me heading up the old drive to the Priory. After that, it's a blur, just flashes of images, with a deafening sound of rumbling stone. The next thing I knew, I came to sprawled on the ground down near the drive with mum sat by my side, her face white. I stood and stared up over the brow of the hill toward Hardacre Priory. I knew I should go and have a look, but I just couldn't. There was no way my feet would move any closer. I wondered about Elliot, what had happened, where he was. Mum was distraught, of course; she has carried guilt all these years. She thinks she failed him just like she did his mother.

Despite that churning feeling in my stomach, I knew I wouldn't find him there, dead or alive. He just wouldn't be there. That place had its grip on him the moment he arrived back in Raynham. When it comes to the Priory, nothing is normal. And as neither of us could go any farther up the drive, we walked back to the car. That's when we saw poor Nick. Mum and I pulled him from the car and tried to resuscitate him, but we were too late. The coroner said it was a massive heart attack, that it would have been instant. I took that as a blessing. His funeral was a small affair, some colleagues, local villagers, and us.

The great oak tree is no more. We found it burned and ripped from its roots, nothing but a charred, twisted mass. I arranged for a tree surgeon to take away the remains. Mum feared we were doing the wrong thing, like touching it would revive the evil. But it's over. Removing the last piece was the right thing to do. Elliot would want that.

No one else walks by the lane; it's almost forgotten. It's only me who visits. I often wonder if I'll glimpse him up there, looking out of the window, wandering the grounds, or writing his latest book. Though, in truth, I can see nothing. But that doesn't mean the Hardacres aren't there. I must live with that hope.

I had a mailbox erected at the end of the drive, next to where the tree had stood. I walked by this morning.

Elliot left mail for me today—two large, brown envelopes. One addressed to his agent, which I shall forward, and a copy of the manuscript for me.

I miss him in a way. He was always a little odd—the boy who wrote funny—but it's what made him special.

He left something else for me too. I heard it before I saw it. I still hear it calling. It sits in my lap, round and heavy, still wrapped in a white cloth. I know what it is, but not sure if I can bring myself to look. So, I keep tracing the carved acorns through the linen.

It came with a little note:

A gift of thanks and love, Elliot and Oliver.

The End
…for now.

Acknowledgements

First of all, I would like to thank you, *the reader*, for picking up this book and joining Oliver on his journey back to the past. If you enjoyed Priory, please leave a review either where you purchased it or on Goodreads (or both); they genuinely are the author's lifeline.

Book 2 in the Oliver Hardacre series is coming late 2022.

Behind every book is a writer bleeding from their fingers ever eager to create something of note. But behind them is a support network who give time and expertise—all to steady the madness.

Firstly, my thanks go to my incredibly supportive husband, James, who is there with me every step of the way, from the stunning cover artwork, book trailer and endless cups of coffee. I couldn't ask for a better wingman, or someone to *help me hide the bodies!*

To the wonderful Sarina at Sparrow Book Publishing for her brilliant proof and editing skills and for generally being fantastic. A great big thank you to Kayleigh at Full Proof Editing for her incredible eagle-eyed final proofread.

My gratitude to my meticulous beta readers, who all had an early copy of Priory—Beverley Lee, GR Thomas, Julia Blake, and Amelia Oz. Thank you for your valuable time, suggestions, and comments; I don't know what I would have done without you.

About the Author

Becky Wright is an author with a passion for history, the supernatural, and things that go bump in the night.

Blessed, she lives in the heart of the English Suffolk countryside, surrounded by rolling green fields, picturesque timber-framed villages, country pubs and rural churches. She is married with children and grandchildren.

Family bonds and the intricacy of relationships feature strongly in her books. With her lifelong fascination for the supernatural, Gothic fiction and the macabre, her stories tend to lean towards the dark side.

For information on all Becky's books, writing and updates, please go to her official website. You can also follow her across all social media platforms.

www.beckywrightauthor.com

Made in the USA
Middletown, DE
03 October 2021

49560679R00154